Elizabeth Craggs – Michael Wood

Elizabeth Craggs

a novel by

Michael Wood

First published in 2023

Publishing services provided by Lumphanan Press
www.lumphananpress.co.uk

ISBN: 9798396023369

Cover photograph: Derwent Isle
Courtesy of Clearview / Alamy Stock Photo.

The Lake District is surely the
most beautiful place on earth
– *Bill Bryson*

PART ONE

Chapter 1

Elizabeth hurried as she typed her sixth property information page of the morning. She was dying for a coffee but had to get one more boring page out of the way first. She typed the heading: *FOR SALE – FOUR BEDROOM BUNGALOW*, then she started on the main script. Long typing sessions had seen her develop from a hesitant plodder into a competent typist and now she got into full swing, her fingers speeding across the keys like those of a concert pianist playing an allegro.

She was describing the wonders of the bungalow's designer kitchen, cringing at the hyperbole she had been instructed to use, when the sudden sound of crunching metal and shouting people stopped her in mid-sentence. She heard the sound quite clearly, her usually noisy office being empty at that moment; it came from the street outside her window. She pushed back her chair and stood up to see what had happened.

She had to stand up because there was a chest-high wooden partition between her and the large window that looked out onto the busy street. On the other side of the partition, facing the street, framed groups of photographs displayed the current crop of properties that Smyth's Estate Agency were offering for sale.

Elizabeth moved to her left to get a better view. Now she could see that a minor collision had taken place between a small baker's van, a large frozen food lorry and a cyclist. The young male cyclist, apparently kitted out to pilot the next space shuttle, sat on the damp kerb with his knees bent to his chin and his feet in the gutter. Two middle-aged women were bent down towards him, no doubt offering their motherly help. The drivers of the van and lorry were alighting from their vehicles, which had skewed sideways and now blocked the street.

"Poor sods," Elizabeth whispered to herself. In the five months she had worked in the agency, she had witnessed the daily struggle the delivery drivers had to offload their supplies in the narrow, overcrowded street in which the estate agency sat. The cramped, twisting streets of Keswick were no different to those found in thousands of old English towns, built to accommodate horses, not the never-ending stampede of hoof-less horsepower that roared along them now.

The street's gutters were all daubed with the usual sinuous yellow threats, but the drivers had no choice but to ignore them as they parked in front of the shops they serviced. Elizabeth thought it was miraculous that there were so few accidents given the congestion and the daily pressure the drivers were under to meet their delivery schedules.

If the tourists, now trapped in the ensuing traffic jam, were expecting the police to arrive and sort the mess out, they were about to be disappointed, government cutbacks having closed the town's police station and sacked a hundred police officers throughout Cumbria. Even now, six years after the financial crash of 2008, Britain's recession continued while other countries recovered.

Elizabeth inwardly cursed the government as she watched the two drivers approach each other shaking their heads in a conciliatory manner. Their whole demeanour said, "sorry mate, what could I do?"

Elizabeth cursed because the scene reminded her about the recession, that creeping, pitiless disease that slowly devoured people's hopes and dreams, including hers. Having recently left university with a degree in Politics and Economics, which she saw as an important means to achieving her long-term ambition of becoming a Labour Member of Parliament, she had been hoping for a job that was relevant to that aim. A receptionist in an estate agency was not one of them. But now, as the economy continued to flounder, she realised that she had actually been lucky to get a job at all.

It had been her mother's friendship with the wife of the agency's owner, George Smyth, that had landed her the job, which had become vacant because of the existing receptionist's pregnancy. The two women had pressured a reluctant George into giving the job to Elizabeth, whereas he had been keen to hire a less qualified person who he believed would stay longer and be easier to mould to his ways. As a result neither he nor Elizabeth were satisfied with the outcome. But while Elizabeth accepted the situation with resignation, Smyth made it clear by his offhand attitude towards her that she was there under sufferance.

Returning to her desk, Elizabeth now found herself dwelling on the contrast between her current life and the life she had been living just a few months ago at university.

There she had regularly been engaged in rational, though sometimes heated, debates about her main interest, politics, and also in the interests and studies of her friends – philosophy, science, medicine, literature, world affairs, and of course, the opposite sex. At times she had been questioned about her career choice of politics when it was seen by many as a thankless, boring profession. In her responses she usually managed to include a quote by Winston Churchill – "Politics is almost as exciting as war. In war you can only be killed once, but in politics many times."

She had also enjoyed a leading role in the university's magazine (frequently contributing articles on a variety of subjects) and a busy social life of nights on the town and house parties. These had resulted in one or two casual relationships, but she had been careful to avoid anything that risked interfering with her studies and her future career plans.

This full and interesting life had now been replaced by a life of mundane office work where the minor crash she had just witnessed was the most exciting event she had seen in the past three months. And after leading an independent life at university, she had found it difficult to go back to living with her parents on the farm, even though her parents were wonderfully supportive. She had hoped to have her own place by now, but that dream had been shattered when she couldn't find a job with a high enough salary to go solo. And even though she loved the farm and all its animals, its location in a remote valley a few miles from Keswick was anything but conducive to an active social life.

She found no consolation in the fact that she had been warned about what lay ahead for her during the recession.

"Your degree has as much value as bog paper," her predecessors had told her. "You'd better practise how to flip burgers."

She had listened to the warnings, of course, but wondered if those warning her had tried hard enough to find a job. There had to be some vacancies somewhere, surely. So she had left university quietly confident that she would find a job somewhere, and hopefully, in journalism, which she saw as her long-term route into politics. She had envisaged starting with a local newspaper then working her way up to a national where she would write hard-hitting political articles and make a name for herself. From there she hoped to progress to radio or television news and current affairs programmes. And finally she would stand for election in her local constituency and win her seat in Parliament.

Then, who knows – Elizabeth Craggs, Speaker of the House? How about Prime Minister? She couldn't do any worse than the last woman who held the post.

Alas, her predecessors' warnings had been right and after three months of contacting every local, regional and national newspaper in the country by letter, email and telephone, she finally got the message – *there are no vacancies.*

Now, prepared to take any kind of work, including flipping burgers, she had set her sights lower. Three demoralising weeks later she was contemplating the voluntary sector when her mother turned up with news of the forthcoming vacancy at Smyth's. Her mother! What would she do without her? Still beautiful, her hazel eyes still those of a young girl, tall, slim, glorious hair, calm, hard-working, best friend, rarely stern, always there, always loving. People told Elizabeth she was her mother's double.

After an initial two weeks training given to her by Susan Jackson, the receptionist who was leaving, she had found the workload hectic but progressively boring and unchallenging. She spent a lot of the time correcting the poor grammar and choice of words compiled by Mr Smyth and his sales consultant, Marcia, a bosomy thirty-something with dyed hair who wore more war paint than a tribe of Apaches and clip-clopped around the office in stiletto heels and tight skirts. They were frequently out of the office at the same time, ostensibly visiting separate clients, but Susan Jackson had whispered that she thought they were having an affair. This could explain why Elizabeth often had to deal with irate and frustrated clients who were unhappy with some aspect of Smyth's service. Not wanting to tell them outright lies, Elizabeth found herself becoming a master of obfuscation. "Perfect training for a would-be politician," she could hear the cynics say.

George Smyth, known to the locals as Gorgeous George, an ebullient, pencil-thin, middle-aged man with long hair, expensive suits with matching waistcoats, pink shirts and bright ties, had run his private estate agency for twenty-four years and in that time had somehow managed to persuade the rich folk of the area to use him when selling their houses, even though he charged more than the other estate agents in town. His business was therefore one of feast or famine, with sales fewer but more profitable than his competitors. This situation had been exacerbated by the recession, resulting in him making a staff member redundant two years ago, which now explained why Elizabeth was always snowed under.

Now, alone once more in the office, and feeling grateful

for the mini-interruption in the street, Elizabeth concluded her typing of repetitive, mind-numbing information regarding a four-bedroomed bungalow in nearby Braithwaite. She clicked the PRINT button, sighed and went in search of one of her daily highlights – coffee.

Chapter 2

One April night, after a particularly tiring day, Elizabeth was sitting in front of the log fire in the farmhouse living room, staring blankly at the flames, when her father came in. He looked slightly older than his fifty-one years due to the lines in his face caused by his constant squinting and scowling against the wind, rain, snow, sun and bank managers. Otherwise, beneath his full head of dark hair stood a man of average height and build, a man who didn't stand out in a crowd. But Elizabeth knew that within this unremarkable facade lived an exceptionally strong man, both physically and mentally, qualities needed to survive as a hill farmer in the Lake District. He was still her hero, her stake in the ground to whom she would always be tethered.

He slumped into the armchair opposite Elizabeth and let out the sigh of a man who had been working hard all day. He was dressed in his corduroy trousers, an Aran sweater and slippers, having shed his overalls, waterproofs and wellington boots in the back porch. Slowly he brought his head forward and looked across at her. "How are you today, lass?"

Elizabeth registered the inclusion of the word "today" in his question, knowing he was referring to the fact that she often expressed her dissatisfaction with the way life had turned out for her after university. She shrugged her shoulders. "Okay..."

"You don't look okay. Your face is longer than Bill Tyson's horse's."

"Do you want me to pretend..."

"No, lass, but this has got to stop." Her father leaned forward in his chair, elbows on knees, and stared into her eyes. "This moping about. It's not good for you. And it's not right. You have nothing to moan about."

Elizabeth was shocked. Her father had always been quietly supportive and encouraging.

"But..."

"Now listen to me, lass. I know you are disappointed that you haven't got the type of job you wanted, and I know that you don't like the job you've got. That's why me and your mother have kept quiet all these months while you've been moaning about the place. We were hoping you would snap out of it and see that things weren't as bad as you made out. But you haven't. You are still feeling sorry for yourself. Well, time is up, young lady. This moping has got to stop. Who do you think you are? Looking down your nose at a job half the lasses around here would die for. Start at nine, dressed in nice clothes, sitting in a warm office meeting interesting people, lunch break, weekends off, no shifts, reasonable pay. Try standing in the bus queue at seven in the morning in all weathers, facing a one-hour journey to Maryport to work as a fish processor, a boss pushing you all day, standing up most of the time, cold and wet conditions, no time to think, the smell of fish always in your clothes, weekend work, shift work, minimum wage, getting home late after another hour on the bus. What is their future? A life of money worries and bad health. These are the people you say you want to represent in Parliament. They don't like their jobs either. Not many people get to work in the jobs they would like." Her father paused, allowing time for Elizabeth's response. None came.

He went on: "Don't you realise that what you are going through now is exactly the training you need to be the kind of politician you want to be. You are learning about the dissatisfaction of most people's lives: you are feeling like they are feeling. Remember it, savour it, use it. Don't moan about it. Do something about it when your chance comes. And I have no doubt your chance will come, lass, because you'll find a way to make it happen. If you are as clever and tough as I think you are, you *will* be a politician one day."

Speech over, her father sat back and rested his head again on the back of his chair.

A silence settled between them, occasionally interrupted by the burning logs shifting in the fire. Elizabeth stared into the flames for a long time.

Finally, she looked up and said, "Thanks, Dad." The lump in her throat stopped her from saying anything else.

Two days later, on a bright spring morning, having walked past leaping lambs and bursting buds, and felt a stir in the town as it prepared itself for the tourist takeover that would last most of the year, Elizabeth found herself alone again in Smyth's office. Spring was also a time when things started to stir in the housing market, and both Mr Smyth and Marcia were out and about dealing with the surge, leaving scribbled messages for Elizabeth to deal with in their absence. Head down, she was dealing with one of them when she heard the door open and felt the presence of somebody approaching her desk.

She looked up to find a man smiling down at her. Late twenties she guessed. Tall, healthy looking, probably more used to a tracksuit than the business suit he was wearing. His tousled brown hair was slightly sun-bleached and, together with his gentle tan, gave her the impression that he was not British. He was a very welcome interruption to her work. She was about to greet him when he said, "*Bonjour, Mademoiselle. Tu es tres belle. Quand pouvoun-nous faire l'amour?*"

With a disarming smile, Elizabeth said, "What did you say?"

The man grinned. "I said good morning, Miss. What a nice day it is."

"No, you didn't," Elizabeth corrected. "You said, good morning, Miss. You are very beautiful. When can we make love? First you patronise me then you lie." Her raised eyebrows challenged him.

"Ah..." the man hesitated. "You understand French."

"Your powers of deduction are remarkable, Monsieur. You must be a detective."

"Ouch! You are so sharp. I bet if I touched you, I'd cut myself."

"If you touched me, you would certainly experience pain."

The man paused and glanced around as if to see if anyone else was in the office, then he turned to face Elizabeth. "I see you have been to that great British school."

"Which school is that?"

"The charm school." He raised his eyebrows.

Elizabeth smiled. "I'm not usually as prickly as this, but I don't like being patronised."

The man frowned and pulled a chair close to her desk. "Is it alright if I sit down?"

"Of course."

The man leaned forward in his chair, as if he was preparing for a long intimate chat. "Patronised." He frowned. "What is this word? I don't think I know it."

Elizabeth hesitated, not sure how to explain it clearly. Eventually she said, "It's when you act towards somebody as if you are superior to them in some way."

"Ah!" the man raised a finger. "We say *condescendants*."

"Condescending, that's it. You came in here thinking you would have some fun with me, assuming I was an empty-headed, uneducated woman. You assumed you were superior to me and could therefore say what you like."

"But what I said to you was complimentary. I said you were very beautiful. Do you not like this?"

"You were treating me like an object and having fun at my expense."

The man sighed. "You are a very serious woman, and I respect what you say. If I have offended you, I sincerely apologise. It was not my intention." He stood up and walked out of the office.

Elizabeth's mouth was still hanging open when he walked in again. "Good morning, Miss," he said. "What a nice day it is."

"Good morning, sir." Elizabeth smiled. "It certainly is. How can I help you? Please take a seat."

The man half-smiled as he sat down and looked at Elizabeth across her desk, his eyes not leaving hers for a moment. Suddenly the smile was gone. "Right, fun over. Let's get down to business. Can I speak to the proprietor or manager? I wish to discuss the purchase of one of your properties and I wish to inspect it today."

Surprised by his sudden change of tone, Elizabeth hesitated before she replied, "I'm afraid the owner and our sales consultant are both out of the office today and probably won't be available until tomorrow morning."

"*Mon Dieu.* Is there anybody else I can talk to?"

"*Juste moi, Monsieur. Ceci est une petite entreprise.*"

"I need to see this property today," the man insisted. "I am flying back to Zurich tomorrow. Can you arrange a viewing in the next few hours?"

Normally, Elizabeth would have called Mr Smyth on his mobile phone and passed it to him to deal with, but today she didn't. "It depends on the property owner," she said.

The man sighed. "This property has been empty for nearly two years and the owner doesn't live there."

"Which property are you referring to, Monsieur?" Elizabeth asked, trying to stay calm while wondering if she was getting in over her head. Clearly, this man was a sharp, experienced operator.

"Arnet...my name is Dominic Arnet."

Elizabeth offered her hand across the desk. "And my name is Elizabeth...Elizabeth Craggs."

They shook hands, Elizabeth squeezing hard to hide the nervousness she felt.

Arnet continued, "The property is called Fell View, situated near a village called Portinscale."

Elizabeth made a note of his name and the property on an enquiry form. She recognised the property immediately. It and its owner had been the subject of local gossip long before she had joined Smyth's, and she had heard Mr Smyth and Marcia discussing it shortly after she had joined. At that point they were deciding to take it off the online advertising schedule because they had already spent too much money over eighteen months without any return. They had not managed to sell any of the eight apartments that now constituted what had once been the Fell View Hotel.

Elizabeth had heard Mr Smyth ranting about the hotel owner, Cyril Porter. Apparently Porter had ignored the advice of both Mr Smyth and the architect when deciding to convert the hotel into apartments after a few years of bad trading. Smyth and the architect had advised that he convert it into twelve two-bedroom apartments. This would keep the price down to a level which would be acceptable to a number of prospective purchasers.

Instead, Porter had insisted that he would make more money by converting it into eight three-bedroom apartments with luxury fixtures and fittings and each with a double garage.

The result was that each apartment was now on the market at almost double the price that the two-bedroom apartments would have been. This took them outside the price range of the usual purchasers and into a range which competed with three-bedroomed detached houses. Needless to say, buyers preferred a detached house to an apartment and Porter's dream of making his fortune had not materialised. Word was that he was getting desperate to recoup his outlay in order to pay off his debts. Sometimes his desperation was directed at Smyth, accusing him of being an incompetent salesman. Smyth was, therefore, also desperate to see the apartments sold.

As Elizabeth recalled these facts, she also realised that Dominic Arnet must be aware of some of them since he knew about the apartments not selling for two years.

"I take it you are aware of some of the history of these apartments, Monsieur Arnet," Elizabeth said.

"Yes, it is my business," Arnet explained. "I am a property buying agent. I buy property for investment companies, wealthy individuals, foreign buyers and others. This one is for an individual. At least that is what the solicitor who hired me told me. I have visited the site and seen the property from the outside. Now I want to see inside."

Now Elizabeth was really worried. She knew she should not be dealing with this professional. Mr Smyth would go wild, probably fire her for not passing it to him. "And which apartment do you wish to see?" she found herself asking in spite of her worries.

"All of them. I am considering the purchase of the whole property."

"All of them?" Elizabeth swallowed. She did a quick mental calculation, multiplying the approximate asking price of each apartment by eight. It came to well over £3 million.

Now she knew for certain that she should hand the matter over to Mr Smyth. Instead, hiding her rising panic, she stood up quickly and said, "Are you able to go for a viewing now? It's only a fifteen-minute drive to the property. I can lock the office up for an hour or so and put the answer machine on." While saying this she had a vague idea that she should be asking for much more information before they went, such as proof of identification, the name of the client he was representing, what kind of time scale he had in mind, and so on.

"Yes, I can go now," Arnet said as he rose. "I'm very grateful, Elizabeth, that you are going to such lengths for me." The half-smile on his face told her that he knew she was totally inexperienced in this kind of work. This and the use of her Christian name only added to her feelings of panic and vulnerability. Deep down, however, she also recognised an emerging excitement.

By the time they left the office together, this cocktail of feelings had brought her close to trembling.

Chapter 3

As they drove out of Keswick, with Arnet at the wheel of a BMW, he explained that he had flown over from Zurich mainly to check out two properties in the Windermere area of the Lake District, with Fell View being a reserve if the others proved unacceptable. He had spent longer than expected at the first two properties and, after much deliberation, had decided they were not quite suitable for his client. Now, having satisfied himself that Fell View was in a wonderful location, with views of Derwent Water and the surrounding fells, he was hoping that his internal inspection would make his journey worthwhile. Otherwise it might become a loss which he would have to bear.

Elizabeth missed some of his explanation, her eyes, and thoughts, distracted by Arnet's tanned left hand regularly reaching towards her thigh as he changed gear.

"Why might you have to bear a loss?" Elizabeth asked, her voice dry and squeaky. "Did your client not ask you to fly over?" Immediately she regretted it. She shouldn't be asking personal questions.

If Arnet minded, he didn't show it. "Yes, of course. It is my job to travel to find a property wherever my client wishes to buy. But the small retaining fee he pays me at the outset may not cover all the costs, and if I don't make any commission from the sale, then I make a loss. This is all to do with a gamble I decided to make when setting the business up. I devised a unique system of payment for my services which my competitors don't offer." He went on to explain the system in detail but lost Elizabeth en route. He finished with, "It is a high-risk, high-reward system which has so far provided me with a comfortable living."

Elizabeth was surprised that he was revealing such detail. "So that means you must be good at finding the right properties and negotiating good discounts," she surmised.

"Absolutely." Arnet smiled. He concentrated on negotiating the A66 turnoff into Portinscale village before continuing. "And that is why I'm glad I have met you today, Elizabeth. I have to confess that I go to great lengths to meet members of staff like yourself."

Elizabeth glanced across at him, wondering what he was getting at. It took quite a while for the penny to drop. "So!" she said, her voice recovering from its squeakiness. "All that business about asking to see the proprietor or sales manager was an act. You already knew I was alone...and you are probably not in a hurry to see the property today...Am I right?"

Arnet smiled. "I knew you were a smart cookie."

"But normally I would have passed you over to the owner. How did you know I wouldn't do that today?"

"I didn't. It is always a gamble. But I have found that a good percentage of junior staff are willing to by-pass the boss. I suspect they are underpaid and undervalued." He held up his hand. "Don't worry. I will not ask you to explain your motives."

There was a long pause as Arnet negotiated past traffic

on the narrow road through the village, and as Fell View was only a few bends further on, Elizabeth decided to leave any further questions until after their viewing. Now she found herself wondering if she was dealing with a professional agent who was open and honest, or a con-man, or some other sort of crook.

Soon they were turning left and entering the grounds of what had once been the Fell View Hotel. Elizabeth had passed this way many times but never had cause to enter. The old painted wood sign had been replaced by a large Lakeland stone sign with the words Fell View chiselled into its surface and coated with gold paint.

The tree-lined drive curved to the right over a distance of about 100 metres, sloping gently downwards towards the lake, before the building was revealed.

It turned out to be an imposing stone mansion, apparently built in the nineteenth century for the sole occupation of a wealthy cotton mill owner. Similar mansions were scattered all over the Lake District, symbols of an era of vast individual wealth. Elizabeth hated them. To her they represented the privilege of the few built on the exploitation of the many. In Arnet's world, she realised, it was obviously still going on.

Elizabeth took a bag full of keys from her briefcase and approached the large front door. As she put the key into the keyhole, an impulse made her turn to Arnet. "How can you work for such people?"

Arnet's eyes widened slightly. "Please explain."

"Don't you think it is obscene that a few people hold all the wealth while the majority struggle to survive? A house should be bought to live in. It should not be a means of making the rich richer."

Arnet smiled at her. "Shall we go inside? The spring sunshine is nice, but the air is still cool."

Feeling like a puppy that has just had its head patted, Elizabeth opened the heavy door and stepped inside.

Arnet joined her and looked around the large hallway. "Ah! This looks promising." He walked quickly, turning into a central corridor, where he stood outside the first door on his right and invited Elizabeth to open it. "Yes," he enthused as he stepped inside.

The whole space was decorated in neutral colours. A plethora of stainless steel and marble glistened in the large kitchen. Four large windows together with French windows overlooking the front lawns brought sunlight flooding in. There were no ceiling or coving mouldings. The rooms had been stripped to the bare essentials. Minimalism was the in thing apparently. Elizabeth's opinion, which she kept to herself, was that it had as much character and homeliness as a hospital operating theatre.

The rest of the apartments on that side of the building were similarly appointed.

At the rear of the building they found the apartments to be very similar inside, but they had the added attraction of a great view of Derwent Water and the fells beyond. The lake, gently disturbed by an easterly breeze, sparkled in the sunshine and Elizabeth noticed that the ferries had started to operate. Sweeping lawns, a lily pond, flower beds, rhododendrons and a variety of huge trees completed the foreground picture.

Arnet didn't speak during his inspection except for a moment when he asked for confirmation of prices. Elizabeth read them out from the sales file she carried in her briefcase. She had also remained silent during the inspection, busying herself opening and closing doors and watching from a discreet distance, recognising that it would be foolish to interrupt the concentration of a man who might be about to spend over £3 million. She had noticed in the file that Arnet had emailed an enquiry eleven months ago asking for a price for the whole property. Smyth had quoted £3.51 million, presumably after consulting Cyril Porter. This was a reduction of £90,000 on the combined price of all the apartments. Arnet had obviously been preparing the ground for his current visit.

While on that side of the building, they had a stroll around the garden. A heron took off as they approached the lily pond, but two mallards continued feeding. A triangle of three new Lakeland stone picnic tables with integral bench seats were arranged around the pond, bird droppings and algae already ageing them.

The garden's perimeter was marked by an old cast iron fence with a gate that allowed them to enter the field beyond. A short walk across the field and they found themselves on the shore of the lake, the water lapping at their feet. The views held them spellbound, their purpose momentarily forgotten and somehow diminished by the timeless, natural grandeur around them.

Breaking the spell, Elizabeth indicated that along the shore to their left, within walking distance of Fell View, was a marina which would be an attraction for boat owners. She then turned and pointed out Cat Bells Fell up to their right, its slopes dominated by bracken still showing its strange winter colour, somewhere between rust and pink, the green shoots of spring not yet bursting through. She explained that it was one of Lakeland's most popular walks, a fact confirmed by groups of Lilliputian figures moving slowly along its undulating ridge.

Finally, they returned to the front of the building and headed for the new garages among the trees. They looked huge to Elizabeth, big enough for lots of sheep – ideal for lambing at this time of year. Arnet, no doubt, was wondering if they were big enough for a Rolls or a Bentley. He inspected all of the garages to satisfy himself that everything functioned okay and soon he was handing the keys back to Elizabeth and escorting her back to his car, thanking her profusely for accompanying him.

Inside the car, which had been standing in the sun and was pleasantly warm, he turned to her. "Now, Elizabeth, you have to get back to your empty office and I have to get back to my hotel. I would be grateful if you didn't mention what we have done today to your boss. I am very interested in pursuing the purchase of Fell View for my client and I'd like to talk some more about it with you. Why don't you come to my hotel tonight and we can talk about it over dinner?"

Elizabeth's alarm bells started to ring again. She knew she should be insisting that Mr Smyth take over from now on. But something told her that she had come too far to turn back, that she would curse herself in the future if she hadn't the guts to see this through to its conclusion. She still didn't know if she was facing an opportunity or a foolish gamble, one that would only be taken by an inexperienced country bumpkin like her. There was also the small matter that she had nothing in her wardrobe suitable for wearing to a dinner in what she felt sure would be a four-star hotel. Hers was a world of sweaters and jeans, fell boots and trainers, waterproofs and wellingtons. The only other clothes she had were those she had bought to wear at the office.

She was still pondering what to do and say when her mouth opened and some words came out. "Which hotel are you staying at?"

"It's called The Swan Inn. It's in the village of Far Sawrey on the west side of Windermere, which is where the other properties were located. You have to take a ferry to get to it. I call it a hotel, but I think you would call it a pub with rooms to let. I can't stand large hotels. I like to relax at the end of the day, not have to get dressed up and be served expensive food by someone looking like an undertaker. Will that be okay for you? I could make an exception if you prefer something else?"

"No! A pub is fine with me," Elizabeth rushed, hoping her relief didn't show. "And I know where Far Sawrey is. I'll soon find The Swan."

Clothing problem over, another quickly took its place. She had no transport of her own.

She had assumed he would be in a hotel near Keswick, forgetting that his priority had been to inspect properties near Windermere. Occasionally she was able to borrow her mother's car, but now she didn't fancy telling her mother she needed the car to go to dinner with a foreign stranger to help him negotiate a multi-million-pound property deal. Nor did she want to mention her predicament to Arnet, thus further demonstrating her peasantry. Her only option was to use the bus for the main journey from Keswick to Windermere and a taxi to take her to the ferry and across the lake to Far Sawrey – a journey that could take up to two hours if you didn't time the ferry right. And she still had to get from the farm into Keswick, and then back again late at night.

There was only one solution – she would not go home from work. She would make the journey straight from work, where she finished at five o'clock, and, ironically, hope she didn't look overdressed sitting in a pub in her office clothes. She would tell Arnet she had had to work late, and phone her mother to tell her she was staying in Keswick overnight to have a night out with Megan, one of her pals who had a flat in town – something that she did from time to time.

"Shall we say seven thirty, for dinner at eight?" Arnet suggested.

"That would be fine, thank you," Elizabeth replied, though ignorant of the bus timetable and suspecting that they only ran every hour or so.

Chapter 4

It was almost dark when Elizabeth arrived at The Swan Inn. The evening air was cold, and she was glad she had brought her old fleece jacket which she kept at the office. The bus journey had seemed interminable, giving her too much time to worry about what lay ahead, and the ferry had been late, adding to her anxiety. However, she was relieved to find that she had arrived just before seven thirty.

The Swan Inn appeared to be a typical Cumbrian pub, the result of redeveloping an old longhouse which used to house livestock adjacent to humans.

Removing her jacket, she took a deep breath and entered the building. After finding her way along a narrow corridor with two doors to negotiate, she eventually emerged into a low-ceilinged bar. She was surprised to see how busy it was so early in the evening and not yet in the peak of the tourist season, but then she began to recognise the sights, sounds and smells of the farming fraternity and she knew there must have been an event in the area that afternoon, such as a livestock auction, a sheep dog trial or a hound trail. The resounding babble and laughter of her own kind helped her to relax as she scoured the room to see if Arnet was among them. When she couldn't see him, she decided to ask one of the men behind the bar to telephone his room.

As she approached the bar, she saw Arnet enter the opposite side of the room. He immediately caught her eye, raised his hand and beckoned for her to join him. Carefully, she made her way through the congestion, the humid air thick with the smell of beer, warm bodies and sprawling collies.

Arnet was dressed in a light blue short-sleeve shirt and dark denim jeans and looked much younger than the suit-clad man who had entered her office. Compared to the somewhat gnarled gathering of cloth-capped farmers, his image was almost exotic. Smiling, he leaned forward, gently placed his hands on both of her shoulders and bent to kiss her on both cheeks. She caught a hint of soap.

"We have a table through here," he said, turning to lead the way beyond a wall which separated the bar from the dining area. Three of the tables were occupied. Arnet led her to a table in the farthest corner of the room. "I'm afraid it's a bit noisy tonight," he said. "This is as far away from the bar as I could get." He pulled out a chair, took Elizabeth's jacket and briefcase from her, placed them on an adjacent seat and helped as she shuffled her seat into place.

As he sat down opposite her, Elizabeth said, "They're mostly farmers in the bar. They are always shouting at their animals and tend to develop loud voices."

Arnet smiled. "Yes, of course."

Elizabeth adjusted her skirt as she made herself comfortable, then found herself fiddling with the cutlery and repositioning a small vase containing a single flower.

His eyes hadn't left her since he sat down. It was as if he was trying to read her thoughts, discover her personality, as if he didn't have time to uncover these things gradually but needed to know right now.

Elizabeth wasn't sure whether to be flattered or worried. She was starting to feel like a laboratory specimen being examined under a microscope. She was also wondering when he was going to comment on the fact that she was still wearing her office clothes. "Can I get you a drink?" he asked suddenly, still looking into her eyes.

Elizabeth was dying for something alcoholic to take the edge off her nerves but remembered to act as if she had driven to the meeting. "An orange juice would be nice, thanks."

"Do you mind if I have a glass of wine? I am the lucky one not driving tonight."

"Of course not." Elizabeth smiled.

Ten minutes later Arnet returned from the bar with their drinks and sat down. Once again his brown eyes searched hers. "Sorry to leave you for so long. It's very busy at the bar." Before Elizabeth could respond he raised his glass and said, "Cheers!"

After they had put their glasses down, there was a long silent spell in which they both waited for the other to start a conversation.

Arnet broke the spell. "So, Elizabeth, you are a supporter of the loony left?"

Elizabeth was caught off guard. She had been expecting to talk about the afternoon's viewing and had spent most of the bus journey studying the file and rehearsing her answers to his questions. Eventually she got to grips with his question. "Er...yes, I suppose I am. I mean yes, I *am* a supporter of the left, but I resent the loony reference."

"Just as I resent being asked how I could work for *such people* this afternoon. I don't work for them. I work for myself. And my ambition is to relieve them of as much money and power as I can."

As Elizabeth frowned her lack of understanding, a beaming smile spread across Arnet's face as he continued, "Relax, Elizabeth, I am also a left-winger. We are comrades. Shake hands, sister." He placed his right elbow on the table and offered his open hand. Elizabeth, caught up in the moment, placed her right elbow next to his and placed her hand in his, as if they were going to arm wrestle.

Elizabeth felt a shock pass through her as their bare arms and hands intertwined, and she wondered if the flush it induced was as noticeable as it felt. Her feelings at that moment were certainly not sisterly, and she found she was in no hurry to break apart. Arnet too seemed to be affected, his eyes continuing to gaze into hers, and his hands making no effort to untie the knot.

Elizabeth finally came to her senses, realised she was behaving like a teenager and withdrew her hands from the tangle. "You surprise me, Monsieur Arnet. I would never have guessed..."

"Dominic...please call me Dominic."

He went on to explain the reasons for his left wing leanings – how as the son of a French worker who had spent his life labouring in the hot vineyards of Southern France, he had seen his father sweat his life away for small wages and a lack of appreciation bordering on contempt from the wealthy vineyard owners.

Later, when he was twenty and working as a ski instructor

in the Alps, he had met and married the nineteen-year-old daughter of a wealthy Swiss investment banker. The banker and his wife had been horrified at the match and had shown him nothing but cold contempt, making it clear to him that he was not good enough for their daughter. The banker had used his contacts to find Dominic a "proper" job as a trainee in an upmarket estate agency in Zurich. To please his new wife, Dominic had taken the job. His in-laws, however, continued to do all in their power to wreck the marriage. The marriage had survived for six years thanks to the good nature of his wife, but eventually she had been worn down by their coercion and threats to disinherit her. An amicable divorce had followed.

During those six years, Dominic explained, he had mixed with his in-laws' friends and their families, most of them connected to the banking industry in Zurich, some of them resident retirees keen to live near their money, all of them rich beyond dreams. With few exceptions, he had been appalled by them. The worst thing was their sense of entitlement. The fact that some of them were rich simply through inheritance or luck did not dissuade them from the belief that they deserved it, that others were either too stupid or too lazy to make money like them. Their main activity seemed to be avoiding paying tax by moving their money around the world. Investing in countries run by murderous dictators was okay as long as the returns were good. Snaps of conversation he was not meant to hear had also persuaded Dominic that some of their wealth was not clean, that it was the result of criminal activity, mostly money laundering.

He went on to explain that those years at the estate agency had given him an understanding of the expensive end of the property market, as well as the habits and preferences of the wealthy. He had learned that most of them were prepared to pay out surprisingly large amounts of money for somebody to do the jobs they didn't like or couldn't be bothered to do. These varied widely, from walking the dog to buying property. Tradesmen and women such as plumbers, electricians and swimming pool cleaners who found favour with the rich in Zurich were earning as much as lawyers.

In his job of selling properties for the rich, he had occasionally come across agents who were buying properties for the rich and found that most of them were simply working for different branches of the same estate agency and had no incentive to negotiate a discount for their clients because they all charged a percentage fee based on the final sales price, thus the higher the price, the greater their fee. Seeing this as a weakness that could be exploited, Dominic had eventually set up his own independent buying agency in competition with them.

Operating out of his apartment in Zurich, he offered clients a choice of three ways to pay for his services, which brought him immediate success.

Over the years he had learned to concentrate his efforts on properties that had remained unsold for long periods. This almost always meant that the seller became more keen, sometimes desperate, to sell and would listen to heavily discounted offers. And this, Dominic emphasised, was why he tried to talk to people like Elizabeth.

During the course of telling his story, Dominic paused to

order food and another round of drinks, and they both took phone calls. Elizabeth's call was from her mother, checking to see if she was okay. Elizabeth used the background sound of the bar hubbub to claim she was in The Royal Oak in Keswick with her friend. Dominic excused himself, taking his call out of the room, and didn't explain the call when he returned.

Elizabeth had listened to his story attentively through-out their meal, but all the while had wondered why he was telling her. She had asked no questions and she could not think of a reason why he should divulge so much detail of his private life and business.

Now, at last, as a waiter cleared away their dishes, she expected to get down to discussing Fell View. Instead, Dominic smiled across the table and said, "So, Elizabeth, would you mind telling me what happened in your life to make you a loony lefty?"

Elizabeth glanced at her watch. It was quarter past nine. All the dining tables were now occupied, the room full of loud, alcohol-induced chatter. She was beginning to feel tired, the tension of playing an unfamiliar role in an un-familiar situation starting to take its toll. She would try to keep it short.

There was no singular event, she explained. Rather, as she grew up on the farm, a slow-burning realisation that there appeared to be little reward or recognition in her parents' life or in the lives of most others who worked hard for a living. When she was fifteen and embroiled in a discussion with her grandfather about the class system in Britain, he had said to her: "Ninety percent of us are working class. Anybody who goes to work for wages, be it a solicitor or a miner, is working class. The clue is in the word *work*." He had his own test of someone's true value. He called it his desert island test. It asked the simple question: if shipwrecked and washed up on a desert island, who would you rather find among other survivors – a solicitor or a miner, a lawyer or a fisherman, an IT executive or a builder, an accountant or a farmer?

Elizabeth went on to take Dominic through her time at university, where she had studied politics and economics and had everything her grandfather told her confirmed. She told him about her bad experiences with the offspring of wealthy parents who displayed a patrician sense of entitlement and superiority.

Finally she pointed out that her present job said everything about the paucity of worthwhile, well-paid jobs, the result of the failings of the latest crop of right wing politicians. She repeated the words her grandfather had said to her as she struggled to find suitable work: "You would have soon walked into a job in my day, lass. Them stupid buggers in Westminster cocked the job up." There had been anger and bitterness in his normally placid voice.

After requesting and receiving an explanation of the term "cocked the job up", Dominic went on to ask, "What kind of work were you hoping to get?"

"I wanted to start off in journalism and eventually go into politics."

"Local or national politics?"

"I want to become a Member of Parliament eventually."

"Really?"

"What does *really* mean?"

"You've just been telling me how useless national politicians are and yet you want to join them?"

"I will be an efficient politician."

"That's what they all say. But here we are hundreds of years after the formation of democratic governments, and nothing has changed. The rich rule the world and it looks as if they always will."

"Things *have* changed, but not enough."

"Okay, I'll give you that. But I think they have gone as far as they are going to. The masters of the world are digging their heels in. They believe they have allowed enough crumbs to fall from their tables. I've heard them say as much. I have witnessed their financial power. You must know that if you try to make things more equal, they will take their money and businesses elsewhere."

"I have to try. Somebody has to."

"A noble sentiment, but I don't think it is possible to change much. I think you will drive yourself crazy with frustration if you become a Member of Parliament."

"So we just give up and let them get away with it?"

"No, we set our sights lower and fight smaller, winnable battles, those that result in improvements for our local society. A good journalist could do this. I try to do my bit by regularly giving some of my earnings to local charities."

"All very reasonable and commendable but too small and safe for me. I feel the need to fry bigger fish."

Dominic smiled at the metaphor. "And what if in your ambition to help others, you fry yourself, Elizabeth? What if you burn yourself out? Where is the sense in that? What about *you*, Elizabeth? What about your brief light?"

"Brief light?"

"Sorry, I sometimes get carried away and quote poetry at people. It's from Catullus – do you know him?"

Elizabeth shook her head.

"Ancient Roman. He was referring to the short period of time we all have to live, which is why we should enjoy it, because death lasts forever. It's one of his short early ones: *Let us live, my Elizabeth, and love, and value at one penny all the talk of stern old men. Suns can set and rise again: we, when once our brief light has set, must sleep one never-ending night.*"

Dominic had been looking into her eyes as he recited the poem. The inclusion of her name and the sincerity in his voice made her believe he was talking directly to her, and meant it. She swallowed and tried to gather her flock of thoughts together, but they gambolled out of control – con-man, seducer, crook, honest, attractive? *When in doubt say something neutral.*

"How did we get from politics to old Roman poetry?" she said.

Dominic hesitated, and as he did so Elizabeth saw the light go out in his eyes, and she regretted her cold question. He looked away from her for the first time and gazed about the busy room. Then he suddenly looked at his watch and said: "*Mon Dieu*, it is after ten o'clock. The last ferry goes at ten. I am so sorry. I forgot to remind you. Did you know about the ferry times?"

Elizabeth's heart sank. Now she would have to admit to not having a car. "No, I forgot to check," was all that came out.

"C'est la vie." Dominic smiled. "At least you have an

alternative road via Hawkshead, but I understand it is longer and slower than the ferry route, so let's get down to talking about Fell View then you can be on your way."

Before Elizabeth had a chance to make her confession, Dominic added, "Look, it is very noisy in here and I think we should hold this discussion in private, so why don't we go up to my room and talk there." He started to rise from his seat as he spoke.

Here we go again. Had he deliberately filled in time until ten o'clock had passed? Had he deliberately taken a drink so he couldn't offer to drive her home? Had he planned to use the privacy line to get her to go to his room? Now her ex-student mind went even further – had he slipped something into her drink?

Chapter 5

Dominic's room turned out to be surprisingly large. Elizabeth guessed it had once been the hay loft from which the farmer fed the livestock below through a trapdoor. Bulging old walls and a sloping floor strengthened her opinion. A double bed, two bedside cabinets, two chairs, a built-in wardrobe, a dressing table on which Dominic's laptop shared space with the tea and coffee tray, and an en suite bathroom via a corner door.

Elizabeth put her briefcase and jacket on one of the chairs.

"Do you prefer sitting or lying?" Dominic asked. Before she could answer, Dominic had flung himself on the bed and lay on his back with his head on the pillow, arms behind his head. "I much prefer lying myself, particularly when I'm thinking."

Elizabeth was speechless. She was tired of trying to second guess his intentions. She played safe and sat on the chair against the wall, facing him.

"Lots of people do it, you know – lie down to think," Dominic explained. "Leonard Bernstein composed all of his great music lying on his sofa. I have my best ideas when I'm lying on my sofa at home. Trouble is sometimes I fall asleep and forget them when I wake up."

Elizabeth smiled, but behind it she was wondering when she should tell him about her being immobile and penniless. While she was hesitating, Dominic stepped in. "Right, let's talk about Fell View. It shouldn't take long. All I am looking for is any information you might have that would explain why the property hasn't sold in nearly two years in such a desirable location, and whether you know anything about the vendor's situation. Is he wealthy and able to wait until a sale eventually occurs or is he keen or desperate to sell? Might he be paying interest on money he borrowed to carry out the project? And finally, what kind of a man is your boss and what is his position regarding this property? He must be getting desperate to see it sold with all that money spent on advertising?"

Elizabeth cleared her throat.

"Before you answer," Dominic intervened, "I am aware that you might not know anything about any of these things, or you might not want to share any information you do have due to a feeling of loyalty to your boss, or your own moral judgement. If any of these things apply, that's fine. We call it a day here and I deal with your Mr Smyth in the usual way. But if you do have information that will help me to make an offer to buy, then won't everybody be a winner? The vendor gets all his apartments sold at once, your boss gets his commission, and I get my commission. *And* I will give you a percentage of my commission depending on how significant I judge your information to be."

Elizabeth had been about to say she was reluctant to tell him anything because she didn't believe it was ethical, when the mention of money made her pause. If she could make a few hundred pounds, she could buy an old banger which would open up a wider area for her to seek new job opportunities. She could feel her dormant ambition rising again. That was the trouble with ambition – it often brushed ethics aside. Before she gave the ethics side of the argument another chance to put its case forward, she found herself saying, "Am I being offered a bribe?"

Dominic leaned over on his elbow and smiled at her. "That is one word that could be used to describe my offer. There are many more, such as incentive or compensation. Don't forget the money would be coming out of the pocket of somebody who can afford a property worth over £3 million. You could call it redistribution of wealth, something I believe you are passionate about. I take it you have some information? Otherwise we wouldn't be having this conversation."

"Yes." Elizabeth nodded.

"Well, it's up to you, Elizabeth. Call it what you will, the offer is there. It's getting late. It's time to decide. Are you going to talk or walk?"

"If my information is very significant, and I know it is, what percentage of your commission are you offering?"

"Fifteen percent. And I will judge the significance."

"What I have to tell you is worth at least twenty-five percent." Elizabeth was surprising herself. She knew she was out of her depth, but she also knew never to accept a first offer. Sheep auctions with her dad had taught her that years ago.

"Okay, twenty-five percent it is. But remember, I will be the judge. You will have to trust me to be fair."

"Agreed." Elizabeth rose and crossed the room to extract the property file from her briefcase on the other chair. She opened the file.

Dominic swivelled over to face her. "I'm all ears."

Elizabeth proceeded to tell him all that she knew about Fell View – how the owner, Cyril Porter, had ignored his architect's advice and finished up with apartments which were too expensive, how he was desperate to sell and would now be pleased just to recover his costs, and how Smyth was equally desperate because of the advertising costs and Porter's accusatory attitude. She concluded with, "I think they would both be delighted if you were to buy only one apartment, never mind the whole building."

As she related the story, Dominic had stirred himself and by the time she had finished, he was sitting on the edge of the bed, directly in front of her. "That is definitely worth twenty-five percent. When I hear that someone is down to the recovering of costs, then I know that things are really desperate. Straight away I can knock £200,000 off the price just on the four more expensive apartments with the views of the lake. Those views didn't cost him a penny. Then I can dig into his profit margin. This is what I call a perfect storm. It could be the best opportunity I have had this year."

"You wouldn't go too far, would you? You wouldn't squeeze him too much?" Elizabeth was beginning to feel sorry for Porter and guilty that she might have started something distasteful.

"No, don't worry. I wouldn't want that. Mr Porter has probably worked hard to get where he is. I have a good idea how much his development costs would be. I would not offer below that. He should still walk away with a small profit."

"What if he doesn't want to accept your offer in spite of all his problems?"

"He will. If he doesn't, he's a crazy man."

"What happens now?"

"You turn up for work in the morning, tell Mr Smyth you couldn't get through to his mobile phone yesterday, so you had no option but to take this demanding Frenchman to view Fell View. Tell him I will arrive at your office at 9.30 a.m. with an offer for the property. That should stop him giving you a hard time. He might even give you a bonus if the sale goes through. We will exchange phone numbers and email addresses and keep in touch after I have left the office and returned to Zurich. If all goes well, in a few weeks I should be paying your commission into your bank account."

"I can't go home. I haven't got a car."

"What?"

Feeling like a naughty child seeking a parent's forgiveness, Elizabeth explained her predicament and why she hadn't told him before. She ended with, "Sorry!"

Dominic stood up and walked towards the door. "Don't worry, there must be some spare rooms at this time of year." He left the room and returned a few minutes later carrying a small plastic bag. He handed it to Elizabeth. "You are in Room Seven at the end of the corridor. The key and a new toothbrush and paste are in the bag. They are used to people turning up here without the essentials. I'm happy to pay for the room, but if you insist, I can always take it off your commission."

"Thanks," was all Elizabeth could come up with. A blend of relief and tiredness was quickly closing her brain down.

Dominic smiled. "And thank you, Elizabeth. We've had a good day together. I'll see you downstairs for breakfast at seven. Okay?"

"Okay."

Elizabeth sat at the breakfast table in the small, low-ceilinged dining room feeling relaxed. She was surprised at how comfortable she felt sharing small talk with the handsome Frenchman who she hadn't known existed twenty-four hours ago. Much of this she put down to his open friendliness, but she also felt a slight swell of pride in herself. He was wearing a business suit and tie again and, as usual, seemed to be studying her as they spoke.

With the scrambled eggs out of the way, they were finishing with toast, marmalade and coffee when he said, "Would you consider working for me, Elizabeth?"

Elizabeth was lifting her cup when the question came. She put it back down too quickly, rattling the saucer. "I..."

"Sorry, that was a stupid way of putting it. Look...I've been thinking for some time that I need to employ somebody in this area to do the groundwork for me. My business is growing, and I am being dragged all over Europe. Sometimes it is essential that I go, but often it is only to carry out initial groundwork which a good assistant could do for me. I am also spending too much time online doing the basic searches for suitable properties, and then monitoring their progress, something else that an assistant could do. The main demand for properties in the UK is in London, the

Lake District and the Scottish Highlands. London is already saturated with buying agencies, so I cover it by passing my enquiries onto an agency in London and earn a referral fee for doing so. But the Lake District and Scotland are much less competitive and with an assistant keeping a close eye on everything that is happening here, I'm sure we could do very well."

Elizabeth told herself to stay calm and focussed. What she said in the next few minutes could change her future. "Do you see it as a full-time or part-time job?" she managed to say, hoping he hadn't noticed the slight tremor in her voice.

"Part-time to start with. You could continue working at Smyth's, which would have some advantages anyway, and work for me in your spare time. An hour or two in the evening and at weekends should cover it. But I do see it becoming a full-time job as time progresses, because most buying agencies offer extra services to their busy clients, such as liaison between the client and local contractors, banks, solicitors, etcetera. You could build up your contacts with all these people and, eventually, there should come a time when I will be able to hand over the negotiation of UK purchases to you. You would in effect become the independent UK branch of my company, which would enable you to make substantial earnings."

Elizabeth was amazed that he was making such an offer when he had only known her for a few hours. She felt it was her duty to give him a reality check. "What you have just outlined is surely aimed at somebody much more ex-perienced than me. I've only been a receptionist for a few months and apart from some bar and waitress work during university, I haven't done anything else."

Dominic shook his head. "You are underestimating yourself, Elizabeth. You told me you had worked on your farm since you were a young girl, so you know what hard work is. You studied for years for your degree. Degrees are only achieved through talent, dedication and determination. Your particular degree, politics and economics, will enable you to converse knowledgeably with the rich and important people who use our services. Our clients will be impressed to see your qualifications on your business cards and stationery. And I have been impressed with the way you conduct yourself. You showed me your bravery and your strong personality. You know when to be quiet and when to speak up. You are thoughtful, honest, pragmatic and inventive. These qualities and the fact that you speak French and look like a film star are precisely the right attributes for the job I am describing. With time and training you will succeed."

Elizabeth gasped. "Wow! You certainly know how to...I didn't realise I was so impressive. Now I think I should have asked for thirty percent."

"And a sense of humour as well." Dominic laughed. "You just got better."

"Seriously though..." Elizabeth paused to take a much-needed sip of coffee. "I'm incredibly flattered by what you've just said and by the job offer, but you know my ambition is to go into journalism and politics. It would be very hard to give up those ambitions."

"Then don't," Dominic insisted. "You must know that some of the best journalists are freelancers who hold down full-time jobs and write in their spare time. And as for politics, would it not be better for you to attempt it after twenty or thirty years in business, with all that expertise and experience to offer?"

"Is there anything you haven't thought of?" Elizabeth queried. "I'd never thought along those lines, and at the moment I can't fault your reasoning."

"So, it's a yes?"

Elizabeth hesitated. "It's a maybe. I'll have to talk to my parents and sleep on it. And by the way, we haven't talked about money."

"Is there anything *you* haven't thought of?" Dominic smiled. "When I get back to Zurich, I'll email you with a formal offer complete with a job description and compensation package. Over a year I would expect you to earn much more than your current income, which I would guess is pretty low."

Elizabeth felt like throwing her arms around him to thank him for his belief in her. He wasn't a con-man after all – he was a thoroughly professional businessman. All that divulging of how his business operated, and all that intense eye searching had been a subtle type of interview. Ironically, she now felt slightly disappointed that his interest had not been more personal. Controlling her arm-throwing emotions, Elizabeth said, "Thanks again for the offer. I promise to give it every consideration and let you know my decision promptly."

Dominic glanced at his watch. "We'd better go. You don't want to be late for work."

Chapter 6

Just after dinner, on a bright spring evening, Elizabeth collected an old outdoor jacket from a peg in the farmhouse porch and wandered outside. She strolled to the end of the building and made her way to an old wooden bench that leaned against the gable end of the farmhouse. The familiar smell of sheep permeated the air, which was alive with house martins flashing in and out of a nearby barn. The bench, which her father had erected for her when she was a little girl, faced south and afforded extensive views almost to the end of their steep-felled horseshoe valley. It was one of her favourite places. When she was a child, she had spent hours on the bench, taking in all that happened around her – the constant coming and going of the sheep and lambs, her tireless father dipping the sheep, driving the tractor, mending the dry-stone walls, working the dogs, helping the shearers, talking with the vet. Now it was the place where she went to think, read, relax.

It had been three weeks since Dominic Arnet returned to Zurich, three hectic weeks which promised to change her life in ways she had never imagined. Dominic had made an offer for Fell View during a meeting with Smyth, and left the office, pausing to thank Miss Craggs for her help. He had shaken her hand with exaggerated formality but winked as he turned to go. A flushed and animated Smyth had immediately invited Marcia into his office and asked Elizabeth to make coffee for them. She could hear their excited voices through the door, but for about a minute all was quiet and she wondered if they were embracing. Perhaps Marcia was whispering the names of expensive hotels in which they could celebrate.

A few days later Elizabeth heard Smyth confiding to Marcia. "That stupid bastard, Porter, has turned down Arnet's offer. He says it is much too low and Arnet is trying it on. He says he expects him to come back with a higher offer after a few days. The man's an arrogant fool. He won't listen to me. Arnet will not do that. I wouldn't in his shoes. Let's hope Porter sees sense when he doesn't hear from him. God knows how long he'll try to hang on."

Smyth was right, Elizabeth reckoned. Dominic was in the driving seat, and though she had helped to put him there, she no longer felt guilty. Porter had brought the situation on himself. As for Smyth – he had not even acknowledged Elizabeth's contribution and had excluded her from all discussions since Dominic left. So much for encouraging loyalty.

None of this helped ease Elizabeth's growing feeling of uncertainty. The sale was on hold and no written job offer had arrived. Dominic had emailed her to say he had been dragged down to the French Riviera on urgent business. Once again she found herself having to trust his word. Her parents hadn't helped either when she told them about her recent exploits and possible future career change. She had to suffer their sermons on lying about her whereabouts, disclosing private business information and trusting the word of a stranger. However, once their sermons were over, they showered her with love and support as they always did and offered to help if she needed it.

Elizabeth's contemplation was interrupted by the call of a raven, causing her to lift her head, and then by a pair of lambs who she had helped to hand rear after the death of the ewe. They seemed to prefer the cobbled farmyard to the fields and often came to her for a scratch and a rub.

Now, as she scratched the lambs, she started to recall the positive events that had happened since Dominic's departure, for which he could take all the credit.

His observation that she could satisfy her desire to be a journalist by becoming a freelancer had hit a receptive chord. She had struck while the iron was hot and approached the editor of her local weekly paper, *The Keswick Tribune*. She pitched her idea of a regular weekly article called Welcome to the Lakes. This would consist of her interviews with people who had recently moved to the Lake District, giving their reasons for doing so as well as a potted history of their previous life and work. She had enthused about the remarkable number of interesting people who came to the area, mainly to retire, quoting someone who had said to her that in Keswick "there's a professor around every corner."

The editor, Sue Burrows, had said she liked the idea but warned that she could not pay a penny, that she would need to see three complete articles before one was published, and would expect consistency and longevity. Needless to say, Elizabeth agreed to everything, asking only that her name appeared on the byline so that she could attach the articles to any future CV.

Two long days later she was invited to a coffee and sandwich lunch at Sue's office, which, fortunately, was a short walk from Smyth's office. Sue told her that she would give the idea a try and specified an article of 500 words plus one photograph, to be submitted once a month rather than once a week. She also asked Elizabeth to submit her first attempts to the scrutiny of journalist Ben Foxley, who worked for the paper. She explained that his experienced eye would spot anything that shouldn't go into the public arena, and he may also be able to offer help and advice on other content. She gave her Ben Foxley's contact details and said he would be expecting to hear from her.

Elizabeth had left the editor's office on a high, feeling like dancing in the rain as she splashed her way back to Smyth's office.

Since then she had managed to produce two articles based on interviews done at weekends with a young couple who had moved from Leeds to work as chef and housemaid at a local hotel, and a couple from Manchester, ex-pharmacist and nurse, who had retired to a bungalow a mile out of town.

Both articles and photographs of the couples had been emailed to Ben Foxley two days ago. This morning she had received a reply from Ben inviting her to his cottage "when convenient" to discuss the articles. After checking with her mother that she could borrow the car, she offered to visit him the following evening after work, and this had been acceptable. Now she awaited the meeting with nervous anticipation.

Chapter 7

Ben Foxley believed that amongst all the magnificent scenery that attracted 18 million visitors to the Lake District each year, the valley in which he lived was the most beautiful. The vista was spectacular and varied, from mountains to meadows, farmland to scrub, caves to crags, streams to waterfalls, marshland to forestry, woodland to heather. Scattered throughout the valley were farmhouses, cottages, mansions, hamlets, villages and one small town – Keswick.

Dominating the valley, the twin lakes of Bassenthwaite and Derwent Water were markedly different even though they had once been a single lake centuries ago, before silting created a gap of marshland and meadow between them. Derwent Water, with its picturesque islands, accessible surrounding fells and adjacency to Keswick, had developed into a tourist hotspot with car parks, ferries, marinas and boats for hire. Two miles to the north, with no islands, and with steep-sided forested fells on both sides, Bassenthwaite was a much quieter lake. Here you found the occasional yachtsman, fisherman and bird-watcher.

It was a valley where everybody, whether they lived in a small cottage or a grand mansion, felt equally humble and equally privileged. Ben put it down to the effect of being permanently in the presence of exceptional beauty, the majesty of the mountains somehow belittling egos, mocking fashion, their permanence a constant reminder of our transience.

It was the peacefulness of Bassenthwaite Lake that had persuaded Ben and his wife, Helen, to buy Scarness Cottage, one of only a handful of dwellings scattered and hidden among the trees along the eastern side of the four-mile-long lake. That had been twelve years ago, when Ben decided to drop out of the rat race to seek a less stressful, more satisfying way of life. Now he worked as a part-time freelance journalist, almost exclusively for the local weekly, *The Keswick Tribune*. When not jumping to the tune of the paper's editor, he could be found in the cottage's conservatory painting landscapes, which he sold through the local art galleries. His income was low, but his satisfaction high.

Helen had become the main breadwinner, her swimming consultancy business taking off as more and more Lake District hotels invested in swimming pool construction, and wild swimming in the Lakes became more popular. The downside was that she was in danger of becoming too busy, the very thing they had come to the Lakes to avoid. Helen never complained about it; it was Ben who felt her absence when work took her away too much.

Today, Ben could be found in the conservatory adding the finishing touches to an oil painting. As he finished he looked at his watch and frowned. It was an hour ago that Helen, who was working at home today, had arrived at his side wearing her wetsuit, stating that she was going down to the lake to take her first dip of the year, the spring sunshine and glass-like water being too difficult to resist. She had said she would be back in half an hour because the water would be too cold to stay in for any length of time.

He had become very protective of Helen ever since he almost lost her a few years ago when murderer, Hector Snodd, brought mayhem to their peaceful valley. He would never forget that feeling of dread when he knew she had been abducted. This now meant he had no choice but to go and check that she was okay.

Before leaving the cottage he put on a thin fleece and picked up his walking companion. His trusty thumb-stick could be a useful weapon in emergencies. Passing through the garden, he was soon on the well-worn track that led down to the lake, only 200 metres away.

On reaching the lake he could see why Helen had been tempted. The pale blue sky was cloudless, and the lake's glass-like surface almost challenged you to plunge in to shatter its perfection. In these conditions it should be easy to spot her, he told himself. But a thorough scan across the water revealed not a single ripple. With a quickening heart he looked along the curving shoreline and behind in the dense trees. He turned and looked out over the lake again. He was considering shouting her name when a thudding weight hit him on his shoulders. He spun around, stick at the ready. From behind a tree a few metres away, a fully dressed Helen emerged, smiling. "Can I have my towel back, please?"

Ben unravelled the wet towel from his shoulders and stepped forward. "You certainly can," he said and swung the towel in an arc, giving her a good swipe on her trousered bottom. Helen turned and started to run back to the cottage. She was slowed down by her heavy backpack containing her wetsuit, giving Ben ample time to run behind her, occasionally swiping her with the wet towel. They arrived at the cottage, panting, their breathless laughter heard only by the wildlife that shared their patch of paradise.

"One of these days..." Ben gasped. "We'll grow up."

Once inside the cottage they reminded each other that there was a visitor arriving that evening, a Miss Elizabeth Craggs, a local lass and would-be journalist. A visitor was a rare event – they would have to be on their best behaviour.

Chapter 8

The evening was sunny but cool when Elizabeth drove along the valley en route to Ben Foxley's cottage. She glanced at a shimmering Bassenthwaite Lake on her left, with the fells in shadow beyond. Nearby, the sun highlighted the fresh spring greenness of the trees. Herefords and Herdwicks were chewing in the fields, swallows flitting and gliding above them. She had travelled that road many times, yet the calming effect of its natural surroundings still worked its magic. She arrived at the cottage in a more relaxed frame of mind than she had expected.

Her knock on the cottage door was answered by a slim, middle-aged woman wearing an apron and a big smile. She was carrying oven gloves in one hand, and she used the other to push her floppy fair hair to one side. "Follow me into the kitchen, Elizabeth," she ordered kindly. Elizabeth obeyed, noting a wonderful smell as she progressed.

Stone-flagged floor, ceiling beams, Aga, storage shelves, Belfast sink, Welsh dresser, old oak table and chairs, pantry, window overlooking the garden, not a flat pack unit in sight – Elizabeth's kind of kitchen.

"I'm Helen," the woman announced as she bent down, opened the oven door and withdrew a tray of lightly browned fruit scones. She placed them on a nearby surface, switched the oven off, discarded her oven gloves and turned to look at Elizabeth. "I think I know you," she said. "I've seen you somewhere before...probably where swimming was involved."

"I sometimes swim in Derwent Water during the summer holidays with a group from Keswick," Elizabeth explained.

"That's probably it." Helen smiled. "I had one or two sessions with them last summer."

"Ah! Yes, I remember now. Somebody said you were an expert, a swimming tutor or something."

Helen nodded. "I used to be. Now I'm more involved with the business side of swimming, advising hotels, mostly on the rules and regs regarding pool construction, staffing and the like. But I still get down to the lake as often as I can. You can't beat it, can you, that feeling of freedom, the closeness to nature..."

Already, Elizabeth felt she had known Helen for years. She was that rare breed who could make you feel at home within minutes. "Those scones smell gorgeous," Elizabeth observed.

"Ben will be salivating. He's a scone-aholic. He's waiting in the garden. I'll take you to meet him and then I'll bring you both some tea and scones, okay?"

"Yes, please."

Helen opened the back door and led Elizabeth out into the garden, which consisted simply of a large lawn, garden shed and log store, all surrounded by yew hedges. Male and female pheasants were strutting all over the lawn, picking up pellets of food. In the hedges dozens of small birds were clinging to bird feeders, an elegant nuthatch catching

Elizabeth's eye. A chorus of quacking announced the arrival of a gang of mallards who appeared from under the hedge and immediately challenged the pheasants for the pellets. Beyond this noisy throng, at the far end of the lawn, a tall, bespectacled man was swinging a golf club.

"Ben," Helen called. "I've brought a beautiful young lady for you."

Half lifting his head, Ben shouted, "That's very kind of you, dear, but I didn't get *you* anything."

Helen gave Elizabeth a knowing look. "He's quite bright really."

Ben walked towards them across the lawn and offered his hand to Elizabeth. Mischievous eyes sparkled in his studious face. "You weren't kidding, were you," he said to Helen. "You'll find your P45 on the hall table."

It took a second before Helen and Elizabeth realised he was referring to Elizabeth's looks.

"I'm off then," Helen announced and turned to go. "I'll pick up my P45 and my scones and I'll be on my way."

"NO! Not the scones," Ben shouted after her. "Okay, you're hired again."

Helen walked away shaking her head. Ben turned to Elizabeth. "Let's sit over there and have a chat." He indicated a wooden seat and table sitting on a gravelled area next to the cottage wall.

They moved to the seat and sat with their backs to the cottage wall. It reminded Elizabeth of her own seat back at the farm. Most of the birds on the lawn ignored them, but one or two mallards came across and moved around their ankles, looking for dropped food.

"Let me put you out of your misery straight away," Ben started. "Your articles are very good. In fact, I struggled to find anything to correct or add. Eventually, I found a couple of adjectives where I think a more common alternative should be used. That is not to say there is anything wrong with your choice. It's more to do with Sue's insistence on not using any words with which a reader might not be familiar. I often have the same battle with her, to which her reply is always, 'If you want to show off your literary prowess, go write fiction.' Anyway, I'll email you tomorrow with these brief alterations, and I'll let Sue know they have my approval."

A long pause followed. Elizabeth had expected him to follow up with other questions or nuggets of knowledge, but Ben seemed to have finished talking. She was relieved and surprised. "Is that it, then?"

"Yep, that's it. You clearly have a grasp of all the basics. Keep it simple, don't disclose personal details, mid-shot photographs. Looks to me like you're a natural. I only asked you to come here so I could say hello and find out what magic powers you have. You see, I've been asking Sue for years to let me write regular feature articles and she always turns me down. Now that I've met you, I think I know why she has favoured you. It's your youth. She wouldn't want to discourage you – she's very supportive of young people. While, on the other hand, I'm an old cynic who can take care of himself and doesn't need a leg up."

"I feel sort of guilty now."

"No. please don't," Ben insisted. "Sue is absolutely right to encourage you. And I'm quite happy doing what I do. Anyway, I'd probably soon tire of having to produce an article every month. Look, I'm genuinely delighted that we have you on our little team and I'll be glad to help you in any way I can."

"Thank you..." Elizabeth was about to continue when Helen emerged from the cottage carrying a laden tray.

"Ah! Scone time," Ben exclaimed. "All business must cease."

Helen laid the tray on the table in front of them and poured two teas. "Help yourself, Elizabeth." She smiled, then turned quickly and returned to the cottage.

"Better get cracking," Ben suggested as he picked up a scone and knife. "The evening is starting to chill."

They ate and drank in silence except for brief observations about the antics of the animals on the lawn in front of them. Elizabeth felt totally relaxed, as if she was sitting beside a favourite uncle rather than a stranger.

When they had finished, Ben picked up the tray. "Let's go inside before we get cold."

Elizabeth followed him along the gravel path and into the kitchen, where Helen was standing, mixing something in a bowl. The smell of scones still hung in the air and the warmth from the Aga made Elizabeth feel suddenly drowsy. "The scone was lovely, Helen, thank you," she drawled.

Helen put down her bowl and turned. "Somebody sounds tired." She looked at Ben. "You haven't been boring our guest with your jokes?"

"Not guilty."

"Sorry," Elizabeth said. "It's been a bit hectic at work today. I was fine until I came in here. The warmth just hit me."

At this point, Ben suggested in a fatherly fashion that she should go home and have an early night. After a few more pleasantries during which Helen invited Elizabeth to bring her swimming gear next time so they could enjoy a quick dip in the lake, Elizabeth was escorted to her car, where the warmth of their goodbyes and the enthusiasm of their waving made her feel like royalty. After driving fifty metres down the lane, she looked in the rear-view mirror. They were still waving. Elizabeth vowed to return as soon as possible.

Chapter 9

Flaming June was living up to its name. The dry spring, which had seen the mountain ghylls stop flowing and the valley streams expose their pebbled islands, was continuing into summer. In Keswick town centre, Smyth's south-facing premises, though situated in a narrow street, welcomed slices of light into Elizabeth's office.

On this first Friday of the month, Elizabeth didn't need the sun to lift her spirits. She had been flying high most of the week. On Monday she had finally received Dominic's formal job offer complete with job description and compensation package. It was all as they had discussed, and she immediately emailed her acceptance. The previous Friday she had submitted her third article to *The Keswick Tribune*, one in which readers were introduced to two thirty-something Londoners who, after ten years working in the hot-house of investment banking, had decided to "retire" and spend their millions buying up and renovating old cottages in the Lake District, using Keswick as their new base. After receiving the go-ahead from Ben Foxley, Elizabeth was subsequently told in an email from Sue, the editor, that her first article would appear in this Friday's edition.

At lunch-time she had walked across the street to the nearest newsagent and bought three copies of the paper.

Trying to remain calm, she had sauntered into a nearby coffee shop, bought a sandwich and coffee, taken a bite and a drink, and put on a show of reading the paper in a routine, unhurried manner, scanning each page slowly rather than scrambling to find where her article appeared. She wasn't sure why she behaved like this. She glanced around. None of the other customers seemed to be taking any notice of her.

When she did find the article, filling most of the top half of page five, her name in the byline, she found herself deeply affected. Whether it was excitement, relief or the recognition that this could be the first step on the road to a new life, she wasn't sure. Whatever it was, it revealed itself as an electrifying tingle throughout her body and warm, slow tears arriving in her eyes.

Through blurred eyes she read the article over and over, surprised to find that her own simple words appeared to be more important because they were now in print. Her next surprise was to find she had finished her sandwich and coffee. She looked at her watch.

Back in the office she put the three newspapers in her desk drawer. She didn't intend showing her article to Mr Smyth or Marcia because they showed little interest in anything she did, and he would probably complain about her doing two jobs. No doubt they would find out soon enough as the town chatter spread, at which point she would nullify his complaint by explaining that it was an unpaid hobby. By which time she would probably be deeply involved in another job which she definitely had to keep secret from him.

As if on cue, as Elizabeth sat at her desk thinking about

her future work with Dominic Arnet, George Smyth rushed into the office and headed towards Marcia's desk. "Porter's changed his mind," he shouted. "He's accepted Arnet's offer. We've done, we've done it."

Marcia rose quickly from her seat and threw her arms around him, and they hugged and grinned unashamedly in front of Elizabeth. She watched them with amusement and played her part by smiling back at them when they looked in her direction.

"Did Arnet offer any more money?" Marcia asked.

"Not a penny," Smyth boasted, in a tone that said, "I told you so."

"Remind me of the total price," Marcia gloated.

Smyth released her from his arms and stared at her. "Exactly £3 million. Don't you remember?"

Marcia hesitated, then found a reply, "Of course I remember. I just wanted to hear you say it out loud."

Smyth went on, "We should be able to exchange contracts and complete within a few days. There is no mortgage involved and Arnet has already had the place surveyed and received a favourable report. It just shows how confident he was that Porter would accept."

Elizabeth realised that Dominic must have deliberately arranged the survey himself, without involving her, so that she continued to look like an innocent bystander. Her mind was still reeling from Smyth's announcement that the agreed price had been £3 million. She recalled that the original asking price had been £3.51 million, which meant that Dominic had succeeded in obtaining a discount of £510,000. Surely not. She did a quick mental calculation. It was about fourteen percent discount. Now she took a calculator from her drawer and, based on the percentages Dominic had told her, worked out how much of the £510,000 would be allocated to the purchaser and how much commission would be left over for Dominic and herself to share.

While she was doing this, Smyth and Marcia hurried off to his office with their DO NOT DISTURB looks on their faces.

Their absence allowed Elizabeth to cry, "What!" when she saw the figures emerge for Dominic and herself. She couldn't believe them. There must have been some horse-trading going on that she knew nothing about, something that Dominic had yet to reveal to her. A more realistic figure would eventually emerge when the deal went through, she told herself. She could not allow herself to rely on the figures she had calculated; the let-down would be too great. And what if the deal fell through at the last minute, as property sales often did. She put the calculator back in her drawer and mentally did the same with the figures she had seen on its screen. It would be business as usual until she heard from Dominic.

Three days later she had an email from him: *Things are looking good on Fell View project. Get the champagne ready, but please don't pop the cork in your office. I know I can rely on you to stay calm.*

At the end of the following week, Smyth, having clearly rehearsed his routine announcement tone, came into the office from the street and said, "The Fell View sale has completed. The money is in our bank." He placed a small box of chocolates on Elizabeth's desk. "That's for looking after Mr Arnet until I got back," he said and stood just long enough to receive Elizabeth's thanks. Then he turned and asked Marcia to join him in his office. Equally rehearsed, Marcia followed him slowly and quietly, as if for a routine meeting.

Elizabeth put the box of chocolates in her bag. She would give them to her parents. They might need sweetening if she had to explain a large windfall to them.

Two days later, while working in her bedroom at home, researching prospective properties for Dominic on her laptop, an email from him appeared on her screen. She opened it with two nervous clicks.

It read, *Dear Elizabeth, Please check your bank account, and please don't feel guilty when you see what is in it. We have profited from the flaws of two rich men; one was greedy and the other gambled and lost. The seller asked far too high a price, which left a lot of scope for a big discount, and the buyer, like all of them, was quite happy to see us walk away with very little should only a small discount be achieved. Nobody got hurt. I reckon Porter would get at least a ten percent profit. I believe we did him a favour. Think of how many years it would have taken him to sell one apartment at a time. Remember there are projects where we make no money, so we need good days like this. Incidentally, this is the biggest commission I have ever earned, and I sincerely thank you for your part in achieving it. Next time I see you, we will open a bottle of champagne together. In the meantime – ENJOY!*

Dominic

Elizabeth stared at the screen for a long time. Her initial impulse to quickly close the window and switch to her online bank account had been overshadowed by Dominic's words. All the way through his email, he had referred to "we" and "us" as if she was his business or personal partner. Perhaps French people related to each other in a more familiar manner than the British. Perhaps it was a clever motivational technique he had learned. However it was meant, she liked it. It made her feel important.

She was about to open her bank's website when she heard her parents' raised voices downstairs. They rarely argued, so it was probably just another routine conversation. Shouting had become the normal way they conversed, evolving over the years because of her father's need to shout at the sheep and the dogs and over the sound of the tractor. As if by some osmotic process, her mother had gradually raised her voice to match him. How *was* she going to explain this to them?

Putting this concern to one side for the moment, she took a deep breath and opened up her bank's website. Another deep breath as she clicked on her current account. A new entry bearing yesterday's date appeared in the credit column. The amount was £31,750. Almost double her annual salary. Exactly the amount she had calculated using Dominic's figures and could not bring herself to believe. That meant that Dominic had earned £95,750 commission, the total between them being £127,500. Then she realised that even the industry's standard commission rate of three percent yielded £90,000 commission. This was crazy. It was as if she had been given entry to another world, a parallel world which most ordinary people could not imagine existed. *There is no such thing as easy money*, her father had preached – *not legally anyway*. Clearly, he had been unable to imagine this world. How was it possible to earn more from a few hours of conversation than he did in a year of hard graft? More importantly, how was she going to be able to move into this world when her ambition was to bring about its demise through political change?

Her mind whirled, looking for answers and finding none. She started to envisage a scenario where she refused to accept the money because of her principles. But could she do this when she knew the farm was in debt to the bank, that her father worried about keeping it going? She didn't think so. Now she recalled Dominic's advice. "Set your sights lower," he had said. "You can't change the whole world. Change what you can change. Help local causes." What could be more local than her own home? And what cause better than the wellbeing of her parents? She took one last "just to make sure" look at the staggering amount of money in her account, made her decision and switched off her laptop.

Chapter 10

A few days later on a cloudy Saturday afternoon, Elizabeth could be found wandering around a small display of second-hand cars parked outside a Keswick garage. She knew she was greatly limiting her choice by not heading for the large car showrooms situated in the coastal towns, but she believed in supporting local businesses. Her plan was to buy a small car for about £5,000, which she reckoned was enough to guarantee a reliable runner for three or four years.

After buying her car she intended to leave £3,000 of her recent windfall in her current account to give her a sense of independence, and to transfer the remainder into her father's account so that he could reduce some of his debts or upgrade some of his farm equipment. As expected, her father had been against her plan, arguing that she should use the money to build a life of her own. But he eventually gave in to her insistent demands. What Elizabeth didn't know was that his intention was to save it on her behalf rather than spend it.

After looking at all the small cars, Elizabeth was about to seek sales assistance to talk about the relative merits of a Honda Jazz and a Fiat 500 when her phone rang. It was Dominic, which meant it must be important, because his usual mode of contact was email.

He came straight to the point. "Can you be at Manchester Airport this time next weekend?"

Without hesitation, she said, "Yes." She didn't want to disappoint Dominic.

"I would like you to meet a Mr Charles Prentice and his wife, Barbara, and disabled daughter Claire, who will be arriving from Zurich. I'll email the flight details later. He is the man who bought Fell View and he wants to see what he got for his money. Normally I would come over with them, but I have appointments in the South of France next weekend which I don't want to miss.

"After seeing the property, they want to spend the weekend in the Lake District, which they have never visited before, and then fly back to Zurich on Monday afternoon. So, can you book them into a good hotel not too far from the property? And if you can't get time off work to take them back to the airport on Monday, can you arrange a quality taxi service for them?"

"What nationality are they?"

"He's English and his wife's American, according to his solicitor. I haven't met them yet. He's an early-retired oil executive who spent most of his working life abroad. Like a lot of them, he retired to Zurich to be near his money. Don't be surprised by his appearance. Apparently he spends most of his time sailing and the solicitor says he looks like a scruffy old sea dog – all long hair and shabby clothes. That's also typical of retired executives, by the way. After a lifetime of wearing formal suits, they can't wait to go native."

After a short pause, Dominic continued, "I forgot to

talk to you about your transport. Please tell me you haven't bought a car yet?"

"Not yet. But I'm looking for one right now. I'm standing in a local dealer's yard."

"Thank goodness I caught you. I won't ask what you were thinking of buying because I'm going to tell you what to buy. It's all about customer expectation and company image. For example, the Manchester pick-up next week of three adults and a wheelchair could only be done with a big car, and the client will be expecting it to be of good quality. You also have to allow for the possibility of some off-road driving. I've decided that you should buy a silver or black four-wheel drive, preferably a Land Rover, which has a British image, and no older than three years. I know it will take a large chunk of your recent commission, but think of it as an investment in your future. And no, I won't supply a company car – they destroy incentive."

For a split second Elizabeth was going to protest that she had given most of the money to her father, but then she realised how immature that would sound, how unprofessional. And now she realised that she hadn't been thinking straight about the car. Dominic was right; a business like his needed to project a smart image and provide comfort for his clients. She would have looked ridiculous turning up at Manchester Airport to meet a millionaire and his family in a tiny Fiat. "That's fine," she said as nonchalantly as she could. "There's a Land Rover garage about twenty-five miles away. I'll go there tomorrow." Looking to add to her newly found professionalism, she continued, "On the subject of company image, is there any particular type of clothes you would like me to wear…you know…like a company uniform?"

"No! No uniforms. Us lefties do not wear uniforms. Anyway, Elizabeth, you will look beautiful whatever you are wearing."

Elizabeth let the flattery go. She had never been comfortable with compliments about her appearance. "Okay, no uniforms. I'm glad."

"And don't forget to get some business cards printed. You've got one of mine. Just copy that, replace my name with yours, call yourself a *property consultant*, add your contact details and your qualifications, but keep the head office phone number on as well." A short pause, then, "Obviously, from a business perspective, it would be good if you could get a place of your own as soon as possible. Otherwise your parents could be pestered with phone calls and our clients will not take kindly to talking to them rather than you."

Before Elizabeth had time to respond, Dominic concluded, "Right, let me know how things go next weekend. I know I can rely on you to look after our clients. Take care, Elizabeth. Bye."

Elizabeth said "Bye" automatically, her mind focussed on the words *our clients*. They sent a warm glow through her. He was either the nicest man in the world, or the best motivator in the world.

Like all motorways, the M6 could be less daunting on a weekend. Gone were most of the heavy lorries, the white vans and the speeding reps. But on a summer Saturday they were replaced by weekend-only drivers and holiday-makers towing caravans. And on this particular Saturday by a young woman driving her big Land Rover for only the second time. However, other drivers need not have worried, because Elizabeth had been driving tractors and old Land Rovers on the farm since she was twelve, and was, therefore, relaxed behind the wheel of her luxurious new beast. Indeed, she was so relaxed as she stared at the tarmac ahead, winding away with grey indifference, that her mind started to drift.

She replayed the relief she felt when her father had seemed glad to return the money to her. Then the excitement of going into the car showroom, being treated like royalty because she was a cash buyer, and the following day driving away in the opulent two-year-old Discovery Sport, with low mileage and every conceivable gadget. All of this, however, tempered by her inherent doubts about the extravagance of it all. The money should have been used for other, *better* things.

Now she found herself thinking about herself and her values. Who was she? What were her values? The events of the last few weeks had only added to the feeling of confusion that had plagued her since leaving university. With her parents, particularly her father, she still felt like a young dutiful daughter. With Dominic, she felt like a naïve teenager, yet with her conquests at university, she had felt like a fully-fledged, confident, calculating woman. At university she had no doubt been influenced by the sensual energy and hedonism that always prevails where young adults congregate. Now her recollection of some of her behaviour filled her with a feeling of shame.

And, in the last few weeks, she had found herself being

swayed by money, compromising her strong left wing beliefs. Would she always remain in this chameleon state, playing a different role to fit each different situation, or would she eventually mature into someone with a consistent, definable charact... Suddenly, she had to brake as the car in front of her came to a standstill at the tail end of a long queue. The signs told her she was nearing Manchester.

Chapter 11

The pick-up at Manchester Airport had gone well. Elizabeth had been in the right place at the right time, dutifully holding a large board bearing the names Mr and Mrs Prentice.

She was glad that Dominic had warned her about Charles Prentice's appearance; otherwise she might have doubted the grey grizzly bear who ambled up to her to introduce himself. He had so much iron-grey wire on his head and face that it was difficult to see any features that could be guaranteed human. It spilled from its uncombed entanglement on his head, over the collar of his polo neck sweater, over his ears, onto his cheeks, and was matched by a dense, untrimmed moustache and beard. Out of this thicket of wire came a deep, warm voice, delivering a precise Oxford accent. *No doubt these cultured tones played a part in the rise of Charles up the corporate ladder.* It was the type of voice that had made her squirm at university. He introduced his wife, Barbara, who was pushing a wheelchair containing their daughter, Claire.

Unlike Charles, who looked as if he had slept in his forgettable clothes, Barbara was smartly dressed, and her short deep-brown hair (probably dyed) made her look much younger than her shabby husband.

Elizabeth noticed that Charles's face seemed to be set in

a permanent frown. Two deep lines between his eyebrows hovered over deep-set, squinting eyes. His right eyebrow had a diagonal white scar running through it, separating the eyebrow into two halves, the outer half being positioned slightly higher than its partner. As a result it gave that side of his face a slightly quizzical look. He looked like a man who had spent his time wrestling real grizzlies rather than attending company board meetings. There was no doubt, however, that he was a man who had wielded power.

So this is how top executives turn out. They let their hair down when they are young and again only when they are old. In between they sacrifice their humanity on the altar of their careers. Is this what my ambition might do to me? Perish the thought.

Daughter, Claire, had a wrap-around blanket over her knees, and wore a hooded jacket that made it difficult to see her features or guess her age. In spite of all the encumbrance, she appeared to be very alert, her head turning constantly.

Typical of situations where strangers are thrown together, the conversation on the drive back to the Lakes from Manchester Airport had been polite, stilted and non-specific. Charles sat in the front passenger seat and only spoke in response to Elizabeth's stimulus. She was careful not to ask questions but to stick to general topics, though she was curious as to what Charles Prentice's plans were for Fell View. She had asked Dominic, but he hadn't known and had pointed out that "people like that don't like being questioned."

The back seat was also quiet, which struck Elizabeth as unusual for a mother/daughter relationship. Glancing in her mirror she noticed that the daughter had removed her jacket's hood. Claire looked about thirty, and had very short, almost military style, blonde hair. Elizabeth wondered if this was a grow-back after some form of medical treatment.

With the silence becoming oppressive, Elizabeth asked if anyone would like some music on the radio. "As long as it's classical," Charles said. She switched on Classic FM and settled back to concentrate on enjoying driving her new car.

When, eventually, Elizabeth saw the familiar swell of the Lakeland fells touching the sky on her north-western horizon, she experienced a feeling of relief. Turning west off the M6 at Penrith, her spirits rose in time with the rise of the fells as they grew larger in her windscreen. And later, when she drove into the sanctuary of the Vale of Keswick, she was sure she felt a hug from her familiar giants.

She dropped the Prentice family off at a four-star hotel overlooking the southern end of Derwent Water. They asked to be picked up at nine thirty the following morning.

Chapter 12

Derwent Water was wearing its best Sunday outfit when Elizabeth arrived at the hotel the next morning. Without a breath of wind and under a clear, deep blue sky, it became a giant mirror reflecting the surrounding fells in perfect detail. Even the taciturn Barbara was moved to say, "Isn't that the cutest little lake," as she entered the car. Charles and Claire restricted themselves to "Good morning" though Elizabeth noticed that they couldn't take their eyes off the lake once they were settled in their seats.

She drove them around the lake via Keswick and Portinscale, planning to return, after their visit to Fell View, via the elevated mountain road on Cat Bells Fell on the other side of the lake, which would give them spectacular views.

Arriving at Fell View, Elizabeth offered to show them around. Charles hesitated for a moment then handed her the keys and said, "Lead on."

On entering the building, she repeated the tour she had made with Dominic, stepping into the background when they had something to discuss. Claire had to remain in the hall in her wheelchair while they inspected upstairs.

Surprisingly soon, they were all gathered in the hallway and ready to leave, the inspection of the house amounting to little more than a cursory glance around each room.

Outside the house, Elizabeth escorted them to the garages and gardens. Throughout the tour the Prentices seemed to view everything with a sense of detachment. There were no bursts of enthusiasm or displays of emotion of any kind. Elizabeth guessed that this was because they were used to living in luxurious houses in exotic locations as Charles's work took them around the world.

It was different, however, when she took Charles down to the lake shore. Here she sensed that his silence did not mean indifference, but awe.

And sure enough, after slowly walking among the trees along the shoreline, Charles turned to her and said, "This is *so* beautiful." There was a quiet reverence in his voice. "It is small yet there is a feeling of grandeur here; it is tame and gentle, yet we are in wild, rugged country. It is almost too..." He tried to go on but, like many before him, couldn't find the words. A slight shake of the head was all that followed. "Are all the lakes like this?" he asked as he continued to stroll along the shore.

"Yes and no," Elizabeth replied. "Yes, they are all quite small. But they are all different. Each one has its own character. Some look wild and inaccessible, others gentle and pastoral. It's because of the variety of their locations. People say that some lakes are feminine and some masculine. Derwent Water is thought of as feminine. It's known as *Queen of the Lakes*."

"Mm, I can see why – gentle, yet majestic." At this point Charles stopped walking and sat on a massive branch of an oak tree which had curled down to within two feet of the ground, just a few metres from the water. His eyes invited

Elizabeth to sit alongside him. "You seem to know the area well?"

"I've lived here all my life," Elizabeth explained. "I've walked around every lake and swam in most of them."

"Swimming…great sport…used to swim myself." He fell silent again, his eyes travelling over the spectacle before him.

Elizabeth pointed to the other side of the lake, about half a mile south of their location. "That's your hotel over there. Has it been okay for you?"

"Yes, it's been fine," Charles said absentmindedly as he swivelled his head to follow her direction.

"I understand you go sailing at home. I assume you have been told about the marina here. It's just a few minutes' walk to our left along this shoreline. And if you go left for a further two miles, you will come to another lake – Bassenthwaite – which has a sailing club where you can sail competitively."

Charles glanced to his left for a moment, then turned to make another visual sweep of Derwent Water and the surrounding fells. He sighed. "Here I am in this amazingly beautiful place wondering what I have missed all my life."

Elizabeth was familiar with this "love at first sight" reaction to the Lakes, and limited her response to, "There's lots more to see." What interested her more was the sudden change in Charles's behaviour. He had become almost gregarious, opening up to a stranger, yet being tight-lipped in the presence of his wife and daughter. Was there animosity between them or was it just the silence of familiarity? Not that it mattered to her. They would be back in Switzerland tomorrow – out of sight, out of mind.

Elizabeth made a mental note to check on the taxi she

had booked to take them back to Manchester. She had not bothered to ask George Smyth for Monday off so she could take them herself; she knew what his reply would be. Suddenly, she found herself oscillating on the tree branch as Charles eased himself off and flexed his legs. "I suppose we had better get back to the others," he said, making no attempt to hide the reluctance in his voice.

On the way back to the house, Charles continued his eulogy on Derwent Water, favourably comparing its intimacy and unspoiled natural beauty with the much larger, overdeveloped Lake Zurich. He also asked Elizabeth to take them back to the hotel so that Claire could have a rest and they could have lunch. In the afternoon he wanted Elizabeth to take them on a tour which contained one or more lakes, and included a place where they could have a coffee break.

Back at Fell View, Elizabeth was once more surprised at the lack of conversation as the family came together again. Charles said nothing about his enthusiasm for Derwent Water and the others showed no interest in what he had been doing. Elizabeth watched as Charles helped Claire out of her wheelchair and into the car. Claire managed this by putting an arm around his shoulder and leaning on him while she walked the few paces to the car. She didn't appear to have much weakness in her legs, leaving Elizabeth to conclude that she must be suffering from some debilitating disease rather than a physical injury.

Once settled in the car, Elizabeth drove them out of the grounds, turning left at the gates. "I'm taking you back to the hotel a different way," she explained. "It's a narrow old road that was cut into the flank of Cat Bells Fell by the original settlers. It's a few hundred feet above the lake and gives you a nice view of it. You'll know we are on it when we start to climb up some hairpin bends."

"Are you sure it's safe?" Barbara asked from the back seat.

Elizabeth glanced at her in the mirror. "Yes, I've driven it many times."

Five minutes later, as she approached the first steep hairpin bend, she put her foot down and felt the smooth power of her new car sweep them up and round without effort. Two more bends and she started along the relatively level section of the road which wound its narrow way along the flank of the steep fell. Soon Derwent Water revealed itself below them on their left. All heads turned to take in the panoramic view of the lake. It continued to dazzle in the late morning sun, its small, wooded islands completing a fairy-tale picture. A few tiny boats wrote Vs in its surface.

"That is really something," Claire breathed.

"Sure is," Barbara whispered.

"Is there anywhere we can stop?" Charles asked, his voice urgent.

"I'll see what I can do," Elizabeth said. "There's only a couple of places where it's safe to stop. Let's hope nobody got there before us."

Shortly afterwards, after manoeuvring around a few sheep who had claimed the road for themselves, Elizabeth pulled into a small parking space that had been roughly hacked out of the fellside. Two other cars filled the rest of the available space.

It was only a short walk to a stone bench, ideally placed to give them a bird's-eye view of the lake. Charles helped

Claire to walk to it, leaving the wheelchair in the boot. Soon all four were sitting side by side, their eyes entranced by the scene below them.

It was pleasantly warm, the humid air infused with the smell of nearby whins dressed for summer in their yellow finery. Small birds sang to each other among the shrubs and bracken, and up above a pair of buzzards glided silently in the thermals. Nobody spoke.

Minutes drifted by, then, "This is like having a seat in heaven," Charles said.

Barbara and Claire remained silent. Elizabeth smiled to herself. *The magic of the Lakes had worked again, turning a hard-headed businessman into a poet.* She imagined his words floating into the air to take their place alongside those of the famous poets who had been inspired to make the Lakes their home. When she was younger she had been surprised that well-travelled people, who had lived in exotic countries, could be so affected by the place she simply knew as home. But now she wasn't. She had heard it all before. "It is special, isn't it?" she said. "It's one of the most popular views in the Lakes. Hugh Walpole loved it so much he came to live here."

"Who?" Charles asked.

Elizabeth was surprised that such an educated man didn't recognise the name. "Sir Hugh Walpole, the novelist. He bought a house just a few hundred yards further along this road. I'll point it out as we drive past. He wrote many of his famous novels there. He called it his 'little paradise on Cat Bells.'"

"When was this?" Charles queried.

"He bought it back in 1923."

"You obviously know your history."

"The schools here are proud of the Lake District's literary connections. They take you on field trips to see where all the poets and writers lived."

"Well, I can certainly see why he wanted to live here," Charles said as he scanned the view again.

Elizabeth kept wondering when Barbara or Claire would join in their conversation or maybe change the subject, but they remained silent, occasionally smiling slightly and nodding their heads, presumably to indicate their agreement.

Now, Charles was pointing downwards in the direction of the south-western shore of the lake. "Elizabeth, do you know whose house that is down there? It's in a wonderful location."

He was pointing to the only house to be seen. It sat on a finger of rocky land which jutted out into the lake, a mini peninsula. The house was located on the northern tip of the peninsula, giving it a superb view down the full length of the lake. It was surrounded by mature woodland, making it difficult to see the whole of its structure. But it was possible to discern a boathouse and a jetty beneath overhanging branches.

"That currently belongs to Señor Pedro Sousa. He's a Brazilian who plays football for a team in Manchester. Apparently he plays for the Brazil international team also and is quite famous as a result. His main home is a mansion in Cheshire. I only know this because last week our local paper reported that he had been sold by the Manchester club to a Spanish club, and that he would be selling his holiday home on the lake. I've added it to Mr Arnet's list of potential purchases for clients, and I'm waiting to see which estate agent he uses to sell it."

"How many rooms are there?" Charles demanded.

Elizabeth hesitated, slightly taken aback by the sudden injection of urgency in Charles's voice.

The relaxed atmosphere had changed. Barbara and Claire both turned to look questioningly at Charles. He didn't acknowledge them.

"The report said it was a five-bedroom house."

"Did the report say anything about the price?"

"Yes, they mentioned a figure of between £1.5 million and £2 million. He bought it for £1.3 million a few years ago."

"Even allowing for the great location, it seems expensive for something that size," Charles declared.

"Apparently, he spent a lot of money modernising it. And the report says the package will include all of the peninsula's land, all the furniture and fittings, and a small island nearby." Elizabeth was beginning to wonder if Charles's questions represented more than just idle curiosity.

"Do you know its history? Who built it, and when?"

"Not in any detail. I remember it was built by somebody who made his fortune out of tobacco. And that must have been before the Planning Act of the 1940s. You wouldn't get permission to build there after that."

"Ah! Regulations, the graveyard of progress."

Or the saviour of an exploited planet.

"How do you get down there?" Charles pressed on. "I presume there is some sort of road somewhere, or is it accessible by boat only?"

"I'm pretty sure there is a small road through the woods further along this road, though I have never been down it."

"Let's go find it," Charles said as he started to rise from the seat.

Elizabeth registered the lack of a "please" and realised that she was beginning to get a glimpse of the real man behind the amiable persona, one who was used to giving orders and expected others to comply without question. Perhaps this explained the reticence of Barbara and Claire. Or were they yet to reveal their *true* personalities?

Back in the car, continuing slowly along the flank of Cat Bells, Elizabeth was so preoccupied with wondering why Charles was interested in the house by the lake that she almost missed pointing out Walpole's house. But she saw it just in time, standing elegantly on the steep side of the fell, and she slowed down to let the others take it in.

It was at this point that the open fell gave way to ancient woodland as the road eased gently downwards towards the valley beyond Derwent Water. Elizabeth concentrated on looking for a small branch road to her left which might take them back and down towards the house by the lake.

Half a mile later she came across it. It was no more than a gap in the dry-stone wall that lined the road, and had she not seen the narrow surfaced road beyond it, she could easily have missed it. On reflection, she realised that she had driven past this gap many times in the past without noticing it. She was about to drive through the gap when she noticed a sign mounted on a wooden post nearby. It read: *NO UN-AUTHORISED VEHICLES.* Elizabeth hesitated, stopped the car and turned to face Charles. Before she had a chance to speak, he said, "More regulations. Ignore it. Keep going."

"But I will be respons—"

"Don't worry, I'll take responsibility. I'll pay the damned fine if there is one."

Elizabeth started up again, passed through the gap and drove along the narrow road which wound its way through a dense wood. There were dozens of bends to negotiate as it snaked around huge trees and rocky knolls. After about a mile she arrived on the southwest shore of the lake. Here the road turned right and followed the shoreline. Soon they could see the peninsula jutting out into the lake, and also the magnificent view up the length of the lake. They were stopped shortly afterwards by a substantial wooden gate blocking the road. To the left of the gate, heavy wooden fencing and wire led across the woodland and disappeared into the lake; to the right the same fencing curled away into the woods. This was clearly the boundaries of the property. A sign on the gate read: *BECALMED*. Alongside, another smaller sign read: *Private Property*.

Charles and Elizabeth got out of the car and approached the gate. "I like the name of the house," Charles said. "Clearly, one of its previous owners was a sailing man."

"*Or woman.*"

Closer inspection revealed that the gate had an electrical security system attached. "Damn!" Charles exclaimed. "This is a 'by appointment only' house. We're not getting to see it today."

Approximately 100 metres beyond the gate, the roof of the house could be seen, but the rest of it was obstructed by a large rocky mound.

"I don't suppose you have a telephone number for the house?" Charles asked.

"No, sorry."

"Do the local estate agents open on a Sunday?"

"Afraid not."

"Some things never change in this country."

Elizabeth braced herself before asking, "Do I take it you are interested in buying this house?"

"I'm very tempted."

"What about Fell View?" The question came involuntarily. "Sorry, I didn't mean to pry."

"You don't think I bought Fell View to live in, do you?" Charles laughed. "That's just an investment. I haven't decided what to do with it yet."

Elizabeth was beginning to dislike Mr Prentice. His tone had intimated that her question was stupid, and his explanation had sounded like that of a boastful teenager. She felt the cold, calculating side of her nature rise to the fore. She decided she would do everything in her power to encourage him to buy the house through Dominic's company, thus relieving him of some more of his money. "Well, this is obviously a wonderful holiday home," she started. "It's in a unique location. I believe it is the only house situated right on the shoreline of Derwent Water, and with all the furniture being included, it sounds as if it would be ready to move into."

"Don't waste your breath on the sales pitch, Elizabeth. I have eyes, I can see. I've bought properties all over the world. If I want your input, I will ask for it. Just stand by."

Suitably chastened, Elizabeth remained silent. She was annoyed with herself; she should never have tried such an amateurish sales pitch with anybody, never mind a worldly man like Charles.

Charles took one last look around the area then turned and walked back to the car. Elizabeth followed behind, determined to up her game.

Charles was in the front seat talking to Barbara in the back when Elizabeth eased herself into her driving seat.

"...but why?" Elizabeth heard Barbara say.

"Why?" Charles scoffed. "How often do you get the opportunity to buy a location like this? Just look at it – it's fabulous. Then there's the boathouse, a marina and a yacht club. It's a perfect package. And it's also excellent from a security perspective."

Elizabeth glanced in her rear-view mirror and saw Barbara frown at Charles, and shake her head, and turn to look out of the window. She didn't speak.

Charles turned to face the front again. Was that anger on his face or just his permanent frown? Elizabeth soon had her answer.

"Here's what is going to happen," Charles asserted, his tone that of a dominant father scolding a naughty child. "We are going back to the hotel for lunch as planned, then Elizabeth will pick us up again at two o'clock and take us on a tour to see some other lakes." He looked over at her and raised his voice slightly, "And I would like the tour to include that yacht club you mentioned."

Elizabeth nodded her agreement while registering that Charles was, unsubtly, letting his wife know that he was serious about buying Becalmed.

Barbara's response was equally unsubtle. "I think I'll give

the tour a miss. I'm tired after all the travelling. I'll have a nap after lunch and maybe use the hotel pool later."

"Fine," Charles snapped. "I'll look after Claire."

Elizabeth took her lunch break just a few hundred yards from the hotel. She sat at an old table outside a farmhouse tea room set back from the valley road. It was swarming with holiday-makers dressed in their colourful walking gear, their abandoned backpacks a familiar hazard on the flagstones between the tables. Pugnacious sparrows and nervous tits and finches darted after dropped crumbs.

Elizabeth felt comfortable amongst these fellow lovers of her home territory. Their holiday mood was always infectious, making her see her familiar surroundings with fresh, appreciative eyes. At one point she thought about emailing or phoning Dominic to tell him about Prentice's interest in Becalmed, and to seek his advice on how to proceed. But she decided the moment wasn't right; nothing definite had happened.

Promptly at two o'clock, Elizabeth arrived outside the hotel. Charles and Claire emerged shortly afterwards, Claire having swapped her dark trouser-suit of the morning for a light fawn suit. A large brown handbag rested on her lap. Charles had not changed anything, and looked deep in thought as he repeatedly stroked his beard. This time, Charles helped Claire into the back seat and then joined her.

"We'll be at Bassenthwaite Yacht Club in about twenty minutes," Elizabeth announced.

"It's as near as that? Good!"

The afternoon went well. Charles thought Bassenthwaite Lake was "very nice", but only a princess compared to the Queen – Derwent Water. He found the yacht club "small, friendly and accessible".

On seeing the twin lakes of Crummock Water and Buttermere in their rugged valley, he became poetic again, describing them as "masculine" and like "two knights protecting their queen".

They stopped for a coffee at a farmhouse cafe in Buttermere village, then continued over Honister Pass into the sylvan valley of Borrowdale and followed the valley road back to the hotel.

Outside the hotel, Charles asked Elizabeth to wait for him while he took Claire inside. Claire gave Elizabeth a sallow smile and thanked her before being wheeled off.

On his return, Charles climbed into the passenger seat beside Elizabeth. He half turned towards her and paused before he said, "Thanks for that tour, Elizabeth. It was enjoyable and educational. Seeing those three other lakes confirmed to me that I hadn't overestimated the beauty of Derwent Water. It *is* very special. So...to get to the point. I intend to buy Becalmed."

He paused again. "Here's what I want you to do. Find out which estate agent is handling the sale. Once you have the details, let me know, via Mr Arnet, on which website I can view the property. If I am happy with what I see online, I will ask my solicitor to instruct Mr Arnet to purchase the property on my behalf, assuming the usual professional inspections and searches reveal no problems. If you accompany Mr Arnet on his inspection, please remind him to look out for any situations that could be hazardous for wheelchairs, and if there are any, make recommendations as to how they can be overcome, and obtain estimates if this involves structural alterations. Likewise with the boathouse and jetty. Any structural problems – get repair estimates.

"After my online inspection I may also ask you to obtain estimates for things like redecorating or recarpeting. And finally, I will need estimates for a security system around the perimeter of the property. This has to be the latest motion detection technology involving invisible infrared laser beams and infrared camera systems. They can use the existing wooden fence posts to hide the hardware in. Plus the usual security systems on the house itself."

Elizabeth hesitantly started to point out that there was virtually no crime in the area, but Charles cut her short. "I'm sure you're right, but we've had some bad experiences abroad and now I simply can't rest at night unless I know we have the best security around us. Now, I haven't discussed this yet, but it may be that we decide to make this our main home, so bear that in mind if it becomes relevant in your dealings. Personally, I'm getting a bit restless in Zurich – it must be the five-year itch. And it would be nice to get back to conversing in my native language again."

This lapse into personal revelation surprised Elizabeth. It was out of character.

"Will you be able to remember all this, or do you need to write it down?"

Elizabeth hesitated. "I'm sure I'll remember it...but I'll write it down in my notebook before I drive away. I assume you will be discussing the price you want to pay with Mr Arnet?"

"Indeed I will. It will be whatever price it takes to ensure the house is mine. I will not be beaten on this one."

Charles opened the passenger door, walked around the front of the car and stood at Elizabeth's window, which was already wound down. "Thanks again, Elizabeth. This visit has been a real eye-opener for me. It might well have set my course for the next few years. With a fair wind I should be seeing you again in a few weeks' time when Becalmed is mine. Goodbye for now." With that he turned and walked towards the hotel.

Elizabeth sat back and breathed a sigh of relief. She was tired and puzzled, but also exhilarated. A little tired by the driving, but mostly by having to concentrate on his every word, and completely baffled by his attitude. He seemed to be disconnected from his wife and daughter. From what she could see, they had had very little say in his decision to change their lives. He talked about the house being his, not theirs. Everything was about *him*.

She couldn't imagine her father planning to move house without consulting her and her mother. At the end he had made no mention of Fell View, the main purpose of his visit. It was as if, in pursuit of his new target, his £3 million investment had been forgotten. Perhaps his mind was slipping. After many years of executive responsibility, it would not be surprising. Or maybe it was a reaction to a life of responsibility. From now on he intended to be deliberately irresponsible, a form of second childhood. One way or another, her first dealings with the rich had also been an eye-opener for her. She had learned how easy it was for them to get things done, even to change their lives on a whim. However, if the Prentices were typical, the old adage that "money can't buy happiness but makes misery easier" appeared to be true.

She was exhilarated because apart from the sales pitch slip-up, she thought she had handled the visit quite well. And she had probably played a major part in achieving new business for Dominic, would probably earn some more commission, and had a few interesting projects to get her teeth into should the sale go ahead. The only cloud on this horizon was Smyth. Where was she going to find the time to work for him and write her column for the paper and sort out all the stuff that Charles asked for? And what if Smyth won the instruction to sell Becalmed? She would have to cross those bridges later, she decided. Right now, she had Charles's instructions to write down. She opened the glove compartment, took out her notebook and pen and started to write.

Chapter 13

Monday morning saw Elizabeth at her desk, staring out of Smyth's rain-spattered window. An army of holidaying families trudged past, their waterproof hoods covering their heads, giving them a uniformity they didn't seek. Why were school holidays held during the wettest month of summer?

Elizabeth wondered if Charles Prentice would have fallen in love with Derwent Water if it had rained like this yesterday; would he have even noticed Becalmed? To decide to change his and his family's life, and to spend that much money after only a short visit, still puzzled her.

She had tried to phone Dominic last night, but he wasn't answering. So she had sent him a long email detailing all that had happened during Prentice's visit. In it she had asked him about the best way to discover the name of the estate agent handling the sale. She had read in trade magazines in her office that some properties never appear on the market because the seller's agent already has people on his books waiting for that type of desirable property. She had to stop that happening if possible, or at least make sure that Dominic's name was on that waiting list.

During morning coffee break she decided to check her mobile phone. Marcia was out of the office and Smyth was in his own office. A long email from Dominic awaited her. Soon her eyes were widening as she read on. After his initial congratulations for a job well done, he more or less ordered her to quit working for Smyth immediately so that she could concentrate on the Becalmed project. He said he would take her on full-time for the same salary as Smyth paid her. Her commission would remain at twenty-five percent as previously agreed. He also reminded her to get her own place as soon as possible.

He went on to explain that he knew about Pedro Sousa being sold to a Spanish club, the cost of his transfer making news all over Europe. Dominic had phoned Sousa's Manchester club, who eventually put him through to their legal team. They had told him that Sousa's house sale was being handled by an estate agent in Penrith, part of a large group whose head office was in Manchester. He had spoken to their manager, who had promised to give him the opportunity to bid once all the details were finalised. Dominic reminded her that he had yet to receive any instructions from Prentice's solicitor and could therefore not make a bid until that came through.

Later in the email he asked Elizabeth to visit the estate agent in Penrith to introduce herself and to confirm their client's keen interest, and to find out if they had taken any photographs of the property for their online advertising. If the property doesn't get advertised online, Dominic pointed out, then Charles Prentice won't be able to see what it looks like. In anticipation of that event, Elizabeth should try to obtain copies of any photographs to email to him.

What a dynamo Dominic is. He had personally dealt with her immediate questions, saving her a lot of worry because of her inexperience, offered her a full-time job and thought through their next moves, all before ten o'clock on a Monday morning.

Keeping an eye out for intruders, Elizabeth emailed an acknowledgement thanking Dominic, informing him that she would visit the Penrith estate agent as soon as possible.

Elizabeth didn't have a contract. Smyth had offered her only a six-month trial period. She decided to tell him she was leaving on Friday of that week and would also need tomorrow off for personal reasons. This would be used to go to Penrith to visit the estate agent handling Becalmed.

The next morning, her half hour's drive to Penrith was taken up mostly with thinking about her parents' reaction to Dominic's offer of full-time employment. They had been pleased because she was pleased, but she sensed that deep down they were worried she was moving from local security, however poorly paid, to take up with a high-flying foreigner they had never met, a man who could be about to lead her off the straight and narrow. She believed that they were wrong, but she still had her own nagging doubts – belief was not certainty.

Smyth had been true to character when she told him she was leaving. He had quickly wiped the initial shock from his face then put on a show of taking the news in his stride. "Ah well," he had said, "it's another call to the job centre for me then." It was clearly his twisted way of trying to belittle Elizabeth rather than thanking her for her contribution. He had not even asked her where she was going. *He'll soon find out.*

Arriving in Penrith, Elizabeth felt nervous as she parked

and set off walking towards the town centre. On reaching the estate agent's office, she stood, hesitant, on the glistening wet pavement. Here she was, still employed as a receptionist, about to present herself as a property consultant. She found herself looking up and down the street, delaying the moment. Cars hissed by. People walked by. The world was not interested in her.

Just do it, you wimp. She took a deep breath, entered the office, smiled at the middle-aged receptionist (Margaret on her name tag), said she had an appointment with the manager and handed over her card.

Her meeting with Robert Thomson (call me Bob), the immaculately suited young manager, went better than expected. Elizabeth suspected that this was because he was taken with her. She had seen that hungry "how can I please you?" look before. Not only would he be pleased to email all the photographs they had taken of Becalmed to Mr Arnet, but he would also send a video made by Mr Sousa himself shortly after he had completed his modernisation programme.

When saying their goodbyes, Thomson had held onto her hand longer than necessary and said, "I hope I can be of service to you in the future. Please don't hesitate to contact me at any time."

Before she left the office, Elizabeth picked up their brochure on properties to rent, and before she left Penrith she picked up more rental brochures from other estate agents in the town centre. She was about to start looking for a flat of her own and knew that flats for rent in the Keswick area were very scarce. She didn't want to move to Penrith, but it was the obvious alternative, being on the west coast main railway line and the M6 motorway.

Back home on the farm that afternoon, she laid the brochures out on her bed and prepared to read through them. Through her half-open window she heard a loud bang and the bleat of a sheep. *Must have kicked one of the sheep-dip containers.* She returned to the mundane job of looking at brochures. Then it struck her. There was nothing mundane about what she was doing. She was about to embark on a defining moment in every young adult's life. She took a moment to close her eyes. *Here we go – new job, new flat. Time to fly the nest.* When she opened her eyes again, they were starting to moisten.

Chapter 14

Elizabeth spent her final three days in Smyth's office working flat out, trying to leave her replacement as clean a start as possible. She restricted her contacts with Dominic to evenings only. On Tuesday evening he had acknowledged receipt of the photographs and video from Thomson, said they were excellent and had already forwarded them to Charles Prentice. He felt sure they would persuade him to buy. As usual, he praised her efforts in obtaining them. He was now waiting to hear from Prentice's solicitor.

She also "cleared the decks" by completing an unfinished article for Welcome to the Lakes. It featured Brendan Miller, a retired theatre director, and his wife Stephanie, retired actress (mostly theatre). They had moved from their rented apartment in central Birmingham to a new block of rental apartments recently erected on the edge of Keswick, specifically targeted at the retirement market. Elizabeth viewed this as yet another example of the indifference of society to the needs of the young.

The Millers had led a colourful life and their anecdotes made completing the 500-word article relatively easy. They had come to Keswick not to walk the fells like most retirees, but to relax in beautiful surroundings, make new friends and hopefully get involved with the town's theatre and many other social groups.

On finishing the article, Elizabeth had the idea of taking it to Ben Foxley's cottage so that he could check it while she went for a swim in the lake with Helen before the summer's warmth disappeared. She felt the need for a dose of physical activity after all the recent car driving and office work. She rang them with the proposition, and they said they would be delighted to see her on Friday evening.

Her last day at Smyth's passed like any other and when it was time to clear her desk and say her goodbyes, only Marcia was present. Smyth had made his usual Friday afternoon absence excuses, but everybody knew he was on the golf course. Marcia gave her a perfunctory hug and wished her well but still made no enquiry as to her future plans. Elizabeth walked away without regret, but she knew she would always remember Smyth's with fondness because of that one day when Dominic walked in and changed her life.

On arrival at the Foxleys' cottage, Helen insisted they fuelled up with a cup of tea and a scone before swimming. Ben, of course, said he needed the same to see him through the arduous task of reading Elizabeth's article.

The recent wet spell had passed, and Helen and Elizabeth walked down to the lake and entered the water on a calm, blissfully warm evening. Neither wore wetsuits and after recovering from the initial cold water shock, they set off to swim around Scarness Bay, keeping reasonably close to the shore. At first they chatted as they swam along, but then the hypnotic rhythm of their strokes took over and both fell silent. Elizabeth, as usual, fell into a trance-like state, feeling so relaxed she could go to sleep. All the stresses and strains of the last two weeks leached out of her and dispersed in her wake, her kicking feet sending them on their way.

Almost an hour later they emerged back at their starting point, and high-stepped ashore with silly grins on their flushed faces. They didn't need to say how much they'd enjoyed it; the grins said it all.

Back in the cottage, Ben had dinner ready, after which they sat and talked. Both Ben and Helen showed a keen interest in Elizabeth's new job, at one stage sounding a little like her own parents as they warned her to watch out for pitfalls. They were up to date on the Sousa story and looked forward to hearing more about the new owners of Becalmed if the sale went through.

When Elizabeth brought up the subject of leaving home and looking for a flat, Helen asked her what her requirements were. "Nothing special," Elizabeth explained. "Just the usual basics – somewhere to eat, sleep, wash, work, relax and park my car. And with good mobile reception and broadband speed."

"Would you be interested in a little cottage?" Helen asked.

"Well...I suppose so...if I could afford it. But cottages to rent are rarer than flats around here."

Helen went on. "There's a two-bedroom cottage just a short distance from here coming on the market to rent at the end of next month. You passed it on the way here; it's part of Cranford Manor. The manor was split into apartments a few years ago. We know the owners of one of them, a Mr and Mrs Andrews. They own a three-bedroom apartment plus an attached two-bedroom cottage which they have rented out for holidays since they moved here. Mrs Andrews told me recently that when this holiday season is over at the end of September, they are going to stop renting it out for holidays because it is quite time consuming. So they are hoping to rent it out long term to somebody local."

Elizabeth shrugged. "It sounds ideal, but in that location and with two bedrooms, it's going to attract couples, possibly with children, so it's bound to be too expensive for me."

"Don't give up yet, Elizabeth. Mrs Andrews showed me round once. The rooms are very small, the kitchen is tiny. It's the sort of place a family can put up with for two weeks' holiday but not for much longer. Long term, I would say it is ideal for one person but no more. Next time I see Mrs Andrews, I'll ask her what rent they are going to charge, and I'll put in a good word for you. Have you worked out what you can afford to pay yet?"

Elizabeth had already done her sums when looking through the Penrith flat brochures. She had based her budget on her basic salary only. "I was expecting to pay about £600 per month for a one-bedroom flat. A two-bedroomed flat would be at least £700, which I could do at a push, but that would be my limit. I'm sure Mrs Andrew's cottage will be much more than that."

Helen smiled. "Leave it with me. I'm sure money won't be the only consideration. After their bad experiences with unruly guests, I'm sure they would be delighted to have someone like you."

Elizabeth thought Helen was being naïve; there would be plenty of decent local couples quite willing to pay the going rate. "Thanks, Helen," she said and left it at that.

The rest of the evening passed in pleasant small talk, and it was dark when Elizabeth walked out to her car, which attracted their admiring comments. As she climbed into the driver's seat, Ben handed over her article. It had not been discussed at all in their after dinner chat, and Elizabeth had forgotten about it. "Perfect as usual." Ben smiled.

Chapter 15

Arriving back at the farmhouse, Elizabeth had a brief chat with her mother, who had waited up for her, her father having gone to bed. She told her about the lovely evening she had spent with the Foxleys, but she did not mention the discussion about Mr and Mrs Andrews' cottage.

Until she signed a rental agreement on a flat, she was saying nothing about leaving home. She needed to be able to walk out on her parents' disappointment, not live with it.

Up in her bedroom, she checked her emails. A lengthy one from Dominic had arrived two hours ago. He had finally received instructions from Prentice's solicitor to go ahead with the purchase of Becalmed. Dominic had insisted that his standard three percent commission must be used in this instance, and the solicitor had eventually agreed. That meant, on a property costing approximately £2 million, the commission would be about £60,000 and her share would be £15,000. Once again, Elizabeth found it hard to grasp that large amounts of money were so easily spent and earned in the world of the rich. If the deal did go through, perhaps she could consider renting Mr and Mrs Andrews' cottage for a year, by which time future earnings should be revealed and she could judge whether to stay there or move on.

Dominic went on to say that he had agreed to carry out

organising Charles's extra requests, such as redecoration and security systems, free of charge. Somehow this made Elizabeth feel better about the money she was about to earn. All this assumed that they would be successful with the purchase, but who knew who else was out there desperate to make this unique location their new home. Finally, Dominic asked if she felt she could cope with negotiating the purchase with the Penrith estate agent. If not, he would be happy to fly over.

Had she not already met Robert Thomson, Elizabeth would have asked Dominic to fly over, but now she believed that she could sweet-talk Thomson into selling the property to her client. She was also keen to demonstrate to Dominic that she was prepared to take responsibility, thus saving him time and expense.

Early the next morning, with the sound of the old tractor coughing into life coming through her window, she emailed her reply to Dominic. She told him she was prepared to do the negotiation and awaited his instructions on how to proceed on price and how to deal with competition.

Her cooked breakfast was ready when she arrived downstairs. It always was on a Saturday, her mother apparently happy to keep up a long-standing tradition. "A proper breakfast," she called it. Elizabeth flashed forward to living alone in a flat. She couldn't imagine cooking a proper breakfast for herself. Perhaps she could call at the farm every Saturday morning, on the pretence that she was doing her familial visiting duty. Maybe she could bring her washing at the same time.

Back in her room an email from Dominic awaited

her. His instruction on price was to offer the asking price immediately, on condition that the agent took the property off the market. If the agent said no, then she was to offer a further £50,000, and if still no, go to £2 million. If the agent still said no, she was to tell him we would have to consult with our client.

Elizabeth was still shocked at the world she had moved into. Bidding in chunks of £50,000? This was the total price of some houses in the poorer areas of Cumbria. Her new world was going to take some getting used to.

She lost no time in telephoning the Penrith estate agent's office. Thomson said he would be delighted to see her at 10 a.m. on Monday morning. He also told her that she was just in time because they had finalised the property details and were about to start advertising in the press and online that very Monday.

In the afternoon, Elizabeth went into town and bought a navy blue business suit comprising jacket and skirt, plus two white blouses, two pairs of tights and a pair of navy blue high heels. Back home she put them on and practised walking up and down the hall of the farmhouse. She was not used to tights, skirts or high heels, but she knew they were a necessary evil in the business world.

Her parents gathered to watch her, teasing her mercilessly as she tottered along. But when she had finished they both said, "You look grand, lass."

Monday dawned to find Elizabeth standing, nervously, outside the estate agent's office at 9.50 a.m. She had risen early, spent the extra time on her appearance, including applying a small amount of make-up, and after a breakfast of porridge and coffee made by her hovering mother, she had left the farmhouse early.

On the drive to Penrith, she kept thinking about the incredible change in her life over just a few weeks. Here she was, ex-receptionist, in a new car, in new clothes, preparing to negotiate the purchase of an expensive property on behalf of a millionaire from Switzerland. All this without experience or training. "Thrown in at the deep end" was an experience she enjoyed in the swimming pool, but she wasn't sure she was going to enjoy this version of it.

Chapter 16

After her meeting with Robert Thomson in Penrith, Elizabeth drove back to Keswick feeling disappointed. The meeting had not been easy. It had been *too* easy. It transpired that Thomson was more intent on impressing her than she him. The difference was she was doing it for business reasons, whereas he was obviously intent on building a personal relationship. He fawned over her, holding her chair while she sat down, serving coffee in china cups, ordering the rest of the staff not to disturb them. Then he tried to guide the initial small talk along personal lines, asking where she lived, what she did in her spare time. Elizabeth had seen where he was heading and eventually managed to steer the conversation on to a business footing.

When she had offered the asking price of £1.8 million for Becalmed, with the proviso that Thomson took the property off the market, he immediately agreed. "No point in making life difficult for each other is there, Elizabeth? My client gets what he asked for, your client gets what he wants, you get what you want, and we get what we want – a quick sale without expenditure on advertising and accompanied viewings. Everybody wins."

They had shaken hands on the deal, Thomson again holding on too long. Thomson thanked her profusely and said he hoped this was the start of a fruitful relationship between their two companies. Before he had a chance to say anything else, Elizabeth had quickly excused herself with the lie that she had another appointment waiting.

Back in the car, she couldn't throw off a feeling of disappointment even though the outcome had been successful. *I didn't* achieve *anything. I didn't have to work hard. It was all too easy. I am going to earn lots of money for doing very little – much less than I did as a receptionist.* Her left wing alarm bells were ringing again.

Had she succeeded simply because of her looks? Thomson was clearly in her thrall. Had Dominic also chosen her because of her looks? Had his highlighting of her academic achievements when he offered her the job just been a smokescreen? If so, what should she do about it? Should she just go along with it? After all, what was wrong with being admired, having an easy, well-paid life?

But it just didn't feel right. She needed to *earn* any success that came her way. Achievement through hard work was in her genes. Could her new life among the rich be leading her to moral perdition?

She waited until she was back at the farmhouse before emailing Dominic with the good news, including Thomson's request for a written offer.

She took some time, and pleasure, in disposing of her business suit and shoes, and sharing lunch with her mother, before returning to her room to check if Dominic had replied.

Tu es magnifique were his opening words. Elizabeth dismissed being called magnificent, putting it down to

Gallic excess. But she was intrigued to see he had used the word *tu* indicating a personal or intimate connection, rather than the formal *vous*. He may have simply been casual with his language, but Elizabeth suspected not. Perhaps this was the beginning of his subtle pursuit of her. If so, Elizabeth suddenly realised, she wouldn't mind being caught.

Dominic went on to say he would keep in touch as the project progressed, including informing her what extras Prentice wanted and when. He ended by reminding her of her need to find a place of her own.

He was always pushing things forward, Elizabeth realised. She just hoped she could keep up with him. For the rest of that day, she decided to, once again, look through the local flat rental market. Now, however, she hoped she could not find anything suitable for the next few weeks. With the prospect of more commission on the horizon, she had now set her sights on the Andrews' cottage.

Chapter 17

Towards the end of September, Elizabeth received a phone call from Helen telling her that, with the final guests about to leave the cottage, Mrs Andrews was offering Elizabeth the chance to take a look at it before she advertised it locally for long-term rent.

Elizabeth thanked Helen and made arrangements to see the cottage the following day. She did not reveal her plans to her parents.

Pine Cottage turned out to be a bit of an oddity. It looked as if it had been added to the main structure of Cranford Manor as an afterthought. It had a series of steps to its entrance because of the different land level in the vicinity. Built of random stone, the manor itself had a somewhat gothic appearance. It had been built in the nineteenth century by a baron who used it as his holiday lodge, for the purpose of hunting, shooting and fishing. He had surrounded the manor with extensive gravel drive areas for the turning of horses and carriages, interspersed with lawns and surrounded by high hedges. Beyond all of this he had imported trees from around the world, including giant Canadian redwoods, and surrounded his little empire with them, giving the manor the appearance of being hidden away in the depths of a mighty forest. He had, however, omitted planting trees at the front of the manor so that he and his guests could enjoy panoramic views over nearby Bassenthwaite Lake. Finally, he had erected a stable block and two large entrance gates.

Pine Cottage had served as the residence of the head butler, with the rest of the servants being housed above the stable block.

All of this history was imparted to Elizabeth by Mrs Andrews as she showed her around the cottage and grounds. Needless to say, it was a history which did not impress Elizabeth, being another example of the excessive privilege she abhorred. She drew some comfort from the fact that Pine Cottage had been the home of a servant, and that people like the Baron had been gradually replaced by people like the Andrews.

The interior of the cottage was also quirky. The main downstairs living area was an open plan set-up, but the lounge, dining and kitchen areas added up to little more than one good-sized room. Within it the floor levels changed for no apparent reason, but who knew what the head butler had had to contend with in his day. There was no room in the tiny kitchen for clothes washing or drying machines, the laundry facilities being housed in a cellar of the main house just a few metres from the cottage. The downstairs was completed with a smallish bedroom into which a double bed had been squeezed and a small, modern bathroom. Upstairs, built into the eaves was another double bedroom with roof windows and a storage area.

Looking out through the downstairs windows, Elizabeth could see huge trees in all directions, the stable block, and a gravelled area where she could park her car. Somewhere beyond the trees she knew Ullock Pike and Skiddaw loomed, but there were none of the open fell views she was used to.

All in all she decided that its pros greatly outweighed its cons. She would be only three miles from Keswick, about eight miles from home, totally secure in a beautiful location with good friends nearby (her parents would like that), have space upstairs to make a perfect office, and best of all, the cottage came complete with furniture, which would save her a lot of time and money.

Mrs Andrews also reassured her that it had good mobile phone reception and broadband speed.

A tall, smartly dressed woman in her sixties, Mrs Andrews had been friendly but business-like throughout, and when she informed Elizabeth that she had taken advice as to the cottage's potential rental value, Elizabeth braced herself for bad news.

"One agent said £1,000 per month, and another said £900 per month," Mrs Andrews told her. By now they were sitting in her lounge, sharing a cup of tea with Mr Andrews, a large, jowly man who sprawled in his armchair like a benign bulldog. "So we were going to put it on the market at £950 per month." She looked at Elizabeth without expression.

Elizabeth tried to hide her disappointment. Mrs Andrews glanced across at her husband and a smile passed between them before she turned to Elizabeth. "Don't worry, Elizabeth, we wouldn't ask a single girl to pay that much, especially not a friend of our good neighbours, Helen and Ben."

"You did promise not to hold drug-induced parties every weekend, didn't you?" Mr Andrews said.

"I do now."

After the laughter had died down, Mrs Andrews said, "How does £800 per month sound? Could you cope with that? That would be fixed for the first year, after which we would review it."

"That sounds wonderful," Elizabeth said, the figure being almost exactly the figure she thought she could manage if she received commission on the purchase of Becalmed.

With the paperwork signed, Elizabeth spent the next two hours going around the cottage again, making notes of the items she needed to bring with her when she moved in in five days' time. She was so excited she found it hard to concentrate, but she knew it would be easy to deal with any oversights.

Before returning to the farmhouse, she called to tell Ben and Helen the news that she was about to become their new neighbour. They seemed more excited than she was, talked of working and swimming together, and offered to help in any way possible.

She drove back to the farmhouse by instinct, her mind a whirlpool of excitement, detail retention and the worry of responsibility.

As she drove into the farmyard, she saw her parents larking about with what turned out to be a wet sponge. They were throwing it at each other as they dodged about the yard, startled hens exploding into the air all around them. Elizabeth smiled.

All she had to do now was tell them she was leaving.

Chapter 18

October started as it often did in the Lake District, with surprisingly dry, sunny weather, giving the swollen lakes time to empty their excess rain into the Irish Sea before the winter storms filled them up again. The rushing mountain ghylls faded to a trickle and finally disappeared, leaving their scars, marking their territory for future use. Migrant birds gathered in flocks before their long journeys, though some travelled alone, secure in their own strength.

Humans also took advantage of this time. Silver-haired tourists seeking peace and space moved in to take the place of school-holiday families.

Locals put away their outdoor furniture, tidied their gardens, enjoyed more parking space in town, and some, like Elizabeth, moved house.

It only took three journeys, using her mother's car and her own to transfer her worldly goods from the farmhouse to Pine Cottage. Her mother revelled in the activity, being one of those women who are happiest when employed. She had in fact been disappointed when, after the shock of Elizabeth's leaving announcement had dissipated, she discovered that Pine Cottage was furnished. Nothing would have given her greater pleasure than to help her daughter furnish and decorate her first home. On seeing Pine Cottage for the first time, she told Elizabeth she was delighted that she had found such a nice place so near to home. Within a few days she seemed to have come to terms with the reality of Elizabeth's new status.

Her father, as expected, had been less enthusiastic about losing his little girl to the big bad world. He didn't say as much, but his silences told his wife and daughter that he was accepting the situation reluctantly. Both knew, however, that his mood would eventually pass, and he would always be there to help.

Dominic, of course, was pleased with the news, and was the first person she contacted when her phone line and computer were installed. He brought her up to date with the Becalmed project, which, apparently, was progressing swiftly, both sets of solicitors keen not to earn the wrath of a rich client.

His main news was that Charles Prentice had decided to make Becalmed his main home while keeping his property in Zurich for occasional holidays, which would satisfy his wife's need for a slice of city life now and then. It looked as though completion could be as early as the end of October, which was why Dominic suggested that Elizabeth made preliminary enquiries now regarding the supply of a security system. He also suggested she compiled a list of local carpet suppliers. Apparently, Pedro Sousa had installed ceramic floor tiling in every room, no doubt to make it feel like the Brazilian houses he was used to. Not surprisingly, Prentice did not think this was suitable for a British climate and intended to have it all fitted with carpet.

Mid-October saw Elizabeth settled in Pine Cottage, all systems functioning. She filled her days working on Dominic's projects and her nights collecting and compiling information for her latest Welcome to the Lakes article. This month's article was to be about Dr and Mrs Kinnear, retired GP and physiotherapist who were still action junkies – cycling, walking, climbing, swimming, sailing, canoeing, hang-gliding, etc. Coming from East Anglia, theirs had been a life-long ambition to retire to the Lakes, where all their action pursuits could be enjoyed "on the doorstep". They planned to climb every Wainwright and swim every lake before their seventieth birthdays. To make sure they were close to the action, they had bought a property in Borrowdale.

As Elizabeth organised her life into what might be loosely described as a routine, she began to realise that she had left little time for herself. The opportunities she had to enjoy her own leisure pursuits of swimming, walking and meeting friends for a drink were now few and far between.

She accepted this situation stoically, realising that this was the burden most young adults had to bear when leaving the nest and starting a career. If, working late at night alone in her cottage, she started to feel just a little sorry for herself, she recalled her father's lecture about the girls working in the fish factory, and she soon pulled herself together.

November, that most dire of months, signalling the start of a downward spiral of bad weather and low morale, with just the slight visual compensation of a last gasp of autumn colours, passed much the same as October for Elizabeth. She had little time to dwell on the discomforts of fog, rain, cold and early darkness as the demands of work filled her days and nights.

The highlight for her had been early in the month when, just before Charles Prentice and his family were due to arrive at Becalmed, she had been instructed to accompany a firm of carpet fitters to the property and oversee the fitting of new carpets. It had taken three days, during which she took the opportunity to have a good look around the house, the grounds and the boathouse. Even the dull November weather could not detract from the magic location, the glorious view. At one point, during the fitters' lunch break, she had walked out of the front door, down the path between the lawns and stood on the wooden jetty above the motionless lake. The low, grey sky had generously shared its colour with all it looked down on, enveloping the whole scene with a soft, grey uniformity and stillness. The atmosphere was one of mystery and other-worldliness. Elizabeth held her breath; she had no choice. This was indeed a special place.

Before returning to the house, she looked around her and imagined, with envy, being the owner of Becalmed. This had been swiftly followed by her usual feeling of guilt at coveting the fruits of the capitalist system.

Although, as requested, she had gathered together estimates for the security systems, when it came to fitting them on site, Prentice had not asked for any assistance. He intended to personally supervise their installation, having had experience of them in other countries.

The Prentices had taken up residence at Becalmed during the first week in November. Elizabeth had not been contacted by them then or since. This had left her feeling disappointed, used. She thought she had made a connection with them. She had seen them not just as clients but as a family moving into her neighbourhood. In her world neighbours usually kept in touch. She had also hoped to interview them for her article series. They, presumably, had seen her as a hired worker and nothing else.

When discussing this briefly with Dominic during a late night phone call, he had laughed and said, "You'll get used to it. In their world you don't make friends; you make money. Console yourself with the money you took off them. Would you rather have their friendship or their money? Goodnight, Elizabeth."

He had put the phone down, assuming he had clarified the situation with a question that could only have one answer. Having recently received £14,250 into her bank account, her share of the commission, Elizabeth could see that the answer did seem obvious.

But was it? She still wasn't comfortable with the ease with which this money was made. She felt as though she was exploiting the rich. "So what!" she could hear Dominic say. "They have been exploiting the poor since time began. And the poor could never afford it. They can."

"Two wrongs don't make a right," she heard herself reply. "We are in danger of becoming them."

Chapter 19

Early on a December morning, a yawning Ben Foxley, wrapped in his navy blue dressing gown, walked down the stairs and into the kitchen where he planned to make a pot of tea and to take a cup up to a still dozing Helen.

The storm-force wind and rain that had pummelled the cottage for two days and nights, and had woken him on a number of occasions, continued to roar and hiss.

For some reason the weather people had recently decided to give storms a name. This one they had decided to call Desmond, a name which for Ben conjured up a mild-mannered, neatly dressed pensioner who enjoyed bowling and afternoon tea dances. A more inappropriate name was hard to imagine as the incessant cacophony continued. If it had to be a D, they should have called it Dante.

As he passed the kitchen window, he glanced out to see if the mallards and pheasants had turned up for breakfast on the lawn. Sure enough, he saw two mallards pass across his vision. But there was something different about them. Where was that rolling swagger of theirs? He took a closer look and blinked in disbelief. They weren't walking across the lawn; they were paddling.

Heart racing, he dashed back out of the kitchen and into the conservatory. Here he opened the door to the garden and looked outside. The cottage now stood on the very edge of the lake. It had risen and expanded by 200 metres during the night and now sat lapping just five centimetres below the step into the conservatory. Looking across the lawn he could see that the water had already claimed the bottom layer of logs in his log store. He closed the door and hurried back through the conservatory, taking some comfort from the fact that he had to take another step up into the main living area of the cottage.

He raced upstairs, two steps at a time, rushed into the bedroom and shook Helen awake. He tried to speak calmly. "We need to get moving. The garden is flooded – the lake is at the door. We need to get those sandbags from the shed. I'll get dressed and see to them, if you could start moving things out of the conservatory into the hall. Wait for me to help with the heavy stuff." He knew he didn't need to say anything else. Helen was always calm in an emergency.

As far as Ben and Helen could tell, the cottage had never been flooded in its long history and certainly the random shape of the original walls suggested as much. But a few years ago the lake had come up to the bottom of the garden and as a result they had decided to carry a stock of sandbags. These were stored in an old coal-house at the back of the cottage.

The slope of the land meant that the back of the cottage was approximately thirty centimetres higher than the front, with the back entrance being almost level with the land. The ground here was covered in Lakeland stone chippings and was where they parked their car. This meant that for the time being they were safe within the living area of the cottage and could eventually retreat via the back door should the water rise further.

Ben dressed quickly, throwing on whatever was nearest, hurried downstairs and picked up his gardening anorak, a cap and his wellingtons in the back porch.

In the old coal-house he loaded two sandbags into a barrow and wheeled it around the side of the cottage to the garden. He planned to build a barrier of six to eight bags, and then leave some more bags inside the conservatory at the step up into the house.

As he got on with this work, Ben could see Helen through the conservatory window. She was busy taking items from the conservatory into the hall.

It took them about an hour to complete their tasks, after which they decided to have some breakfast. The seating had yet to be removed from the conservatory, but they reckoned, because it was light, they could swiftly move it if needed.

They soon had their cold hands wrapped around cups of tea and they sipped and said nothing until the cups were empty.

As Helen dished up two large bowls of porridge, Ben switched on the local radio station. Its normal programmes continued as usual but were perpetually interrupted with news of the storm and its effects. As the statistics and tales of disaster built up, it soon became clear that this was no ordinary winter storm, but one that was breaking statistical records as well as people's hearts. There was, however, some good news. Forecasters predicted that the rain would cease in Cumbria within the next two hours.

Ben and Helen looked at each other across the breakfast

table. Experience told them that their troubles might not yet be over. The rain might stop, but the rivers and mountain ghylls and saturated fells would continue to release millions of gallons of water into the lakes for some time to come. It was now a race. Could the lakes empty themselves quicker than they filled up?

Ben reached across and took hold of Helen's hand.

Chapter 20

A few days later Ben and Helen were once again sitting in their conservatory, having just finished replacing all the furniture. They had been lucky. The lake had continued to rise until it was just over the outside step, but only a trickle of water had penetrated the sandbags and reached the floor of the conservatory. They had been able to contain the wooden floor's dampness to within a metre of the outside door, after which the water receded. Hot air blowers had restored the floor to near normal.

During those few days Ben had also been extremely busy, along with other local and national media journalists, revealing the full horror of the storm. Cumbria had been at the centre of what the weather people called an extratropical cyclone. Record amounts of rain had fallen, causing damage on an epic scale, creating scenes reminiscent of Third World catastrophes.

Major and minor roads and railways were flooded and blocked by landslides, 5,000 homes were flooded, 40,000 homes lost electricity, 140 major and minor bridges collapsed. Villages at the foot of fells had been severely flooded and suffered considerable damage as hundreds of tonnes of rocks, boulders and trees were swept down once quiet streams. Some villages had been cut in half as centrally situated bridges collapsed. Towns such as Keswick and Cockermouth suffered major damage as the rivers running through them breached existing flood defences and deposited mud, trees and boulders throughout the streets and parks. Shops and supermarkets were inundated. Farms were particularly badly hit as sheep, cattle and other animals were drowned, bridges washed away, walls collapsed, fields filled with rubble, trees and mud; landslides filled their yards. Forest trees situated on steep, saturated slopes lost their grip and keeled over. Caravan sites saw vans swept away, the vans progressively breaking up as the water carried them downstream.

The event was headline news for days and brought rescue agencies, the army, volunteers, insurance assessors, medics and even the Prime Minister into the region. The cost of damage was estimated at £500 million, the time taken to fix it at five years.

In those first ten days, one fatality had been reported – an elderly man knocked off his feet and overpowered by a swollen river. Tales of human suffering were ubiquitous, particularly among those whose homes were flooded. Rescue centres and food and clothes depots were set up in village halls and leisure centres.

There was so much to report, so many human stories, that Ben felt overwhelmed. Which one deserved priority, the local human story or the political "blame game" story about the lack of money spent on flood defences in the past and promises regarding the future?

He was, in any case, limited by the fact that his was only a small weekly paper with little spare room for such a massive story.

Eventually, Sue, the editor, decided that in order to serve the public, they needed to produce a separate four-page "Storm Special" pull-out for the next few weeks.

To assist Ben and to help fill the special, she asked Elizabeth to forego her usual articles and go out to the farms in the area and come back with their stories and photographs. Sue was aware that farmers were an independent lot, not the kind of people who would ask for help even though they might need it more than others.

Elizabeth, who had come to no harm in the storm, her cottage being on higher ground than Ben and Helen's, and who had the benefit of her four-wheel drive vehicle to negotiate the sodden ground, relished the prospect of visiting the farms to report on their problems. This was the kind of purposeful journalism she had dreamed of at university. She was so keen she almost decided not to seek Dominic's approval. After all, she could easily do her company work at night; the internet never went to sleep. Dominic would never know. But her conscience decided otherwise. She wrote him a long email, detailing the calamity and seeking his permission to do as Sue had asked.

Dominic's reply was prompt.

Dear Elizabeth,

The floods of Cumbria have been on our TV screens for the past few days. Here in the Alps we are familiar with natural disasters, mostly avalanches and floods, and so are familiar with the devastating effects they can have. When I was a ski instructor, I lost two good friends to avalanches. You have our sympathy and best wishes.

With regard to work, the decision is yours. How you plan

your time has always been up to you. All I am interested in is results. I trust you implicitly.

 Please don't take any risks.

 Dominic

 p.s. You might want to check on the Prentices.

Chapter 21

To start with, Elizabeth visited the farms in her immediate vicinity, on the eastern shore of Bassenthwaite Lake. She soon established that the damage in this area, though grim, was little more than a larger version of floods farms had suffered in the past. It had been the same on her parents' farm, which she had checked on the day after the storm subsided. Lots of water in the wrong place, but no great structural damage. She began to realise that the topography of an area had a big influence on the effects of the storm.

In the following weeks she visited farms surrounding Keswick. This had to be done on a random basis as some roads were inaccessible due to landslide, flood, bridge collapse or other structural failure. Even when roads were passable, some of the minor lanes and dirt tracks that branched off to the farms were blocked. She often had to abandon her car and walk, climb walls and fences and wade across streams to reach the farms.

Many of the stories she returned with were harrowing, some heartbreaking. Some farms had been hit in every conceivable way – stock drowned, bridges gone, walls down, fields completely covered in rocks, stones and mud. Many trees were down, miles of fencing hopelessly entangled in wire, timber, branches, marsh grasses and other detritus, the farm buildings half covered in metres of mud from landslides.

On most of the farms, Elizabeth found the farmer and his family outside, working together to try to restore some order to the chaos, their stoical attitude a tribute to years of adversity. Most looked exhausted but up for the challenge.

On one of the worst hit farms, no one answered the door when she knocked. The ankle-deep mud in the yard was covered in footprints. A few dead sheep had been stacked in a corner.

She opened the door and found the family sitting in the living room. They looked like statues – heads down, eyes dead, silent. Their clothes were filthy, their faces, hands and hair smeared in mud. They were obviously in a state of shock, probably overwhelmed by the scale of the damage and the impossibility of dealing with it. They were beyond stoicism. They were beaten.

Elizabeth had realised the gravity of the situation immediately. The suicide rate among farmers was high. When she introduced herself they barely raised their eyes to look at her.

She stood in silence, not knowing what to do. They made no attempt to speak. She felt herself starting to stare, as if being dragged down to join them in their shock.

Then she snapped out of it. She tried to give them hope by promising to bring help, but her words brought no reaction. They carried on staring.

She made tea for them and tried to cheer them up with chatty local anecdotes. Their continuing stares seemed to emphasise how stupidly trivial she sounded.

Finally, she gave up, went outside and explored every area of the farm. She took photographs of all the different types of damage. Before leaving she reiterated her promise of sending help.

She compiled her article as soon as she got home, emphasising the impossibility of the farmer and his family dealing with the disaster on their own. She took the matter further by suggesting to Sue that she should ask the local television stations to visit the farm to highlight their plight. Sue agreed and also said she would pass Elizabeth's excellent article to the nationals.

Within two days Elizabeth's article and photographs appeared in some of the national newspapers, and the whole nation saw the plight of the severely hit farm on their television screens.

The result was dramatic. From all over the country, volunteers turned up at the farm offering to help. Haulage, plant hire and engineering companies offered their earth-moving and lifting equipment free of charge, charities and individuals raised money. Other farms were also being offered help as more volunteers came to the region.

Elizabeth was amazed and delighted that just a few words and pictures could have such a profound effect. It confirmed to her that journalism was the profession she wanted to follow. The work had been deeply satisfying, unlike her work for Dominic.

Her farm visits throughout January ended each day when darkness descended around 5 p.m. After that she spent most of her time on her research work for Dominic, often working until midnight.

Her journalistic success did not go unnoticed. She was interviewed by local press and television stations, and even had the offer of a junior reporter's job with a Carlisle paper. A year ago she would have jumped at the offer, but now she felt she could not walk out on Dominic. She also convinced herself that the very small salary on offer had nothing to do with her decision.

She was showered with praise by her proud parents, her circle of friends, Ben and Helen, Mr and Mrs Andrews, and Dominic, to whom she had emailed the names of the nationals carrying her articles. He had replied:

Dear Elizabeth,

Would an MP have achieved so much? I am very proud of you.

Dominic xx

Elizabeth noted the pointed reference to the MP, but she still believed that as an MP she could achieve much more than help to alleviate the occasional natural disaster. Her attention was more taken by the language Dominic had used. *I am very proud of you* was the sort of thing said by a parent or husband or brother. It indicated a close personal relationship. *Congratulations on your success* would have been more appropriate for a business relationship. Then there was those two 'x's after Dominic's name. Were they just the customary French kisses on both cheeks or a genuine message of affection? She hoped for the latter.

After the storm the entire Vale of Keswick had been submerged in water. The twin lakes, Derwent Water and Bassenthwaite Lake, had risen to record heights and spread across the two-mile stretch of flat land that separated them, ostensibly recreating the single lake they had been thousands of years ago. The River Derwent, which flowed across this land from Derwent Water into Bassenthwaite Lake like an umbilical cord between the two, could no longer be seen.

Covered by the water was a central area of marshland, encircled by a number of sheep and cattle farms. Although practically on her doorstep, Elizabeth had yet to visit these farms.

Eventually, when the land was dry enough, she paid her first visit to a farm which sat close to the edge of the River Derwent, now contained within its steep-sided banks.

She received a warm greeting from farmer John Garston, who told her that the river had never burst its banks in the thirty years he had farmed there. Fortunately, his fields and farm buildings had not been invaded by enough water to drown stock, and he had come through the ordeal left with financial problems but not too many physical ones.

He did, however, express concern about the future ability of the river to flow properly because of a number of large log-jams along its length, caused by fallen trees and the like. Elizabeth took photographs of John and his family and of various areas of the farm buildings where water damage had occurred and then said her goodbyes.

On leaving the farm she made her way along the river bank to look for the log-jams. She intended to photograph them and add them to her article. A blocked river needed freeing quickly, before the next big rains came.

About 200 metres upstream from the farm, she came across the first log-jam. It had clearly been initiated by a large birch tree which had fallen when the river bank had been undercut by the swollen river. It had fallen straight across the narrow river, its top branches now resting on the bank opposite. The main trunk lay just above the water, like a bridge, with dozens of its branches entering the water below it.

This web of branches had trapped a myriad of objects as they flowed down the river, including shrubs, timber of all shapes and sizes, sundry items of plastic, various parts of destroyed caravans, footballs, netting, garden furniture, clothing, tarpaulins, rope, marsh grasses, etc. Some of the plastic sheets and clothing, draped over the branches above and below the water, had eerily taken up the approximate shape of human bodies.

Elizabeth started to take photographs, some long shots, some close-ups. It was usually the close-ups which were chosen for the paper, a mud-covered child's doll being more poignant than a panorama of destruction.

Now she zoomed in on the most lifelike of the body-like shapes hanging from the branches, its arched back out of the water, its head, legs and arms gently swaying in the peaty, slow-moving current. As she adjusted the lens, bringing the subject closer, her pulse quickened. It was *too* lifelike. She lowered the camera and took another look. There were light shapes under the water, but they were blurred by the current and the peaty colour. Could those things that looked like wriggling worms really be fingers? Surely not.

She swallowed, raised the camera again and concentrated on bringing the subject closer. Slowly, it came into focus. Now she had it, clear and unmistakable.

The lighter colours under the water were bare hands and

a face. The rest of the body was covered in a black wetsuit, which had become camouflaged with marsh grasses, dead leaves, green algae.

Elizabeth took the photograph then lowered the camera. Her hands were trembling slightly.

Chapter 22

Ben arrived on the scene as the light was fading. He had passed a number of police cars and an ambulance parked in the farm lane, and found their occupants gathered on the banks of the river. Area searchlights had been erected, their beams now focussed on the river.

Down in the water, Ben saw one man sitting in a rigid inflatable rescue dinghy which was tied to one of the beech tree's main branches. A short distance away, two men in wetsuits were in the water, wrestling with the tangle of branches and other impediments, trying to free the body.

Elizabeth appeared at his side, now fortified with her hooded anorak, which she always kept in the boot of her car. The temperature was close to freezing. She had also been fortified inside by John Garston's wife, Mary, who had provided her with soup and a hefty bacon sandwich while she waited for the police and Ben to arrive.

"Are you alright?" Ben asked.

"I think so."

"Bit of a shock, eh!"

"Yes."

"Long time no see," said another voice from somewhere behind them.

They turned to find a tall, middle-aged man half-smiling

at them. Elizabeth didn't recognise him but sensed a military presence. Ben said, "Hello, Peter," and held out his hand. While they shook hands, Ben continued, "Still slicing them?"

"I wish," Peter said. "I haven't had a game of golf for ages. No time these days. You know how it is with the cuts."

Ben had known Detective Inspector Peter Murphy since he was a uniformed constable in the Keswick police station. Somehow, Peter and Sergeant Bill Unwin had become Ben's golfing buddies over the years, a fact that always puzzled Ben since he had nothing in common with either of them. Their differences didn't seem to matter when they were absorbed in hacking a golf ball down a fairway, but sometimes came to the fore when they found themselves involved in local crime cases.

In spite of these differences, their co-operation on two major cases had resulted in successful conclusions. On one of the cases, in which a demented forest ranger had imprisoned a woman in his house in the forest, Ben's life had been saved by an incredible act of bravery by the now retired Bill Unwin. The case had become national news and Bill Unwin had received a substantial amount of money from a tabloid newspaper for exclusivity on his story.

Bill had spent it on a holiday apartment in Menorca, where he now spent most of the year, apparently happy to spend the rest of his life perfecting his golf swing.

Peter, meanwhile, had concentrated on climbing the promotion ladder, treading on a few toes along the way, including Ben's, and had eventually become top man in Keswick station.

Unfortunately Peter's moment in the sun had been short

lived. The Keswick station had been closed due to government cuts and he had been moved to County Headquarters in Penrith.

Being a smaller cog in a large organisation did not suit Peter's temperament, and that plus the ever-increasing workload due to continuous staff cuts had turned him into a somewhat embittered individual.

Peter was about to start talking when Ben interrupted him and drew his attention to Elizabeth, still at his side. "This is Elizabeth. She also works for *The Tribune*. You may have read some of her wonderful articles about the plight of the farmers after the floods."

Peter shook his head. "Haven't got time to read the papers these days. Hello, Elizabeth." He didn't offer to shake hands.

"Elizabeth is the person who found the body and reported it to your office," Ben insisted. His raised voice clearly indicated his annoyance at Peter's indifferent attitude towards Elizabeth.

"Right…" For a moment Peter seemed to forget their presence as he turned away and surveyed the scene. "This is all we need, a bloody floater on top of everything else."

"Is there something particularly unforgivable about a floater?" Ben teased.

"Yes! The pathologists often have trouble identifying the time of death or even the cause of death due to the physical effect of the water and its temperature over the period of immersion. And unless a relative or friend comes forward in the first week or so to identify them, or we can match them to the missing persons list, then the case can drag on forever."

Ben wished he hadn't asked.

By now they could all see that the men in the water had succeeded in freeing the body and were loading it onto the rescue dinghy.

Peter and Ben moved forward to get a closer look as the dinghy arrived at the river bank. Elizabeth started to follow. Peter turned. "Stay there, Elizabeth. This is not something you want to see. Believe me. By the way, did you take any photographs of the body?"

"Yes."

"Well, you know you can't put them in the paper, don't you?"

"Yes, she does," Ben pounced. "We spoke about it before you turned up. Anyway, I'll be handling the report on this, so you can stop worrying about procedures."

Peter turned and walked towards the river. Ben stayed behind to talk to Elizabeth. "Don't think too badly of him. He's obviously stretched to the limit work-wise. I suppose he's a classic example of where ambition can lead. Thank God I got out of the rat race in time."

"So you think ambition is a bad thing?"

"Not in all cases. Some people seem to thrive on it as responsibility grows. But others are not cut out for it and can finish up stressed and dissatisfied, like Peter. Are you ambitious?"

"Yes...at least I was when I came out of university...very ambitious. I think I still am, but I'm not certain anymore."

"Well, that's good, isn't it? There's nothing as unreliable as certainty. I wouldn't worry about it. Just keep ploughing on and one day you'll know whether to jump on the ambition train or whether to sleep in and miss it."

While talking they both noticed that the body was being lifted from the dinghy onto a stretcher. "Shall we go take a look?" Elizabeth started to walk.

"No! Peter was right about you not seeing the body." He paused. "I assume you haven't seen a dead body taken from water before?"

"No."

"I've only seen two. I won't even attempt to describe them. But I threw up both times. I wouldn't look at this one if I didn't think I should for reporting purposes. I'm only going to take a quick glance and then I will be retreating as fast as I can. Promise me you will stay here until I come back."

Elizabeth sighed. "Okay."

By now it was almost dark and getting very cold. Elizabeth stood with her hands deep in her anorak pockets and looked around. The lights were still shining on the river, highlighting the log-jam; ghost-like figures were moving about on the river bank. A host of voices produced a single indecipherable babble; a light breeze brought a diluted smell of putrefaction from the direction of the body. It was like a scene from a TV police drama, but this was real. This was real life and death, and she loved it.

Once again doubts swam into her mind. Did she really want to earn a living by simply looking for properties for the rich and privileged, when there was the challenge and satisfaction of being involved in the dramas that journalism threw up every day?

Ben was back at her side within a few minutes, a handkerchief held to his face. He stood silently, head down, breathing quickly as if he had just sprinted.

"Are you alright?" Elizabeth asked.

"Just..." Ben gasped.

"Have you been sick?"

"I'm still fighting it..."

Elizabeth brought a tube of mint sweets from her pocket and offered it to Ben. He took two and put them in his mouth. Elizabeth took one.

"Let's get out of here," Ben urged.

Ben had brought a hand torch with him, and he used it to negotiate a wide berth around the police and medics who were still examining and photographing the body.

By the time they arrived back at Ben's car, he seemed to have won his fight with nausea. He invited Elizabeth to sit in the car with him, switched on the engine and the heater, but didn't drive away.

"It's a man," he said. "Unrecognisable, of course. All I picked up on was his short black hair and the fact that his wetsuit had a knife sheath attached and there was a knife in it. That's a bit unusual for swimmers around here, isn't it?"

"It is. I've never seen anybody swimming in the Lakes with a knife in their wetsuit. You usually find ocean divers, not swimmers, carrying knives. They take them as a precaution in case they get caught up in nets and the like when they are underwater. What happens next?"

"I'll write a brief report for the paper – you know, just the basic facts that we have. And I'll ask readers to contact the police if they have any information that could lead to the victim's identification."

"Will the police let you know if and when they obtain an identification?"

"Yes, and if they don't come up with one, I have a promise from Inspector Murphy that I'll get a copy of the pathologist's post mortem report."

"Why would he do that? I thought the reports were made available to the press anyway?"

"Summaries are made available, but not full reports. He lets me see them when he has a case he is struggling with because in the past I have helped him to solve cases using the analytical strengths I developed when working in industry."

"So you are like a private eye, working for the police under cover of being a part-time journalist and painter?"

Ben laughed. "No, I'm no Sherlock Holmes. I'm an amateur, more like Miss Marple or Lord Peter Wimsey. Sometimes when Helen is frustrated with the amount of time I spend on a case, she likens me to Inspector Clouseau."

"Are you working on anything at the moment?"

"No, I haven't been asked to help for quite a while. It would be good to get cracking again."

"So, you would be glad if the police don't get an identification on this body?"

"I wouldn't say glad, but if they ask for help, I won't turn them down. Anyway, enough of this conjecture. It's been a long day for both of us. Why don't we get ourselves home and see what tomorrow brings."

"Good idea. Will you let me know what happens on this case? I'm really interested."

"Yes, of course. There wouldn't be a case if you hadn't found the body."

They wished each other goodnight as Elizabeth exited

Ben's car. She found her own car with the aid of Ben's head-lights and soon she was driving home. Home? She liked her cosy little cottage, but she still didn't think of it as home, not yet anyway. Home was the farm and her parents and the animals, and on this cold, dark night of death, she really wished she was heading there.

Chapter 23

For three weeks after the discovery of the body in the river, *The Tribune*, along with all the other newspapers in Cumbria, received requests from the police to report their appeal for any information which might lead them to an identification of the body. Local TV and radio stations were also asked to report.

During the first two weeks, the police released the only clues they had. These were the approximate height and weight of the man, the approximate length of time he had been in the water, the colour of his hair and the name of the manufacturers of his wetsuit and knife. Cause of death was described as *unknown* at this stage.

As with all bodies recovered after a period of immersion in water, facial photographs were out of the question. Nobody could put a name to a face with blue/green/black skin, grotesquely bloated lips and protruding eyes and tongue.

On the third week the police released the news that DNA genetic analysis tests pointed to the likelihood that the man was of South American origin, probably from the northern part of that continent.

By now the national newspapers had picked up on the story. Headlines such as *WHO IS THE MAN IN THE WETSUIT?* appeared in the tabloids.

At the end of the fourth week, while working in his office, Ben received an email from Detective Inspector Peter Murphy enclosing a copy of the post mortem and DNA analysis. He wrote that they had received only a few leads, none of them fruitful, and invited Ben to take an initial look at the case if he was interested. Ben immediately downloaded paper copies of the documents and opened a file, feeling that stir of excitement he always got at the start of a case. It was of course early days, but already he had a feeling that this one was going to be special.

The opening page of the five-page post mortem started with what appeared to be a standard preamble. Under the heading *Bodies Recovered from Water*, he read: *It is not always possible, due to the effects of immersion, to determine whether all or some of the injuries present are ante/peri/ or post mortem in origin. Marine animals/fish may cause damage, and injuries caused by contact between the body and submerged objects, structures, rocks, gravel, etc. are frequently seen in some bodies of water.*

This was followed by a long, detailed description of the body which put the man's height at approximately five feet seven inches and age range thirty-five to forty-five.

Under a sub-heading, *Length of time immersed*, there was a long paragraph explaining the difficulties of calculating this due to the presence of the wetsuit and temperature variants, which were unknown. Three to eight weeks was given as a rough guide.

Next came the type of injuries present on the body. The head had suffered *cranio-cerebral injuries, with linear, comminuted fracture of left side of skull*. There was also a *linear pattern of contusions of left cerebral hemisphere, abrasion of left cheek, sub-arachnoid and subdural haemorrhage. A lacerated wound measuring 16 x 4 mm beneath the left eye.*

Reading on, Ben ascertained that the torso, while displaying all the discolouration and deterioration expected of an immersed body, did not appear to have suffered much physical damage.

Two more pages giving the findings of the dissection of the internal organs were mostly beyond Ben's understanding, but there were no indications that any of them were malfunctioning at the time of death.

Finally, he reached the summary. *Based on the above observations, it has not been possible to give an opinion as to the cause of death.*

Medical Cause of Death: Indeterminate.

The report had been signed by two people, one with the title Pathologist, the other Forensic Pathologist. This indicated to Ben that a very thorough post mortem had taken place.

Ben surmised that both pathologists had been unable to tell whether the severe head injuries or drowning or both had caused death, or whether the head injuries were caused before or after entering the water. Or whether the injuries were accidental or inflicted by persons unknown, or even by the man himself (suicide). If you ruled out the unlikely possibilities of foul play or suicide (who would put on a wetsuit to commit suicide?), then the head wounds might easily have been caused during the floods when large trees and other structures were floating at speed down the rivers. Or the man may have tripped and fallen on rocks before entering the water. The possibilities were starting to look endless, and Ben could see why the pathologists had been unable to come up with a plausible explanation.

The report also carried a photograph of the knife in the wetsuit sheath, followed by the knife on its own. Although apparently used by divers to get them out of trouble under-water, Ben thought that it was one of the most deadly-looking weapons he had seen. With a dagger-like point and two sharp edges, one serrated, it looked like something the military would carry into action.

Ben put the report down, glanced out the window and watched a lone pheasant do its comical strut across the lawn. Then he picked up the DNA analysis. The detail was totally incomprehensible, but the conclusion was clear: *The subject's genetic signature is commonly found in the northern countries of South America.*

Ben understood that "commonly found" did not mean it was certain the man came from that area; it was only a guide to his shared ancestry. He had seen the man's black hair when they hauled him out of the river, but presumably the original colour of his skin, which might have been olive or black, could not be ascertained. Ben found this perplexing. Surely skin pigmentation would show up somewhere under the microscope? The fact that it wasn't mentioned on the report meant that, for the moment, Ben could not rule out that the man was of Caucasian origin.

At this stage the case looked quite intriguing – an un-identified body and an unknown cause of death. But Ben knew that at any given moment some simple explanation could appear, and the case would be closed. However, until that happened he intended to continue with his normal routine of listing, then investigating, all the possible causes of death, and the information (clues) that could lead to the man's identity. It was this pedantic attention to detail which had been the basis of his success on previous cases.

After typing his lists he decided to check on the population of ethnic minorities in his local council area. If the man was of South American origin, he could belong to a local family who, for yet unknown reasons, had not come forward to identify him. He assumed the police would have already done this, but he wondered if the cuts in police numbers might have affected their efforts.

He was surprised to find that there was only a 0.6 percent ethnic minority population in the area, which meant that a town like Keswick, with a population of 5,000, had approximately thirty residents of ethnic minority, and the whole council area about 120. Only a small proportion of this number were likely to be of South American origin, so even with a smaller workforce, he assumed the police would have visited all these families by now. He could find out if he phoned Peter Murphy, but he knew Peter did not like him questioning him about such routine procedures. For the time being, therefore, he would make a note of this question on file. While doing this, his phone rang.

"Ben, it's Peter."

Ah! The case is closed already.

"We have another floater."

Chapter 24

A few weeks after the storm, Sue Burrows asked Elizabeth to stop visiting the farms. Their immediate crisis was over as far as she could tell. Many farmers had contacted her office to thank Elizabeth for her efforts on their behalf, and some even brought in small tokens of their appreciation – flowers, chocolates, eggs, etc.

Sue was experienced enough to know that the effects of the floods would last for years, particularly where major bridges and flood defences had to be rebuilt, but these were things that Ben could cover as time unfolded. She asked Elizabeth to go back to writing her articles, though she suspected there would be few newcomers to the area over a winter period which included massive floods.

Because of the sparsity of newcomers over the winter, Elizabeth decided to turn her attention to the Prentices. They were potentially an excellent subject for a Welcome to the Lakes article. Readers would be very interested to know their background and why they came to the area.

With the intention of phoning them to make an appointment, she looked up her records but was unable to find a number for them. She had the number the footballer used when he owned Becalmed, so she tried that, but to no avail. She checked with Directory Enquiries and was told there was no number listed under the name of Charles or Barbara Prentice. There was nothing for it but to go cold calling and hope to find them receptive.

It was a sharp, early March morning when she set off to drive to their house. The trees were still naked, the blue sky still anaemic, the bracken still a rusting scrapyard, but a few snowdrops had pushed through, a sure sign that spring was flexing its muscles, ready to break out of its cold prison.

She retraced her last visit to the house, via the Cat Bells mountain route, and soon she was on the snake-like minor road that twisted through woodlands as it approached Becalmed. The road was littered with twigs and small branches, no doubt the result of heavy winds about a week ago. When she had to stop to remove one or two branches, it told her that nobody had been along this road for at least a week. She wondered if they had gone back to Zurich to see out the winter, a winter dominated by floods. Who could blame them?

She pressed on until she reached the gate that spanned the road. The old wooden gate had gone and in its place stood a new steel gate. She stepped out of the car and approached the gate. It was made of such a thick gauge steel that it looked as though a tank would have problems breaching it. There was no obvious way to open it, no handles or bolts or keyholes. Nor was there any system of contacting the house to announce her presence.

On either side of the gate, the old, dilapidated wood and wire fence still stood, apparently yet to be replaced by the new security system that Charles had wanted to install himself.

Having decided that the fence would be easy to climb, and that she was suitably dressed for the job, in jeans and walking shoes, Elizabeth returned to the car and retrieved her backpack, which contained her interview materials, camera and a belated housewarming present in the shape of a bottle of whisky from the local distillery.

After hefting her backpack onto her back, she returned to the gate, stepped off the road and was about to start climbing the fence when, from the corner of her eye, she saw the gate open slowly. It was completely silent. The effect was quite eerie. She stepped back onto the road and walked through the open gateway, feeling as if she was being lured into a world of science fiction.

As she walked towards the house, it occurred to her that she must have been observed by hidden cameras near the gate, and that the gate had only been opened when she began to climb the fence. She concluded that the Prentices would not have opened the gate had she not attempted to climb the fence. In other words, she was not a welcome visitor. The realisation made her want to turn round and drive off, but this impulse was countered by her natural inquisitiveness. While dithering between the two, she saw the front door of the house open and Charles step out to greet her.

He was dressed as scruffily as ever, his baggy blue chords topped by a grey polo neck sweater apparently knitted with rope. His hair and beard looked wilder than before, leaving her to conclude that he had not had them trimmed since they last met. Through all the grey hair, she detected a slight smile as he held out his hand to shake hers.

"Hello, Elizabeth?"

"I tried to phone..."

"Ah! Ex-directory, I'm afraid."

"Yes..."

He stood barring the way, as if waiting for Elizabeth to explain the purpose of her visit.

"I came to see if you and the family had suffered any problems during the floods."

"That's kind of you, Elizabeth. Now, while we're out here let me show you my new boat – it's down at the boathouse. Follow me."

Though taken aback by the sudden suggestion, Elizabeth followed obediently. They made their way through an untended garden and down a rocky slope until they reached the boathouse sitting on the edge of the peaceful lake.

Once inside the boathouse, Charles prowled around the boat, extolling its virtues. Elizabeth registered the words: solid red cedar, clinker, thwarts, transom, deep keel, rowlocks, sternsheets and gunwale. Next it was the two outboard motors, one electric for fishing, one petrol for speed. She tried to look interested and say a few positive words when the time seemed right, but she was relieved when he brought the tour to an end with, "Let's go in and say hello to the girls."

On the way back to the house, he told her that he kept a small racing yacht moored at the Bassenthwaite Sailing Club.

As she stepped into the house, Elizabeth couldn't throw off the feeling that Charles had been keeping her outside for as long as possible in order to give those inside time to do something. Maybe tidy up or get dressed or change their clothes. *And why not? Haven't we all been caught out by a surprise visitor?*

Charles took her through to the spacious lounge, where Barbara and Claire greeted her with smiles that were polite rather than warm. At first glance it looked as if none of the furniture which the footballer left had been removed.

Claire, as usual, was in her wheelchair while Barbara sat nearby on a luxuriously cushioned pale blue sofa. Suddenly, Barbara rose from the sofa and approached Elizabeth, holding out her arms in front of her. Elizabeth thought she was about to be embraced, but just as she was about to lift her own arms, Barbara said, "Let me take that backpack from you, then you'll be more comfortable."

Elizabeth had little choice but to stand still while Barbara removed the backpack from her back. "I'll put it near the front door." Barbara walked away before Elizabeth could object. She had hoped to give them the bottle of whisky as soon as she arrived, but that would now have to wait until she was ready to leave.

Charles invited Elizabeth to take a seat, while he went to sit on the sofa. Barbara had not yet returned from her trip to the front door. *Probably popped into the kitchen to make tea or coffee.*

The wait for Barbara to reappear seemed interminable as nobody offered to speak while she was gone. Finally, she walked in and sat down beside Charles. She had not brought any tea or coffee or any explanation for her long absence. Elizabeth found herself noting that there was no sound of a flushing toilet either. Then she wondered why she was having these ridiculous thoughts. There could be any number of reasons why Barbara had been delayed. Was she becoming paranoid, or was there really something a bit strange about these people?

With three pairs of eyes staring at her, Elizabeth felt obliged to break the silence. "This room looks much larger with the carpet fitted than when it was tiled. Were you happy with the carpet fitters' work?"

"Oh, yes!" Barbara replied. "They did an excellent job. And they cleaned up afterwards. We've had trouble on that score before."

"And I take it you survived the storm okay?" Elizabeth went on.

"Nothing serious happened," Charles said. "A few fallen tree branches had to be moved and the rising lake buried the jetty and half the boathouse, depositing a lot of rubbish along the way, but I think we got off fairly lightly. I quite enjoyed it. I've always enjoyed severe weather, particularly tropical storms with all that dramatic lightning. The girls are not so keen though." Barbara nodded her head in agreement, while Claire made a shuddering motion.

"What about Fell View?"

"Same thing. Tree branches all over the lawns, but no water problems. It's too far back from the lake for that."

"Have you decided on your plans for Fell View yet?" Elizabeth asked. To her, it was an innocent follow-on to the previous question, but when she saw Charles hesitate to answer, she realised she had probably gone too far. Questions about the weather were one thing, questions about his business plans another.

"Still in abeyance. We've been too busy settling in here and getting my boats ready for spring."

"Did you manage to get your new security system installed? I didn't see much sign of it when I arrived...apart from the new gate." Again, she wondered if she had gone too far, but this time Charles smiled condescendingly.

"That's the whole point of it, Elizabeth. Invisibility. These new laser alarms send an invisible infrared beam around the whole perimeter of the property. The hardware is hidden in the bushes and trees. Anyone passing through the beam sets off a warning signal which, hopefully, frightens them off. This is particularly useful when you are not at home. And, if you are away from home, you can phone from a distance and check on the state of security. You will have gathered that it is also backed up by hidden cameras."

"Yes, I assumed that when I saw the gate open. So, I presume if I had climbed that fence, an alarm signal would have sounded?"

"Normally, yes. But in this instance, when we saw it was you, we turned the signal off."

"What about animals – deer, foxes? Are they not constantly setting off the alarm?"

"No. Don't ask me how they do it, but the beam is not affected by animals or rain or snow."

"Amazing."

She wanted to go on and push him about his need for such an expensive, high-tech security system, but thought better of it. His previous explanation about having experienced bad situations abroad seemed a bit implausible to her, given the absence of serious crime in this area. However, she couldn't

160

blame him for playing safe. He hadn't lived in the area before, so he wasn't personally aware of its safety record, and he had a vulnerable daughter to protect, and most important of all, he could afford it.

She was dying to see the control room for the security system; no doubt there was a room full of monitors and pulsing lights somewhere in the house. But she demurred. Charles might not like the intrusion and she needed to keep him sweet because she was about to ask him to do an interview for her Welcome to the Lakes article.

When she did ask him, his reply was short, loud and not so sweet. "Absolutely not!"

Elizabeth saw immediately that there was no point in pursuing the matter – his reply had had so much finality in it.

"By the way," she blurted suddenly, pleased to have thought of something to change the subject. "Have you heard about the man in the wetsuit?"

Three puzzled expressions told her they hadn't.

"It's been all over the local and national news for weeks now," she pointed out.

"Ah," Charles said. "We don't purchase any newspapers and we rarely watch television, and never watch the news. We are trying to create an oasis of peace and relaxation here."

Again he had given only bare facts and then clammed up. There were never any reasons or explanations. None of them appeared to be interested in learning about the man in the wetsuit; not a single question was asked. Elizabeth had been ready to recount the exciting story of the body in the river, but since they didn't seem interested, she was at a loss as to what to say next. She sat for a while, hoping that somebody else would start talking, but they didn't. As the seconds ticked by, her discomfort grew, until she thought *I need to get out of here.*

"Right...well...I'll be on my way..." As she spoke she rose from her seat. "I hope you didn't mind me calling in without an appointment."

A chorus of "no" and "not at all" answered her, but she doubted their veracity.

As she made her way out, Charles rose from his seat to accompany her. Barbara stayed behind with Claire. Elizabeth noticed again that they had contributed very little by way of conversation.

At the front door, Elizabeth paused to retrieve her backpack, but neither she nor Charles could find it. Instead of returning to ask Barbara where she had put it, he said, "Let's look outside."

They stepped outside, and there it was, on the pavement, leaning against the wall of the house. Charles picked it up and handed it to Elizabeth. "She was protecting Claire," he said. "Sorry."

Again no further explanation. By now, Elizabeth was in no mood to seek explanations. All she wanted was to get away from these weird people. She opened the main compartment of the backpack, took out the bottle of whisky and handed it to Charles. "A small housewarming present. To wish you and your family well in your new house."

"Well, thank you, Elizabeth, that is very thoughtful of you." He studied the words on the bottle label. "We might enjoy this after dinner tonight."

For a horrifying moment Elizabeth thought he might

invite her to stay for dinner, but she should have known better. What did please her was the fact that they drank whisky – they might be normal after all. She turned to leave. "You have my card. If you need any help, please don't hesitate to phone me."

"Thank you for coming."

Elizabeth set off walking towards the gate. As she walked she glanced at all the trees and bushes and fence posts, looking for the hidden security hardware and cameras. Nothing caught her eye. She watched the gate open as she approached it and turned to watch it close behind her, still finding its total silence a bit spooky.

On reaching her car she clicked the boot open and of-floaded her backpack. Only now did she notice that the two side pockets were zipped shut. She was sure she had left them open as she always did when they were empty. Barbara! Was this why she took so long to return to the lounge? Had she spent the time searching through the backpack then closed all the zips when finished? Why? This was taking security to another level, an obsessive level. Charles said that Barbara had been protecting Claire. From what?

Elizabeth climbed into her car and drove off, still looking for the answer. It was not until she arrived home and was unloading the backpack that a possible explanation struck her. The only connection she could make between a backpack and fear was terrorist bombs. They were often delivered in backpacks left in stations and airports. Could Claire's disability be the result of a bomb explosion? Had all three of them suffered from a bomb explosion, which they didn't wish to talk about? A common response to severe trauma. This could explain their unusual behaviour, their silences.

But why all the security now? It was as if they were *expecting* to be attacked. Why would terrorists be seeking them out? Perhaps they weren't. Perhaps the Prentices had simply been in the wrong place at the wrong time and had no connection to terrorist organisations.

Elizabeth had a vague recollection of oil companies being in conflict with local natives in Third World countries, being accused of damaging their land, polluting their rivers. Some of these conflicts were violent. Perhaps the Prentices had been involved in one of these conflicts and had been threatened with death no matter where they went, their enemies bent on revenge. But did they seriously think she was a potential threat? Could they now be suffering from paranoia after numerous attacks? Could they be pouring her whisky down the drain right now, fearing it might be poisoned?

It was all conjecture, Elizabeth realised, and she had often been told that she had a lurid imagination, but she felt it must be something similarly traumatic that caused the Prentices to behave the way they did. She decided to discuss it with Ben the next time they met. He, no doubt, knew where to look to find records of historical clashes between oil companies and native populations. Perhaps he might even be able to unearth the very event in which Mr Charles Prentice and his family were involved.

Chapter 25

Ben sat at his desk, looking out the window, taking in the expansive view of Bassenthwaite Lake and its surroundings. Beyond the bare trees a blanket of morning mist hung above the lake. A flock of Barnacle geese emerged from the mist and, like a well-drilled RAF squadron, flew in a wide semi-circle over a lakeside field before landing in it, their honking calls just audible to Ben's ears.

Five minutes ago he had carried Helen's briefcase out to her car and waved her off. She would be gone most of the day, her main appointment being in Windermere to discuss staffing levels and operating procedures for a new swimming pool nearing completion. She planned to pick up some milk, oatcakes and tissues on the way home.

He liked these quiet mornings when nature seemed to invite you to copy it, to slow down and recharge your batteries before spring arrived and put its foot on the accelerator.

He had been in between paintings for over a week now and normally would be thinking about starting a new one. But not today. Maybe not for quite some time. Whenever he got involved with a case, it was always his painting that had to go, his work for *The Tribune* taking priority.

He swivelled his chair away from the window and looked at his blank computer screen. Time to enter new details on the file headed *Floater*. After that he intended to contact Elizabeth to let her know about the second body.

The first thing he did was add an *s* to the word *Floater*. From the brief details given to him by Peter Murphy, it sounded as if the word *floater* was inappropriate in this case, the second man's body having been found trapped under a tree on the *bottom* of the river, just a few hundred metres further upstream from the first body.

This body also wore a wetsuit and carried a dive knife. Having been in the water longer than the first man, the body was in an advanced state of decomposition and was therefore unlikely to reveal the cause of death. Police expected an autopsy and DNA report within two weeks, which Peter promised to pass on to Ben.

Ben's next entry was interrupted by the ringing of his doorbell, a rare occurrence at this time of day. Hurrying downstairs, he opened the door and found Elizabeth standing well back, smiling apologetically. "Sorry, I hope I'm not—"

"Stop!" Ben demanded in a mock serious tone. "You are a journalist now, a master of the English language, yet you bring the language of the street to my door. I know everybody does it, but they shouldn't. You can't start a sentence with 'sorry.'"

"Sorry..."

"That's better." Ben smiled. "You had a reason to be sorry that time."

Elizabeth knew Ben well enough now to know that he was having fun with her, although she also knew that he was passionate about the correct use of language.

"Come in, come in," Ben invited. "I'm glad you're

here. I've got some news for you. Let's go through to the conservatory."

"And I've brought a new conundrum for you," Elizabeth said while following Ben inside.

"That's a big word for a Tuesday morning."

"Somebody told me I was a master of the language."

"Would you like some coffee? Helen left a brew in the coffee pot."

"Mm, yes, please."

Soon they were sitting opposite each other in the conservatory, close to the windows in the hope they might see some wildlife.

"You go first," Ben said as he leaned over and picked up the notebook and pen he always left on his coffee table.

Elizabeth set the scene by reminding him that she had spoken to him some months earlier about being involved in the purchase of Pedro Sousa's house. She went on to introduce him to the new owners, the Prentice family, his oil executive background and where they came from. And continued with anecdotes about their unusual behaviour, their claims of suffering some kind of trauma when working and living abroad, causing their obsession with security. She included the story about her backpack as an illustration. She mentioned their reluctance to answer questions or offer information or be interviewed for *The Tribune*.

She concluded with her own theory, however outlandish, that their trauma might have been caused by some form of attack, perhaps by native people of a Third World country angry at the oil company's mistreatment of them or their environment.

She had related the story slowly so that Ben could make notes. When she saw him lift his head from his notebook, she said, "I was wondering if it would be possible to trace historical records of conflicts between oil companies and the foreign countries in which they operated?"

"Anything's possible if you spend enough time on it," Ben said. "Which oil company did your Mr Prentice work for?"

Elizabeth smiled sheepishly. "I don't know."

Ben glanced at his notes. "You say he was an executive. Was he a director, a member of the Board?"

Another sheepish smile.

Ben grimaced. "It's all down to language again, a lack of clarity. The word 'executive' lacks clarity. Somebody selling double glazing is called a marketing executive these days."

"He is very rich."

"Well, that is significant. It points to a high salary plus bonuses plus shares. And that points to a member of the Board. We can assume that for the time being. Of course, he might just have inherited his wealth."

"But if he had, why would he be working for an oil company?"

"Can we not ask him?"

"Not a chance. He's like the proverbial..."

"Clam?"

"Mm. Anyway, it doesn't really matter. I just thought it would be interesting..."

While Elizabeth was talking, Ben seemed to be lost in thought. Suddenly he interrupted her. "It could be *very* interesting, Elizabeth," he enthused, then carried on thinking. He did this by staring into a space just in front of him, apparently listening for something creeping up behind him.

Elizabeth resisted the temptation to look over his shoulder. Instead she looked out the window and saw a woodpecker go from total stillness to sudden, head-banging violence when it pecked at the nuts inside a bird feeder.

Turning back to Ben, she found him waiting to talk to her. "I take it you didn't see the possible connection?" he said.

"Er...no," Elizabeth admitted. "What have I missed?"

"Before we go on to that, let me first tell you my news. Another body has been found in the River Derwent, in a wetsuit, with a knife. Peter Murphy phoned me yesterday. They are doing a post mortem and DNA tests as before – results in about two weeks."

The news and its relevance both hit her at the same time. "Wow!" was all she managed to say as she processed the information.

"You see the possibility now, don't you? The Prentices installing an expensive security system, behaving as though expecting to be attacked, and two men with knives found dead."

"I do, but the bodies were four miles from Prentice's house?"

"True. But four miles is nothing. The bodies could have been taken there by car or boat, or even carried there by the floods."

"They have a boat."

"The two things might not be connected, but the possibility certainly needs investigating. Look at it this way. The police investigation on the first man has drawn a blank, which is why Peter passed it to me. I could spend months investigating this case and draw a blank like the police. So far I don't have much of a starting point, other than the first man might come from South America. Then along you come with the Prentice story, and you put forward your theory that the Prentices might have been attacked in the past by people in a Third World country. Parts of South America are designated as Third World. You happening to know these people might be the luckiest coincidence in the history of investigation or cause the biggest waste of investigative time in history. Only time will tell."

Elizabeth wasn't sure what to say. Ben's reasoning was plausible, but she remained to be convinced. "I just can't associate the Prentices with anything that might lead to murder," she said at last. "I think you might feel the same if you met them. He's a retired pen pusher turned hippie who told me he is trying to create an oasis of peace, his wife looks as though she would struggle to burst a balloon, and the daughter is in a wheelchair."

"And Shipman was a caring doctor."

"Shipman?"

"Sorry, Elizabeth, I keep forgetting how young you are. You would have been a little girl at the time. Doctor Harold Shipman was one of the most prolific serial killers in history. He murdered about 250 of his patients, mostly elderly women who thought he was charming."

Elizabeth frowned. "There is something vaguely familiar about that. I probably heard my parents talking about it. Anyway, what can I say? I take your point. I did ask them if they had heard about the body in the wetsuit, but they all looked mystified. Apparently they don't buy the newspaper and never watch or listen to the news."

"A likely story is a phrase that springs to mind."

"Perhaps I'm too gullible?"

"Which is exactly what you should be at your age. The job of investigating people like the Prentices should only be done by old cynics like me. Over the years we've learned that there is no limit to the wickedness and goodness of our species and that the wickedness hides within the same facade as the goodness. It doesn't announce itself. It has to be discovered. Leave this with me, Elizabeth, and I'll let you know as soon as I find anything interesting about your peace-loving Prentices. I don't suppose you have any photographs of them?"

"No."

"When you get home can you email me a full description of each of them?"

"Yes, of course, though I'm not very good at guessing people's ages."

"And I thought it was just us oldies that had that trouble. Helen and I are convinced that our GP is no older than eighteen."

"What about me?"

"Fifteen. Definitely no more than fifteen."

Changing the subject, Elizabeth announced that she would be away in the Scottish Highlands for a few days to do an initial survey of some mansions and a castle for a German client who fancied the idea of being a laird. He wanted to be able to shoot, fish and have a view of a loch on his estate.

"Don't tell him about the midges."

"What midges?" Elizabeth rose from her seat. "Time to get back to my day job. I'll catch up with you when I get back. Thanks for the coffee."

Ben rose from his seat and accompanied her to the door. "I might have some info on body number two by then. That's something for you to look forward to, isn't it?"

"I can't wait."

Chapter 26

"We have routine news, good news and bad news. Where would you like me to start?" Ben said.

He sat in a window seat in his conservatory, and Elizabeth sat opposite him. Three weeks had passed since they sat in identical seats. An April breeze spat rain against the windows, harassed the daffodils in the garden border.

Elizabeth had already had her say, briefly outlining the highs and lows of her trip to the Highlands, one of the highs being her first visit to the village of Plockton, where Wainwright used to holiday. "*So* beautiful." One of the lows was being exhausted and soaked due to difficult topography and persistent rain. Since returning she had been busy catching up with her local work and her articles for *The Tribune*.

She had been brief because she was eager to hear whether Ben had been able to uncover information about the Prentices. She assumed there would be nothing earth shattering; otherwise he would have contacted her on her mobile. "In the order you just mentioned," Elizabeth said.

Ben lifted his notebook off the coffee table, glanced at it and started, "The routine news is that the second body in the wetsuit also carried no identification. He might well have been the brother of the first. Same approximate height, weight, etc. and also probably from northern South America. His body had suffered similar head wounds to the first, but, as with the first, the pathologists could not specify the cause of death. The only difference I could see between the two was that the death certificate of the second one gave cause of death as 'Unascertained', whereas the first one said 'Indeterminate', which is clearly just a question of semantics and not relevant to us."

"And both are still unidentified, I take it?"

"Yes."

Elizabeth went on. "I've been wondering where their clothes might be. You don't go wandering about in wetsuits longer than necessary. There's probably a car parked somewhere with their clothes in it. I suppose the police must have thoroughly searched all the area around the river."

"Don't count on it. According to Peter Murphy a lot of routines are no longer being carried out. And of course there are numerous other possibilities regarding their clothes. For example, the men may have been dropped off by a third person driving the car, who has since left the area with their clothes in the car."

"I think I might take my walks along that river bank in future."

"Good luck. Are you ready for the good news?"

"Fire away."

Ben turned a page in his notebook. "Your theory that the Prentices might have been the victims of an attack by people angry at the activities of his oil company looks plausible, particularly when linked to oil company activities in northern South America, where our wetsuit men might come from. The big oil companies have been operating in Venezuela, Ecuador, Peru and Bolivia for many years. Each government offers its own licence agreement, and they differ enormously. Some insist on strict controls on location, taxation, environmental care, etc. while others are much more careless about these things.

"Peru, for example, was the most laissez-faire country of all, more or less letting the oil companies do what they want, where they want. There, the government leased out three quarters of its Amazonian forest for oil exploration and extraction. And it's in Peru where there has been the most trouble between the locals and the oil companies for the past twenty years.

"The locals accused the oil companies of dumping millions of tonnes of oil sludge in their rivers, killing the fish, causing animals to run away, wilting their crops and making their people sick, with some dying.

"In 2006 they eventually took direct action. Armed with shotguns and spears, they occupied and held the wells. They forced one of the biggest oil companies, Occidental, to pull out eight years ago, but another oil company has taken their place. Now the locals have taken legal advice and have filed a class action lawsuit against this company, result as yet unknown. You can see from this example that if people have seen their relatives die and they have not had justice for them, they might well seek their own revenge. So, your theory is a good one. However, time for the bad news."

Elizabeth remained silent.

"I can't find Charles Prentice anywhere."

"What?"

"I've checked every oil company operating in every South American country for the past twenty-five years and his name does not appear at executive level. I've also checked all the British and American oil companies and most other companies operating in Third World countries all over the world. Nothing.

"I then put his name through all the usual search engines. There are plenty of Charles Prentices but none connected to the oil industry. It's possible, of course, that I may have missed him somewhere, or that his status was not sufficient to be listed at executive level. Then there is the possibility that he is using a false name. If he is on the run from people intent on killing him, who can blame him?

"Another alternative is that Prentice is his real name and he has invented his title of oil company executive to cover up the real way he became rich. Perhaps he made his millions from something like scrap dealing, or drug dealing, or bookmaking, or a lottery win. People desperate for social status will go to great lengths to hide the means to their wealth."

"Well, he looks more like a scrap dealer than an oil executive," Elizabeth said. "But he does talk very posh."

"Very posh could indicate that he is trying too hard."

"I think the first scenario is more likely – he is some sort of executive using a false name. Leaving aside his scruffy appearance, his mannerisms seem to me to be those of an executive rather than a scrap dealer."

Ben replaced his notebook on the coffee table and settled back in his chair, nudging his glasses up the bridge of his nose. "So, we are left with a mystery man in our midst, who could be using a false name, who seems to be living in fear of his life, who might already have killed two men."

"This is getting exciting."

"If any of it is true, it could be dangerous."

Chapter 27

The next morning Elizabeth felt tired as she crawled out of bed and drew back the curtains. The sky that greeted her was as grey as her mood. She had slept fitfully, her mind constantly replaying Ben's theories about Charles Prentice.

Later that morning, as she put the finishing touches to a long email to Dominic, reporting on her trip to the Highlands, she suddenly remembered that Prentice had been a client of Dominic's. How could she have forgotten?

Now she realised she should tell Dominic about the possibility that Prentice was not the real name of his client. Half an hour later she clicked "send" on her second email of the morning to Dominic, in which she did just that. She then introduced him to Ben, explained their relationship at the local newspaper and pointed out that it was Ben who had looked into Prentice's background, after she had planted the seeds of doubt. She then listed some of the theories that Ben had come up with.

Dominic's reply to the second email came back surprisingly quickly.

This could be very interesting. Prentice (or Mr X) settled his account with me using a bank which is in the group owned by my ex-father-in-law. I believe my old father-in-law's banks are involved in providing a safe financial haven for money launderers and fraudsters and I would love to find a way of proving it.

If it transpires that Prentice is a dodgy character and has changed his name, then I suspect it will not have been done using the usual legal documentation, which would list his former real name, but rather through documentation provided by a skilled counterfeiter. So if you continue your investigation into this area, don't be surprised if you don't find legal documents.

Could you please try to persuade Ben not to take this matter to the police yet? I think you should continue with your investigations and test some of Ben's theories. Meanwhile, I will contact a private investigator I know in Zurich and ask him to start digging at this end.

I will reply to your Scottish email in the next couple of days.
Dominic

Elizabeth read the email twice to make absolutely sure she understood Dominic's wishes. She had not been expecting him to show such intense interest, but she was delighted that he had. His hatred of his ex-father-in-law must run very deep, she concluded.

Now she intended to meet with Ben as soon as possible to discuss how to take the investigations forward. She was already sure that Ben would agree to leave the police out of it. He preferred to solve mysteries by his own means, then hand the solved case over to the police.

Before picking up the phone to call him, a creeping darkness in the room took Elizabeth's eyes to the window. The morning's grey sky had been replaced by one of brooding black and a distant flash of lightning told of trouble ahead.

Chapter 28

At their next meeting in Ben's conservatory, during which Elizabeth told Ben of her recent contact with Dominic, and his wish that they should continue investigating Prentice, they came to an agreement about the best way to proceed. Ben would do most of the indoor, sedentary investigation online, by phone, etc. while Elizabeth would do any outdoor, physical investigation required.

Ben decided to start with a return to his probing of the big oil companies' executives, but this time to saturation level over a longer period. Elizabeth felt that if Prentice had been attacked by the men in wetsuits, he might be thinking about taking flight. Elizabeth, therefore, was going to try to find a way to keep an eye on him. She also decided she would try to cover some of the ground that the police may not have had time to cover, such as along the river banks where the bodies of the two men were found.

As Elizabeth explained her plans, Ben could see how enthusiastic she was. Before she left he asked her not to make the mistake of neglecting her other work. "Remember, most fishing trips end with nothing."

That night, undeterred by Ben's parting words, Elizabeth lay in bed trying to think of an elevated location somewhere around the shores of Derwent Water from where she might be able to observe the front elevation and garden of Becalmed. It was better than doing nothing; it was a start. She might get lucky and see something significant or, heaven help her, the next wet-suited assassins creeping towards the house.

The next day, having done some routine work for Dominic in the morning, Elizabeth drove along the east shore of Derwent Water. She was on a reconnaissance mission. She was heading for a tourist hotspot called Surprise View. It was a small clearing on top of a vertical, wooded crag which afforded great elevated views of Derwent Water, and hopefully of the area containing Becalmed.

She came to a small signpost announcing the village of Watendlath, turned left and started the narrow, winding climb up the tree-covered fell. After a harrowing fifteen-minute drive, which saw many tourists turn and go back, she arrived at the Surprise View car park, which was simply a small clearing in the woods.

It was only a short walk to the edge of the crag, where she found a group of tourists gazing at the views. Some were noticeably quiet, the captivating scene apparently too beautiful for words. Others whispered, as if in a cathedral. "To think," she heard an American man whisper, "yesterday we were in New York." His companion didn't reply. There was something akin to reverence in the almond eyes of a Japanese group. Then, relatively loudly, a Yorkshire voice said, "Beats Huddersfield," and a wave of gentle laughter swept through the gathering.

Elizabeth found a place amongst the clicking cameras and raised her binoculars. It took her a few sweeps of the shoreline to find Becalmed, tucked away among the trees. From this angle she couldn't see all of the front elevation because of the trees, but she could see most of the roof and the garden and the boathouse.

There was no activity to be seen around Becalmed, so Elizabeth withdrew from her position and started to look for a more private location. After walking a few metres, she found a good viewing spot between two trees and was pleased to see that the ground was not trampled, indicating that the tourists did not tend to venture away from the main viewing area.

Satisfied that she had found a good spot, she was walking back to the car park when something about her encounter with the tourists made her stop. They had come from all over the world to see this wonderful place, but she had quickly turned her back on it in her dash to some sort of achievement. Slowly, she turned and walked back to the edge of the crag and looked again, as if for the first time, and let the beauty before her work its wonders on her busy mind.

Two days later, on a warm afternoon, Elizabeth took up her position between the trees and settled down for her first "spying" session. She had come well prepared, her metal-framed backpack folded into a seat, and she had filled it with a snack, some water, waterproofs, spare pullover, laptop, and notepaper and pen. Fortunately spring was the driest season in the Lakes, so she didn't expect to use the waterproofs very often.

The only activity she saw that day was a pair of mallards landing on the jetty, waddling along it to the lawn, where they nibbled at the grass before flying off.

At her next spying session, two days later, she found Prentice's daughter, Claire, already sitting in her wheelchair in the centre of the lawn. She had a pair of binoculars resting on the blanket covering her lap and every time a boat on the lake approached her vicinity, she followed it with her binoculars until it moved on. While the binoculars were in her hands, she then proceeded to scan all the slopes of the fells surrounding Derwent Water. She did this for about three hours then wheeled herself back into the house. Elizabeth thought it a bit strange that Claire had been left alone for so long and that nobody had brought her a drink during that time.

Three more uneventful spying sessions passed, Elizabeth using her non-binocular time to work for Dominic on her laptop and using her notepad to draft her next article for *The Tribune*.

When she arrived for her next session, she found the garden empty again. But as she lifted her laptop out of her backpack, she spotted some movement. Raising her binoculars she saw Claire, once again taking up her position in the centre of the lawn, and Prentice pushing a lawnmower. This in itself was informative as it confirmed the Prentice family's obsession with privacy and security; why else would a millionaire cut his own lawn? Barbara also turned up and sat on one of three wooden seats which were spaced out around the perimeter of the lawn. She appeared to be reading a book.

Elizabeth watched this idyllic scene for about ten minutes and was reaching for her bottle of water when she heard the sound of a helicopter. A common sight in the skies of the Lake District, she presumed it would be the

Air Ambulance Service helicopter, which is called in by the Mountain Rescue teams when a rescue involves a person with serious injuries. Instinctively, she lifted her binoculars to watch it.

She spotted the small yellow dot approaching from the north. It soon grew larger as it flew over the centre of Derwent Water towards the Borrowdale valley. It flew past her at about the same height as she was, giving her a clear view of the crew. Its course was taking it over the area where Becalmed sat among the trees. Elizabeth scanned her binoculars over towards Becalmed and was just in time to see Prentice running off the lawn into the house, gesticulating urgently to Barbara to follow him, which she did. He had left the lawnmower behind, Barbara had left her book, and both had left Claire sitting in her wheelchair.

"They were scared," Elizabeth declared. They were running scared because they thought they were being attacked from the air. But why had they not included Claire in their dash to safety? Did they assume that nobody would attack someone in a wheelchair?

Five minutes later, the skies now quiet, both Prentice and Barbara reappeared. They had a brief word with Claire, then continued with their mowing and reading. Elizabeth collected her things and called it a day. She was now convinced that the Prentices were in danger, that some enemy from their past was intent on taking their lives. She hoped that Ben and Dominic's investigations would lead them to that enemy.

PART TWO

Chapter 29

Carlos De Leon was born in a country destined for tragedy. Situated on a major Central American fault line, Guatemala was prone to regular earthquakes and volcanic eruptions. Over the centuries this had left the country with a dramatic landscape, including thirty-seven volcanoes, and a capital city, also called Guatemala, with an incongruous mix of traditional dwellings and tower blocks, the tower blocks having been built to house the people who survived the 1976 earthquake, which had killed 23,000 people.

The regular violence of its land was occasionally matched by its people as they fought each other in civil wars and, in current times, in street gangs. However, Guatemala City's murder rate was seen as relatively low compared to the capital cities of the country's neighbours, such as Mexico to the north and Honduras to the south. Unlike its neighbours it was not involved in the manufacture of drugs, though drug supply within the country was the main cause of gang violence.

Carlos was born in a single-storey dwelling in a poor outer suburb of Guatemala City. His father, who like many others had moved into the city to escape the poverty of the countryside, had turned one of the rooms into a slaughter-house and another one into a butchers shop. The remaining two rooms were given over to domestic use.

Carlos's father worked hard but only made enough money to send his son to school, his three daughters having to miss out on education.

The school teachers reported that Carlos was a bright kid who did well at English language lessons and on the sports field at baseball, soccer and athletics.

Carlos shared a bedroom with his three younger sisters. His abiding memory of their childhood together was that of comforting them during long nights as they listened to their mother being beaten by their father in the adjacent room. The beatings usually took place on a Sunday, his father's day of rest from his long hours in the slaughterhouse and butchers shop. On Sundays he drowned his money worries and responsibilities with tequila, which had the effect of turning this peaceful man into an aggressive drunk.

At the age of twelve, Carlos started to try to stop his father from beating his mother but usually finished bruised and bloody as he was no match for his muscular father. Being held in his vice-like grip, breathing his alcoholic fumes and feeling the anger emanating from the man who, yesterday, laughed and played with him, was a trauma that would live with Carlos for the rest of his life.

Outside the home, Carlos spent his childhood playing soccer and baseball in the dusty streets, dreaming like most of his pals of becoming a professional when he grew up.

At the age of thirteen, Carlos killed his father.

After a Sunday afternoon game of soccer with his pals, Carlos had returned home to find his father attacking his mother. She had fallen to the floor and his father had knelt down over her to continue the onslaught. Carlos had witnessed similar scenes many times, but something about the dull look in his father's eyes and the fact that his mother had stopped struggling with him triggered Carlos to pick up a nearby baseball bat and aim a swing at his father's back. As Carlos swung, his father tried to swivel his body to avoid the blow. The result was that the bat connected with the side of his father's head, just above the ear. He keeled over onto his back, apparently unconscious.

Carlos helped his mother to a chair and brought her a drink of water. Five minutes later he checked on his father and found no sign of life. "I think he is dead," he whimpered to his mother. His mother knelt down beside her husband and felt his pulse and opened his eyes with her thumb. For a few moments she was silent as she stared in disbelief and shock. Then she turned to her son.

"You must go, Carlos. You must run away, or the police will arrest you," she croaked.

Carlos ran to his bedroom, where he found his sisters huddled together, crying. He put all the clothes he possessed into a plastic bag, said goodbye to his sisters, hugging and kissing each one, then returned to say goodbye to his mother. She thrust some coins into his hand. "This will pay for a bus to the city centre," she cried. Carlos felt her warm, plump arms wrap around him and crush him and he felt his heart pump in his throat as she pushed him away and said, "Go quickly."

Two years later, having learned how to survive on the city's streets, a knife being an essential defence weapon, he returned to the house to find it occupied by strangers.

After two more years on the street, he joined up with insurgents in the civil war, where he learned how to handle weapons and kill with his bare hands. By this time he had grown into a powerfully muscled young man.

He gradually became disillusioned with the insurgent movement and, during a lull in operations, walked out and headed north towards the Mexican border, thumbing lifts from truck drivers. His ultimate aim was to cross from Mexico into the United States, there to start a new, stress-free life.

Chapter 30

Carlos entered Mexico through the border town of Gracios A Dios (Thanks to God), a notorious smuggling hub used by thousands of migrants as they made their hopeful way north to the USA. Here there was no formal border crossing, just a line of white stone obelisks marking the border. Fields of corn and beans grew on the Guatemalan side, while cattle roamed the hills on the Mexican side. The truck driver giving him a lift used it frequently, sympathetically giving lifts to travellers like Carlos.

When asked by Carlos where he might make some money as he travelled north, the driver offered to introduce him to the boss of the wholesaler's warehouse where he was off-loading his cargo of boxes of bananas. This was in the town of Comitan just twenty miles inside the Mexican border. The driver explained that the boss usually had work for truck drivers going north as long as they didn't ask questions.

They arrived in Comitan in the late afternoon. The driver introduced Carlos to the boss, a burly man called Diego Alfara. He was about fifty years old, with receding hair, large gut and a missing small finger on his right hand. The boss asked Carlos what trucks he had driven in the past and Carlos gave him the names of a number of trucks, failing to mention he had driven them during his time with the insurgents. In answer to further questions, Carlos said that he could cope with delivering a load of pineapples to Oaxaca, an eleven-hour drive, and bringing a return load back to the warehouse by late afternoon the following day. The boss, who insisted on being called Señor Alfara, offered to give him a few days' trial, told him how much he would be paid and said he could sleep in the truck and use the warehouse facilities until his early start the next day.

Carlos set off at 6 a.m. the next day and returned the following day by 4 p.m. He had enjoyed the freedom of the open road, seeing new places, meeting new people, the prospect of earning a wage, however small. The inevitable loneliness and tiredness had to be accepted.

After another eight days of delivering and returning loads to and from the north, always within schedule, the boss offered him a full-time job. Carlos gratefully accepted and began calculating how long he would have to stay there to earn enough money to pay for accommodation and meals on his planned journey north to the USA, a trip of some 2,000 miles.

A month later Señor Alfara called Carlos into his office, told him he had performed well and as a result was now being transferred onto a different roster, one that covered the same journeys to the north, but carried other products alongside the fruit and vegetables. On this roster he would be paid three times his existing wage. This was classed as danger money because the trucks were occasionally attacked by small-time gangsters intent on stealing the other products. He would have to carry a gun to defend the cargo and himself.

Carlos didn't need to ask what the "other products" were

because he had heard from other drivers that his company was known to ship drugs manufactured by their southern neighbours Honduras and El Salvador to the north of Mexico and into the USA. Apparently there were seven more wholesalers like his strategically located on the long journey to the US border. Word was that state governors and police chiefs were all being paid to look the other way as the trucks drove through their states.

Carlos accepted the new job and was given a Beretta 90two pistol and ammunition. He was familiar with the gun and confident that he could defend himself with it. He had no great desire to take part in the drug running business but had no major objection to it, the drug trade being so commonplace in Mexico and other Central American countries. More importantly, the increase in wages now gave him options on how he could travel north to the USA. Now, instead of hitching lifts and sleeping in cheap lodgings over the 2,000-mile journey as originally planned, he could buy himself an old motorhome or van and sleep in it as he drove the whole way. All he would need to do is work a few more weeks than originally planned.

During the next two months, Carlos learned that he was now indirectly employed by the Sinaloa Cartel, the largest drug cartel in Mexico and the biggest criminal organisation in the world, involved in money laundering and other crimes as well as drug running, and having international ties with the Mafia and the Chinese Triads. He was told that other Mexican cartels were too afraid of the Sinaloa to attack their convoys, so any attack on his truck would probably be done by naïve individuals or local gangs trying their luck.

Carlos experienced two attacks during those months. In the first one, two teenagers confronted him in the dark as he left a roadside truck-stop cafe. They threatened him with knives and demanded he hand over the truck keys. His past experience told him that their tone of voice and body language were not those of seasoned criminals and that they were no real threat. He simply pulled out his Beretta and watched them run for their lives, glad of the darkness.

The second attack was more serious. He had pulled off the road in a remote, forested area to have a short sleep break, having eaten too many enchiladas for lunch. Before going to sleep he had locked the doors and windows and placed his Beretta on the seat alongside his right thigh, his right hand resting lightly on it.

A forceful bang on his driver's-side door woke him up. His hand automatically took hold of his gun. Looking out of the window, he saw a man standing five paces away from the door, pointing a gun at him and gesticulating an order to open the door. Quickly glancing at the passenger side, he saw another man at that window also pointing a gun at him. Both looked middle-aged and had a hard history engraved in their features. Carlos reckoned that once he opened the door, they would kill him, and if he did not open the door, they would shoot at him through the windows. Men like this did not leave witnesses to their crimes.

Quickly, as though compliant, he raised both hands and showed them to the man on his side, then lowered them, and with his left hand he eased the door open. He saw the man's body tense and aim the gun at him. Now with his Beretta in his right hand, below the window level, Carlos pushed the door slowly open, and when he judged it was sufficiently open to give him a shot, he fired his gun from hip level, aiming low. The man gave a gasp and fell to the ground clutching his left thigh and dropping his gun. Carlos leapt out of the truck, ran to the man, picked up his gun, then ran around the back of the truck to tackle the other man. He was standing with his back against the passenger door, listening to the shouts of his injured partner, clearly unsure of his next move. From the back of the truck, Carlos shouted to him that he would not shoot him provided he left and took his partner with him.

There was a pause then a lot of shouting between the two men. Finally, the man shouted to Carlos saying that they wanted to leave. Carlos told him to go ahead but leave his gun on the ground. After a few seconds Carlos poked his head around the corner of the truck and saw the man leave his gun as instructed and walk quickly around the front of the truck towards his partner. Carlos followed him and saw him help his partner into their nearby car and drive off.

Once again Carlos felt grateful for his military training. He had learned that once a leader was down, the follower rarely carried on, and it was better to give the follower a chance to quit than to engage in further shooting. He had shot the leading man in the thigh because he took no pleasure in killing, particularly people who had probably had a bad start in life like himself.

Now, a week after the last attack, Carlos reckoned he had earned enough money to buy an old vehicle and head for the USA. He told Señor Alfara his plans and thanked him for the job. He had been a good employer. Used to drivers coming and going at short notice, Señor Alfara wished him well, and told him about a small garage in town where he would pay a fair price for an old vehicle. He also advised Carlos to take the west coast route north, which finished on the border with the USA at the city of Tijuana. This was the main crossing place into the USA, the Californian city of San Diego a short distance away. He gave Carlos the name and phone number of a man in Tijuana, a member of the "wholesalers" organisation, who would probably help Carlos to cross without a passport. This man would want payment for his service.

Two days later, now the proud owner of an old Volkswagen T2 camper van, Carlos left Comitan and headed north on his 2,000-mile drive to a better life.

Chapter 31

Two weeks after seeing Charles and Barbara running scared off their lawn at the approach of a helicopter, Elizabeth decided to call off her spying sessions. In that time she had seen them, occasionally, in the garden, reading or pottering, apparently taking advantage of the improving weather. On one very sunny day, she saw Charles and Claire bring his boat out of the boathouse and take a leisurely three-hour trip around the lake, Claire spending most of her time looking through her binoculars.

This spying business was not achieving much, Elizabeth decided. And it was very boring and time consuming. She needed to be more productive. It was time for another update with Ben.

The following day she found Ben sitting on his garden seat, pen and notebook at the ready. "Well, if it isn't the new Mata Hari." Ben smiled.

"Who?"

"I've done it again, haven't I? It seems these references from the past don't travel as well these days. She was a Dutch woman who was accused of spying for the Germans in the First World War. She was eventually executed by a French firing squad. For some reason her name became synonymous with spying by females."

"I don't mind the spying association," Elizabeth said. "But I'm not so keen on the execution thing."

Ben patted the seat beside him. "Let's just sit for a while and give our busy little brains some time off."

"Yes, please."

The sun was pleasantly warm, the pheasants and mallards were scrapping on the lawn as usual, and a horde of smaller birds took turns on the bird feeders, fluttering like butterflies while they waited their turn.

Elizabeth watched them for a while then turned her face up to the sun, relaxed, and closed her eyes. It wasn't long before she drifted towards sleep. Just before she succumbed, a sudden, loud bang woke her up. She opened her eyes and looked for the cause.

"Shotgun," Ben said. "Local farmer probably. Just when I was reliving a birdie on the ninth I got a couple of days ago."

"I thought it was the local firing squad warming up," Elizabeth joked.

"Perhaps it was the starting gun for our chat...I suppose we'd better get started. Do you want to go first?"

"Okay," Elizabeth said and went on to tell Ben about the results of her spying activities.

"Nothing very sinister there," Ben observed. "Are you sure Prentice and his wife were running into the house because of the approaching helicopter?"

"It looked that way to me."

"What if they had simply heard their phone ring and were running in to answer it? Or they had heard a noise at the front of the house and went to investigate? There could be lots of reasons why people run into their houses. And, if they thought they might be under attack, why did they not take their daughter in with them?"

"Yes, that last question had me wondering too. And I don't have an answer to it. But I am ninety percent certain that it was the approach of the helicopter that made them run in. They were turning and looking up at it as they ran."

Ben pushed his glasses up and scratched his ear. "Okay, let's assume you are right. What can we learn from it?"

Elizabeth jumped in quickly. "That whoever wants them killed has plenty of money. Prentice believed that the helicopter contained his enemies. That means he knows they can afford to rent or buy a helicopter. And assuming the two dead men in the river, both from South America, were hired to kill them, that also speaks of big money."

"Hired professionals would not have been deterred by a security system. The property is in a very remote location; nobody would see them. They could barge down the gates with a suitable vehicle or climb a fence, do their worst, and make their escape long before the police could respond to the alarm system. Maybe they were using a quiet approach from the lake because they *don't* want to kill them. Maybe their objective is to interrogate them. That could take a long time, which would make it essential that the security system had not been activated by their intrusion."

"But surely they could remove the Prentices from the house and take them away with them to interrogate them elsewhere."

"Too risky. Better to do the interrogation in the house without the police or anybody else being aware of it, rather than alerting the police and trying to escape their inevitable blockades."

"Have you heard anything else from the police?"

"No. I spoke to Peter, Inspector Murphy, a few days ago and he had nothing new to tell me. His whole tone indicated that the case no longer had any priority. Probably because they had not been able to identify the men and no obvious crime had been committed. We must never forget that the men could have been having an innocent day out and suffered an unfortunate accident. We could be wasting our time on this."

"God! I hope not. I know it's mostly about my suspicions about their strange behaviour and heavy security and linking that to two men found dead in the vicinity. I know it's a thin thread that joins them, but what if we abandon our investigations and one day they are all found murdered? I would find that hard to live with."

"So would I, Elizabeth. Anyway, I enjoy doing this sort of thing, so let's keep digging, eh?"

"Yeah, let's. How have your investigations been going?"

"Well, I've just finished a world-wide search of the last fifteen years of overseas operations of all the big oil companies and there's still no sign of Prentice, whether an executive or not. The same goes for all the big company headquarters around the world – no Prentice. He has probably stolen somebody's identity at random or paid somebody to steal it for him."

"You make that sound easy."

"It is easy, if you know how to use the information that is readily available online. Social media hands it to you on a plate. People talk to each other quite openly online and share lots of routine, innocent information. Online security people reckon it is possible to steal an identity in forty-five minutes of online research, plus the time it takes to make a few phone calls."

"Frightening."

"Anyway," Ben went on, "I'm not going to waste any more time hunting for Prentice in the oil industry. It doesn't really matter where he worked or what his name is. The important thing is establishing that this man is responsible for the deaths of the two men in wetsuits, and if so, answering all the whys that follow on from that. Assuming he killed them in self-defence, as we suspect, we need to find out if they were paid professionals or operating on their own. If they were professionals, then we know we are dealing with money people, and that the wrong he did to them must have been big to warrant his execution. What kind of people hire professional killers? Gangsters, businesses, governments, rich individuals."

"My guess would be one of the first three," Elizabeth offered. "If it was a government, perhaps it was a foreign one. Perhaps Prentice worked for our Secret Service and became involved in anti- Islam operations, and now he has become the target of Islamic terrorists?"

"Who knows," Ben said. "We have so little to go on at the moment. I'm going to start on a different tack. On the basis that it might have been a major crime Prentice committed, one that made the headlines, I am going to search for them over the last fifteen years in the UK and America."

"Why America?"

"Because he is married to an American. Perhaps they lived there for a while. I know it's a needle in a haystack job, but often I've found that just the act of searching can trigger something else – a new idea or thought, that eventually brings results."

"Good luck."

A long silence followed and when the conversation switched to the amusing behaviour of the wildlife on the lawn, it became apparent that the serious stuff was over. Elizabeth started to rise from her seat, and Ben did likewise. They walked together towards the cottage.

"I'm finally going to walk the length of the river where the men in wetsuits were found," Elizabeth announced. "The spring weather has dropped the water level considerably. Here's hoping I can find something helpful to our cause."

Ben turned to her. "Be careful near that river. There's a lot of exposed mud when it's low; you can get stuck in it. I would take a stick to test it before standing on it."

"I always take my stick when walking," Elizabeth reassured him, appreciative of his concern.

They entered the cottage together, where Ben insisted Elizabeth must join him for tea and scones before she left.

Chapter 32

Seven days after leaving Comitan, Carlos drove into the city of Tijuana. His old camper van had proved to be reliable on the long journey and it was going to have to continue providing him with a place to sleep for the foreseeable future because he had only seventeen pesos left in his pocket.

He was not looking forward to spending time in Tijuana, known internationally as the most violent city in the world. Gang murder had accounted for over 100,000 deaths in the last ten years, with another 35,000 people missing, presumed dead. The Sinaloa Cartel bore most responsibility.

It shared a fifteen-mile border with San Diego on the US side, and it was the main crossing point between the two countries, handling over 50 million people each year. These numbers made it impossible for the border authorities to apprehend all the drugs and people that were smuggled into the USA in an endless twenty-four-hour stream of traffic. It was via this stream of traffic that Carlos, aided by the contact Señor Alfara had given him, expected to be smuggled into the USA. Unfortunately he was going to have to find work in the city in order to pay the contact for this service.

That evening he parked on wasteland on the city outskirts and went to sleep early as the long journey had taken its toll.

The next morning he phoned his contact, Señor Mateo Perez, and was relieved to find him available. Perez invited him to come to the warehouse, which was located on a large industrial estate close to the city airport.

Mateo Perez was very un-Mexican in appearance, being tall and thin, his clothes hanging as though on a coat hanger. He was younger than expected, about thirty-five. A hooked nose and turned-down mouth made him look parrot-like.

Señor Alfara had already informed Perez of Carlos's wish to cross the border into the USA without a visa or passport. Carlos asked Perez how much money it would cost and told him he needed to find work to raise the money. Perez immediately offered him a job. But it was not a driving job or a job in the warehouse. It was in security, which entailed personal bodyguard work for senior staff when travelling on business, and general warehouse security when not otherwise employed. It included escorting Perez himself on his daily journey to and from work. Perez explained that Señor Alfara had told him that Carlos was very reliable, could handle a gun and was capable of dealing with dangerous situations.

Carlos already knew about the situation in Tijuana, where rival cartels were constantly at war, fighting for control of the vast drug market that existed in the city because of its proximity to the USA. He had no desire to become involved in it.

Carlos told Perez he was not interested in getting involved in dangerous situations. He would rather do something else, like driving.

Perez snarled, "You don't get to choose. You do what I say."

"So, I'll find somewhere else to work," Carlos said and turned to go.

He had only taken two steps when two men he had not previously noticed stepped out of the shadows and pointed guns at him.

"Nobody walks out on the Sinaloa," Perez hissed.

Carlos stood still, keenly aware that if he tried to fight or run, he would be shot. One of the men stepped forward and frisked Carlos for weapons. Finding none, he stepped away, shaking his head.

Suddenly, Perez's manner changed. He smiled at Carlos. "Look, we are brothers. We all work for the Sinaloa. I hear you are a good man. We need good men. We pay good men well. You work for me, you do well...Where is the problem?"

Carlos stared at him. "How long do I have to work before I can go across the border?"

"Six months."

"Six months?"

Perez sneered. "If you have 100,000 pesos, you can go tomorrow."

Carlos took a few seconds to run through his options. Finally, he said, "When do I start?"

Chapter 33

Lakeland's warm, dry spring had performed its usual blotting paper effect on the landscape, soaking up the rains of winter, drying out the mud-splashed fields, calming the roaring rivers. The once skeletal trees, drunk with excess water, had sprung into leaf at astonishing speeds. The insects and birds had appeared from nowhere and filled the air with sound.

Although Elizabeth was on a serious mission, she could not help but enjoy her favourite time of year as she walked along the river bank close to John Garston's farm, the place where the two wet-suited men had been found dead. As expected, the river level had dropped considerably, exposing its muddy banks and in some instances its bed. From the exact location where she had found the first man, she planned to walk the bank until she reached its conclusion at Derwent Water, a distance of about one mile.

It wasn't long before she was scrambling down the river bank to examine something on the river bed reflecting the light of the sun. It turned out to be the top of a food tin, probably discarded by careless campers.

The next shiny item peeping out of the mud turned out to be a brown beer bottle, no doubt campers again.

And so it went on as she walked along the bank

– numerous eye-catching items turning out to be innocent everyday objects, their discarders not so innocent.

She was about 200 metres from the end of her walk when something else caught her eye. This time it didn't shine, but its dead black, engineered shape told her it was man-made. Picking it carefully out of the mud, Elizabeth realised, with an ever-increasing heartbeat, that it was a small handgun. She assumed it wasn't a toy because it had some weight about it. On rinsing the mud off in the slow-moving river, she saw the words *M&P Bodyguard 380* embossed on the main metal casting. She was very careful not to touch the trigger or any other bits that looked moveable as she placed it, gingerly, in her backpack.

She completed her walk without finding anything else and turned to go, her pace picking up to match her heartbeat.

Realising she was not far from Ben's cottage, she decided to call in to show him her find.

Ben was delighted to see her, as always, and soon they were sitting in his conservatory. Helen was out at work.

"I've found something interesting lying on the river bed," Elizabeth said while lifting the gun out of her backpack.

"Good heavens!" Ben exclaimed as Elizabeth lay the gun on the coffee table.

"Do you know anything about guns?"

"Not a thing." Ben leaned forward and carefully lifted the gun by its handle. He examined it, turning it over. "It's a Smith & Wesson," he said, squinting at the name lightly etched on the opposite side to *M&P Bodyguard 380*.

"I hadn't noticed that. Does the name mean anything to you?"

"Only that it often came up in Hollywood westerns years ago. Maybe it's an American make. This one looks quite new, doesn't it?" Ben started to rise from his seat, still holding the gun. "Why don't we go to my office and check it out online."

They made their way upstairs, where Elizabeth looked over Ben's shoulder as he searched the web.

"Here we are," Ben said eventually. "Founded in 1852, headquarters in Springfield, Massachusetts, USA. It's obviously still going strong – they have over 2,000 employees."

He scanned down the first page under the heading *Revolvers* and found no reference to the Bodyguard range. Under the heading *Pistols* on the next page, he eventually found the Bodyguard range. Designed for personal protection, it claimed to be compact, lightweight, simple to use and ideal for concealed carry. Next came lots of incomprehensible technical stuff, including the fact that its capacity was 6 + 1 rounds.

"Looks like the men were carrying more than knives," Elizabeth suggested.

"Yes, I agree. It's very unlikely to have been anyone else, and it's just the sort of lightweight gun you would choose to carry while swimming. I wonder if they both had a gun and one is yet to be found? I wonder how they got the gun into the country?"

"Maybe they got it from contacts already living in England."

"Or maybe they didn't enter the country via the usual legal means."

Elizabeth sighed. "At least we can now discount the possibility that the men were harmless swimmers."

"Agreed," Ben said, "and that is important. We now know we are not wasting our time. But at the moment I can't see that finding the gun answers any other questions; it just adds to them. I think by law we have to hand this over to the police, but before we do, we should take photographs of it for our reference."

Ben stood up and laid the gun on an A4 sheet of white paper and proceeded to take a few photographs using his phone. "I'll ask Peter to drop by and pick it up."

"Do you think the police will get more involved now?" Elizabeth asked.

"Maybe...but I don't think we can rely on them. I think we should continue to do our own thing. I suppose they might contact the American police to see if the gun is traceable, but don't hold your breath – you can buy a gun as easy as a tin of beans over there."

Ben switched off the computer and rose from his chair. "I'll let you know what Peter has to say about it. Meanwhile, I think it's about time we had a cup of tea and a scone."

Half an hour later, Elizabeth left Ben's cottage and made her way home.

On entering her cottage, she headed straight for her computer to ask Dominic if his private detective had un-covered anything useful.

Chapter 34

As Elizabeth began to email Dominic, a now familiar frisson swept through her. She had noticed for some time that the way they communicated had become more relaxed, less business-like, at times warm and familiar. She now regretted the barrier she had erected around herself when they first met, when she didn't know whether he was sinner or saint. At that time she had thought it important to appear business-like and professional and certainly not to reveal her attraction to him, something that had occurred the instant she looked up and found him standing in front of her in Smyth's office. Now every time she heard his voice or simply typed his name, she felt a hopeful surge of anticipation. Unfortunately it was usually followed later by disappointment as their moment of contact ebbed away in a pleasant but platonic manner.

Dominic had clearly got her message when they first met. All she could do was hope that he was now picking up her new signals. Her worse fear was that he had already picked up her signals and wasn't interested, something that wouldn't surprise her. After all, he had previously been married for six years and might not be keen to get involved again. He was also seven years older and had established his own business while she was just a student. That made him much more mature and worldly than she was, so he probably viewed her as too immature for him. Perhaps she was simply not his type. Perhaps he already had a girlfriend in Zurich? Until she knew the answers to these questions, she had no choice but to carry on being warm and friendly towards him and hope for the best.

She clicked on her email app and found five emails awaiting her attention. One was from Dominic; she immediately gave it priority.

Dear Elizabeth,

She loved the old-fashioned way he addressed her. No American destruction of the language here. She dare not hope that he actually meant she was dear to him, and assumed it was simply the way people still addressed each other on the continent.

Our German client (Mr Felix Schafer) is starting to ask questions about the castles in Scotland that you visited. I have answered many of them using the report you provided after your visits, but there are quite a few that I couldn't answer, e.g. he wants estimates of how much repair work or upgrading would be required to bring the castles up to modern standards.

Out of the four castles on your list, he has already dismissed the one in the Highland region, the small tidal island being too remote for his family.

I need to see these properties for myself now, so could you please make arrangements to meet me at Glasgow Airport and take me on a tour of the other three? Please, therefore, make appointments with your contacts at the castles and let me know dates ASAP. Please also arrange accommodation for us en route – you know the type we prefer.

If any of this upsets plans you have already made, let me know and we can discuss priorities.

Yours

Dominic

Elizabeth read it again and her eyes settled on the addition of "Yours" when signing off. If only that was true. She also noticed the inclusive "we" regarding choice of accommodation.

Once again she could not stop a hopeful surge of anticipation sweeping through her at the thought of spending two or three entire days and nights together. The probable let-down afterwards was, for the moment, placed firmly in her denial tray.

Six days later Elizabeth stood in Glasgow Airport's arrivals zone waiting for Dominic. The mid-day sun flamed through the large glass windows, giving the area an unusually bright, warm glow. It mirrored the way Elizabeth felt at the prospect of seeing Dominic again.

Dominic arrived, casually dressed in an open-necked navy blue shirt, fawn chinos and sandals. He was carrying a holdall. He looked quite serious yet ridiculously boyish. When he saw Elizabeth an instant smile appeared and remained until he reached her and bent to kiss her on both cheeks.

He took a step back and stared at her for some time. "Elizabeth..." he started, but didn't go on, and continued staring at her.

Puzzled by his behaviour, Elizabeth eventually said, "Dominic..." then she also found herself lost for words.

More staring at each other took place until Dominic said, "Big chatterboxes, aren't we?"

They both started laughing at the same time. "How are you?" Dominic asked as the laughter faded.

"Fine..." Elizabeth said. She searched for something to add but couldn't find it. She became embarrassed as the silence that followed seemed interminable.

"Right, lead on, Elizabeth," Dominic said finally, rescuing the situation by switching to business mode. "Let's get out of here and hit the high road."

A relieved Elizabeth turned towards the exit. "Follow me," she said, pleased to hear her own voice was working again.

Soon she was driving over the River Clyde via the Erskine Bridge, taking the road that led to the Highlands.

She was heading for a castle on the Isle of Skye, a long drive which would last until evening, leaving them no time to visit the castle that day, but giving them all the following day to inspect it, with enough time left over to drive to their next overnight accommodation back on the mainland.

The long drive north seemed to pass quickly as they both found their voices again. The conversation centred mostly around business matters with the occasional switch to the Prentice family conundrum, Dominic confirming that his private detective had yet to come up with anything useful.

They also talked of their love of the Scottish wilderness as they swept through it and swapped stories of other wild places they had enjoyed or would like to visit. Dominic's favourite place was southeast Australia, which he had visited when on a skiing holiday in the Snowy Mountains. Elizabeth's was closer to home – the Hebridean islands.

Throughout the journey Elizabeth was on high alert, all her senses in their starting blocks, ready to respond to any word or movement from her passenger. She also sensed that Dominic was not his usual relaxed self. At times, Elizabeth thought that the air between them carried some sort of electric charge, though that could have been wishful thinking.

Inevitably, the long drive took its toll and long before they reached their destination, they had lapsed into silence.

Eventually, as evening approached, they arrived at their accommodation, a small hotel near the centre of Portree, Skye's main town. After booking in, neither felt like eating dinner, and they settled for a light supper and an early night. Elizabeth felt a tug of disappointment as they wished each other goodnight and went to their separate rooms.

After breakfast they were soon on their half-hour journey to Loch Dunvegan to inspect Kilcraig Castle. It was on the market for £3 million. "Doesn't seem much for a sixty-room castle," Elizabeth observed.

"All these old castles are relatively cheap to buy," explained Dominic, "because they need large sums spending on them to modernise them and they cost a fortune to heat and maintain."

On arrival at the castle, Dominic asked Elizabeth to make notes on the number and condition of the electric services to each room, while he concentrated on the volume of the rooms, for heating purposes, and the condition of the windows.

Five hours later they thanked the estate manager for showing them around and took their leave. They headed back to the mainland, where Elizabeth had arranged for them to spend the night in the beautiful Ross-shire village of Plockton, overlooking Loch Carron. Tomorrow they would inspect nearby Dunchoan Castle.

After booking in to the Highland Stag Inn, a small pub with five letting rooms in the heart of the village, they went up to their rooms to shower and change before meeting again for a bar meal at seven thirty.

The bar was relatively quiet when they sat down and ordered their meals, including a bottle of French wine which Dominic recommended. They started to discuss the results of their day at the castle, with Dominic announcing that his estimated price for a new central heating installation, plus new double glazed windows and a complete electrical rewiring, was approximately £290,000.

Although he hadn't been asked by the client to provide the information, he was also going to advise him that such a large estate would probably cost in the region of £500,000 per year to maintain based on wages for ten staff plus materials.

Elizabeth tried to assimilate all the information while sipping her wine but was glad when Dominic eventually stopped talking and sat back to enjoy his wine.

Soon they were tucking in to local venison while their conversation slowly changed from work to other matters, from local news to world events. They became so absorbed in this discussion that it was only when they took a breather to order another bottle of wine that they noticed an hour and a half had passed and the bar was heaving with people, a raucous birthday party starting to rev up.

After finishing their meal they both sat back, taking in

the sights and sounds of the bar. Talking was clearly over for the moment. Elizabeth glanced at Dominic. Was he happy in his single life? Did he have a girlfriend? What did he want in the future?

Before Dominic had the chance to start another safe conversation, Elizabeth decided to take the initiative. Otherwise she saw the night drifting into another pleasant but platonic memory.

She needed to tread carefully, so she started with an innocent question. "Do you still go skiing, Dominic?"

"Yes, occasionally, though not as much as I would like."

"That's understandable considering your work commitments. When you do get the chance, do you ski on your own or with friends?"

Dominic stroked his chin, a potential beard making an appearance because of the late hour. "I have two long-standing friends from my instructor days. We relive our youth every time we take to the slopes together...great fun."

"I wish we had ski slopes in the Lake District." Elizabeth sighed. "I'm told there isn't enough guaranteed snowfall to make a commercial slope viable."

Dominic looked into her eyes. "I take it you would like to ski?"

"I would absolutely love to."

"Why don't you come over to Zurich one weekend and I'll teach you the basics," Dominic said, making it sound as easy and routine as popping to the corner shop. "If you like it, I'm sure we could fit a few weekends in combining business and skiing."

Elizabeth floundered, the thrill of the sudden offer catching her off guard. "Are you serious?"

"Yes, of course."

Elizabeth hesitated. "I wouldn't be treading on anybody's toes, would I?"

Dominic looked puzzled. "Is that one of your strange English expressions or are you really concerned about standing on people's toes? Aren't you confusing skiing with dancing?"

Elizabeth laughed. "Your English is so good I often forget you're not English. The expression means: I hope I am not in danger of disturbing any arrangements you already have, particularly with the opposite sex."

The sudden laughter that came from Dominic made her jump and caused heads to turn in the noisy throng filling the bar. "You English." He scoffed. "You have alternative expressions for everything. I wonder why? What is wrong with plain speaking? If you want to know if I have a girlfriend, just ask."

Though now feeling embarrassed, Elizabeth stuck to her task, looking Dominic in the eye as she spoke. "We use them because we don't want to be considered as rude and superior as the French."

Dominic held up his hands, an admiring expression on his face. "Touché. *Tu es formidable, ma cherie.*"

Elizabeth smiled, enjoying the words "my dear" but remaining determined not to be side-tracked by compliments. "So what is the answer, Monsieur?"

Dominic leaned towards her across the table as if about to reveal all, then he hesitated, lifted his head and looked around the bar. "It's too noisy and crowded in here. Shall we grab a nightcap and go up to my room...or your room, and I will reveal all my secrets to you."

"How can I resist such an invitation?" Elizabeth spoke playfully, trying to hide the drama playing out in her head.

Dominic led the way through the cacophonous crowd and stopped at the bar. "I'll order a nightcap and bring it up," he shouted in her ear. "You don't need to wait...I'll see you upstairs."

Elizabeth asked for a whisky. If the night went badly, it would help drown her sorrows. If the night went well, it would be drunk in celebration.

Chapter 35

Elizabeth sat on a chair in a corner of Dominic's disappointingly small and not very well-appointed room. The Highland Stag had been the only establishment with vacancies in the popular holiday village of Plockton. She could see why.

The noise from the bar came up through the floor, indicating that the bar was directly below her. She would ask Dominic to relocate to her quieter room when he came up.

While waiting for Dominic she spent her time looking at the old paintings on the room's walls, mostly misty mountains and strutting stags, and tried to follow the intricate pattern on the dull wine carpet, wondering whether it was dye or spillage that had produced the colour – anything to take her mind off the bad news that was surely on its way.

She closed her eyes to black out her thoughts and found her head starting to spin. She realised she had drunk too much. But she didn't care. The worse that could happen would, tonight, be the thing that she wanted to happen.

Dominic arrived carrying their drinks. Before he settled she persuaded him to move on to her room, which was slightly larger than Dominic's and better appointed. On entering, she carried her drink to a chair adjacent to the dressing table, but Dominic headed straight for the bed, as he did at their first meeting. He put his drink on the bedside cabinet, fluffed up a pillow against the headboard and sat on the bed with his back to the headboard.

"Cheers," he said, raising his glass.

Elizabeth reciprocated. She paused, waiting for him to invite her to join him on the bed as he had at their first meeting.

When the invitation didn't materialise, Elizabeth thought she knew why. That first invitation had been a frivolous display of bravado by Dominic, a gesture of no consequence between strangers, with the mutually expected result of rejection. This time there could be consequences, and Dominic knew it. They were no longer strangers; there was an indefinable closeness between them, and they were both drunk. These were good reasons for Dominic not to repeat the invitation. But if he was really interested in her, would he not have asked and laughed it off if she rejected him again?

"Do I not get an invitation this time?" Elizabeth's words were out before she could stop them, no doubt propelled by alcohol.

Clearly surprised by the question, Dominic was slow to reply. "Er...yes...of course...sorry..." Then he smiled and tried to make light of the situation. "Anyway, it's your bed. You don't need an invitation." While speaking, he turned and placed the pillow beside him against the headboard. He patted the bed. "Your seat awaits, madame."

Elizabeth rose slowly from her chair and clambered onto the bed, resting her back against the pillowed headboard. Sitting side by side, their upper arms occasionally touching,

Elizabeth started to tense, and she wished she had not drunk so much.

"Welcome aboard." Dominic smiled as he raised his glass. He appeared to be very relaxed, and slightly distant.

Elizabeth now had the growing feeling that he saw her as a work colleague first and a friend second, someone who shared his views and made a good companion after work. She now felt embarrassed by her actions. She had been too forward and placed him in a difficult position. He was probably hurriedly thinking of a funny way to diffuse the situation, and a kind way to let her down. She sat in silence, unable to think of anything to say.

Dominic put his glass on the bedside cabinet and half turned to face her. "So, you want to know if I have a girlfriend."

Elizabeth stared straight ahead, braced herself, but said nothing.

Dominic went on, "The answer isn't yes or no. It's maybe."

"I don't understand," Elizabeth blurted.

"Well...strictly speaking I don't have a girlfriend in the full meaning of the word...but I recently met a lovely lady. We have only seen each other a few times because of work commitments, but she seems interested in me and I am certainly interested in her. I think there is a good chance that our relationship will eventually become a long-term one. Hence the maybe."

The news crushed Elizabeth. Dominic was lost to her, and she had made a fool of herself. She gritted her teeth, determined not to show her feelings. "Do you think she would mind if you gave me some skiing lessons?" she managed to ask in a level voice.

"Why don't we ask her?" Dominic said. He had a silly grin on his face, the look of someone who had told a joke and was waiting for his audience to get it.

Elizabeth wondered if he was making fun of her. Surely not? She remained silent.

Dominic turned to her and saw the perplexity in her face. Instantly, he reached over and took hold of her hand. "I am so sorry, Elizabeth. I thought you understood. It's you, Elizabeth...it's you. You are my lovely lady."

Elizabeth couldn't remember what was said immediately after those words, but she would never forget the hugs and kisses, the tears and laughter, and the blissful climax to their first night together.

Chapter 36

Three years after arriving in the Mexican city of Tijuana, Carlos De Leon was still living there. His boss, Señor Mateo Perez, had turned out to be a cunning, ruthless man, a master at manipulating people and situations so that they almost always did as he ordered. Those that didn't risked a gruesome death or a life of permanent fear, wondering if or when he would mete out his punishment. If they did a runner, they were still destined to a life of fear, of looking over their shoulder to see who followed them. The Sinaloa Cartel appeared to have a special department whose job was to seek out runners, anywhere in the world, and exterminate them. Hence their fearsome reputation and the reason why Carlos was not yet in the USA.

Like many others, Carlos had fallen into Perez's traps. During the first few months, he carried out his bodyguarding job to the best of his abilities. But when Perez ordered him to find and kill a member of an opposition cartel, Carlos refused. "I was employed as your bodyguard, not a hitman," he snapped.

"Killing this man *is* being my bodyguard," Perez hissed. "People tell me he is planning to kill me. You will end him first." He finished his sentence with a malignant smile.

"Why don't you fight your own battles," Carlos demanded.

This was met by an even more unsettling smile. "You are new, so you get one chance. But next time..." He used his hand to make a slashing action across his throat. "The rules are simple here. I tell you what to do and you do it... *Comprendo?*"

One of Perez's armed henchmen appeared from nowhere and stood beside Perez. Carlos realised that Perez must have some kind of signalling system arranged between them.

"Understood," Carlos seethed, fighting to hide the rage he felt.

Perez calmed down. "Good. I want this man gone *rapido*. Get on with it."

Carlos had managed to track the man down within two weeks. In that time he learned that the man, Adan Romero, was the local hitman for an Ecuadorian cartel called Los Choneros, one of the gangs constantly fighting the Sinaloa for control of the drug smuggling route from Ecuador to Central America.

From a distance the man looked terrifying, his shaven head, face and neck completely covered in snake tattoos. But when passing him in the street, something Carlos had deliberately arranged, he saw that beneath the tattoos was a furtive, frightened teenager. Carlos had noticed early in his time in Tijuana that most gang members were young, indicating that only a few of them survived into middle age.

Carlos started to follow Romero. He soon found the place Romero called home, one of three peeling red paint doors down a narrow, unlit alley.

Carlos had no intention of killing Romero. He planned

to confront him in the alley, tell him to quit town and threaten to kill him if he returned.

On the chosen night, dark and cool following a day of rain, Carlos saw Romero leave the bar he had seen him enter two hours earlier. He followed him along the main, glistening road and into the alley, its darkness now diluted by some of the light from the main road.

A few paces from Romero's doorway, Carlos closed in. He drew his gun and shouted, "STOP! Don't turn round..." Before Carlos had time to continue, Romero had started to turn and reach for his gun at the same time. Carlos shot him in the leg, hoping to save both their lives, but even as Romero's leg collapsed, sending him stumbling to the ground, he managed to twist and get a shot away. Carlos felt the bullet flick his trousers as it hurtled past. Now he had no choice. He called on his God to forgive him as he shot Romero in the chest. It was all over in three seconds.

Carlos stowed his gun, turned and walked away. As he was about to turn onto the main road, he heard an alley door open. He turned and saw a young woman come out of the doorway, pause as she took in the scene and then walk quickly and quietly to bend over Romero. The absence of screaming or other dramatics suggested to Carlos that she was not surprised to find him lying dead, that she had been expecting it to happen one day.

During his first year in Tijuana, Carlos was ordered by Perez to carry out one more single assassination and to team up with two other gang members in the killing of three enemies as they exited their car.

His single mission went almost the same as with Romero.

This time he managed to explain his full deal to his target, that he would not kill him if he left town and didn't return, but his target still went for his gun, an act which turned out to be his last. Carlos was learning that Tijuana had become a town where trust had been annihilated, a town with one simple rule – kill or be killed.

During his team mission, Carlos deliberately aimed above the heads of the targets as his team opened fire on the three men leaving their car. He gambled that his companions would kill the defenceless men without his help. His gamble paid off.

Over the next eighteen months, Carlos was involved in four more killings, each one increasing his hatred of Perez and his desire to escape. Every time he returned from a killing, Perez seemed to be surprised but pleased. Carlos guessed that this was because Perez now saw him as a reliable hitman, a valuable rarity given the short lives of most of them.

It was during this time that Carlos found, to his horror, that he had also become a target. Enemy gangs had become aware of him and now sought their revenge. He now understood the frightened, furtive look he had seen on Romero's face. His life had now become like Romero's, one of daily fear, watching, mistrusting, hiding, moving.

This was not the hitman's life as depicted in Hollywood films. Most of their hitmen were presented as anti-heroes, highly paid professionals, usually middle aged, experts in armaments, cool and smart, enjoying classical music and the company of intellectuals while lounging in their luxurious apartments.

In real life they were mostly young, macho, slum dwellers, often on drugs and desperate for the money to pay for them. They lived short, heightened lives of fear, and with many ready to take their place, they were expendable.

Carlos had managed to survive not because he was clever or good with a gun, but because he was not as stupid as his enemies – so far. They didn't take precautions; they took risks. They behaved in a careless, macho way, no doubt fuelled by drugs or alcohol.

In comparison, Carlos was nothing more than a steady operator, someone who didn't take drugs or alcohol and who was painstakingly careful, as any sane person would be when death was threatened. He saw every death he was involved in as an act of self-preservation. If the enemy didn't kill him, Perez would if he tried to escape.

Proof that Perez now saw him as a reliable member of his team came suddenly one day when he asked Carlos to drive him to an industrial area just outside Tijuana's airport perimeter. Here, he led him into a relatively small, newly built industrial unit, which required a password to enter.

The unit turned out to be just another wholesale business, with the floor covered with aisles of stacked pallets of vegetables and men with forklifts moving them about. Perez ushered Carlos to a distant corner of the unit, where Carlos was surprised to find two heavily armed men standing guard while others lowered plastic bags containing a variety of drugs down a hole in the concrete floor measuring approximately one metre square.

"Our tunnel is down there," Perez said, a touch of pride in his voice. "It is half a mile long and it takes our products to the American side of the border, to San Diego." A big grin was followed by, "There are no customs officers down there."

Carlos thought it would be wise to appear interested and impressed. "How do the bags travel along the tunnel?" he asked.

"There's a railway line. The bags are loaded onto flat carriages."

"Isn't there a danger of the tunnel walls collapsing?"

"You have much to learn." Perez smirked, shaking his head. "The Sinaloa do things properly. The tunnel walls are all lined with reinforced concrete. Our civil engineers know what they are doing."

"It must have cost millions."

"No problem," Perez boasted, as if he was personally responsible for the project. "Sometimes the Americans find our tunnels and we have to build a new one. No problem."

Carlos began to appreciate the massive scale and wealth of the Sinaloa Cartel's operation. He wondered why Perez had brought him here. Was he hoping to instil some pride and loyalty in him? If so, he was wasting his time. He hated the fact that Perez was revealing some of the cartel's secrets to him. The more he knew about them, the more certain it became that they would not let him go.

Perez continued to reveal more details. "We ship about 200 tonnes of product a year through this tunnel – not bad, eh?"

Carlos continued to feign interest. "And San Diego distribute it around the States, I guess?"

"No, San Diego ship it on to our main hub in Chicago. They distribute it."

Carlos couldn't be bothered to ask any more questions. He stared at two small lizards scurrying up a wall.

Perez went on. "When you drop through that hole, the space opens up and there's a steel ladder down to the tunnel. The hole is small so that it can be quickly hidden under a pallet of vegetables. The tunnel is used to transport people as well as product into the States..."

Suddenly, Carlos was excited. He looked at Perez. "You are letting me go..."

The sickly grin on Perez's face told him the answer. "You disappoint me, amigo. I told you already – nobody leaves the Sinaloa. We are sending you through the tunnel, but you will be coming back."

Carlos was past caring now and stared blankly at the floor. He refused to feed Perez the questions he was obviously waiting for.

Eventually, an irritated Perez said, "The San Diego operation is controlled by us in Tijuana. The boss over there has reported that one of his men has been stealing stock and selling it privately. He wants the man ended to deter others from doing the same, and he doesn't want the others to know who ended him. This is to increase their mistrust of each other and make them easier to control. That's why you have been chosen for the job."

"When do I go?" Carlos whispered, his head down, his staring eyes as dead as his spirit.

Chapter 37

On returning from Scotland, where she had kissed Dominic goodbye at Glasgow Airport, Elizabeth found herself in a daze. Dominic had told her that he had fallen in love with her at their first meeting in Smyth's office and that his first words to her had come directly from his smitten heart. He had found her cool response disappointing but understandable. He was a stranger; she was right to be wary.

Later, his despair at the thought of not seeing her again after their business had concluded had led him to offer her the job he had already planned to create. Leaving aside his personal reasons, he said he had no doubts that she was the right person for the job, possessing all the qualities and qualifications he was looking for.

Later still, when they knew each other well, his own self-doubt had stopped him from telling her how he felt. Why should she, he reasoned, a beautiful young woman just starting her adult life, be interested in him, an older divorced man? He had resigned himself to worship her from a distance but leave her free to live her life.

When, in the Plockton inn, she had revealed that she also had been holding her feelings back due to self-doubt, the joy that he felt had been indescribable.

Between them they had messed things up, wasted precious time, and now they had months of pent-up feelings aching to be released. The night had ended in a mutual eruption of emotion, an explosion of passion.

Before Dominic returned to Zurich, they had arranged their first skiing weekend together, with the ambition to make it a regular event, and to meet as often as possible on personal as well as business matters. Dominic thought it wise not to make too many commitments until they had spent more time together, and Elizabeth agreed, recognising that he was talking with the benefit of experience.

Now, floating about in her happiness cloud, she was reminded of the expression "love is like a drug" and she knew it to be true. She carried out her daily routines on auto-pilot, enjoying a thoughtless world which kept reality at bay.

It took a phone call from Ben to bring her down to earth. After initial niceties, he invited her to his cottage to bring her up to date with his investigations.

Elizabeth found Ben sitting on his garden seat enjoying the sun. He was his usual jocular self, enquiring if she had enjoyed her trip to the land of midges. Elizabeth joined in his mood by telling him she had indeed been bitten while in midge-land, but not by a midge, by a love-bug, and went on to tell him about her new relationship with Dominic.

Ben expressed his great pleasure at her news, then, eventually, got down to business. He explained that he had concluded his search for details of major crimes in the

UK and America in the past fifteen years and had found thousands. He said there were far too many to investigate in detail until he knew the exact type of crime he was dealing with, and in which country.

He was now going to concentrate on the two conclusions (accurate or not) they had reached so far and start to dig down into them, namely:

The people intent on killing the Prentices were wealthy, rich enough to hire hitmen and helicopters.

The fact that the hitmen could have ignored the security system, stormed the house and shot the occupants, but didn't. This meant they did not want to kill the Prentices, yet. They wanted information from the Prentices before killing or capturing them.

"So," Ben went on, "what could that information be? Usually, it is the answer to the question: what have you done with the money, or the jewellery, or the state secret, or the formulae, etcetera, etcetera?

"If we ask ourselves where is the best place to hide any of the above, the answer, surely, is not in a hole in the ground, but in a bank. And which countries are best known for allowing illegally obtained money or goods to be deposited? The Cayman Islands and Switzerland. And where have the Prentices come from? Switzerland."

Ben paused and looked at Elizabeth. "Agreed?"

"Yes. Tell me more."

"Not much more to tell, I'm afraid. That's about as far as I've got…theories about theories."

"Did Inspector Murphy say anything about the gun?" Elizabeth asked. "Does he think they can trace where it came from or, better still, the person who bought it?"

Ben made a snort of disapproval. "He contacted the American police who, apparently, took down the serial number etcetera and said they would send it to their National Tracing Centre. However, the police told him that the centre's success rate was only sixty-five percent because of their archaic system, which is frequently overwhelmed by the millions of guns sold each year in their 55,000 gun shops and the vast number of shootings they are asked to assist with. The system is not computerised, and the paper records are kept in each individual shop, so you have to trace the shop first. Peter is still waiting to hear from them."

When Elizabeth didn't comment, Ben went on. "I find it strangely comforting to know that the American authorities are as inefficient as ours."

"So, what do you think our next step is?" Elizabeth was keen to know if she could help him.

"There are still too many variants," Ben explained. "I need to narrow it down to the exact field of activity our protagonists were or still are involved in. I think, because of the Switzerland connection, I will start with money. I will search for crimes involving big money over the past fifteen years. Then, if I find nothing that fits, I'll move on to espionage, then jewellery and so on."

Elizabeth thought for a while. "Perhaps we should let Dominic know what you are doing, because of the Switzerland connection. He might want to ask his investigator to do the same thing at a local level."

"Good idea. Can I leave that to you?"

"Yes, I'll get straight onto it."

A knowing smile spread across Ben's face. "I thought you might. You can't wait to talk to your beloved again."

Elizabeth smiled. "True!"

Chapter 38

Although he had read about San Diego, and had seen lots of American cities in movies, Carlos was still unprepared for the contrast between San Diego and Tijuana, even though the two cities were joined together along a distance of fifteen miles, and only separated by a border fence.

He had read about the higher wages, the better roads, the bigger houses, the average home having two cars, no slums or squatter areas, but to see it in reality was still a shock.

This was why most Central Americans risked their freedom and sometimes their lives to cross the US border. This was why he had headed north from Guatemala.

Now that he had crossed the border via the drug tunnel, now that he was in the promised land, all he wanted to do was to keep going, to disappear into the vast hinterland of the USA, never to return to Mexico. But he couldn't. He had company in the car the Sinaloa had provided for him on arrival at the San Diego end of the tunnel, also located inside a vegetable warehouse on an industrial estate.

Sitting in the driver's seat was Dwayne, seventeen stone of tattooed muscle, obviously educated in Hollywood judging by his demeanour and vocabulary. When introduced to him as his guide to the city by Jose Garcia, the boss of the San Diego operation, Dwayne had given the game away by saying, "You gonna behave yourself, Beaner? I can be a pussycat when Beaners behave...that so, boss?"

Jose Garcia had shaken his head in dismay. "Sure, Dwayne, sure."

Carlos ignored the Beaner slur. He, like most Hispanics, was used to it.

It was obvious to Carlos that Perez had told them to keep an eye on him, that Perez thought he might do a runner once on the US side of the border. But Carlos had already decided not to run this time. He planned to fulfil his mission and return to Tijuana to gain more trust, then to make his escape the next time they sent him through the tunnel.

Carlos had arrived in the San Diego warehouse early that morning in order to not be seen by his target, who didn't start work until the afternoon. He was a local delivery man named Roy Mitchell. His job was to pick up stock from the warehouse in his white "vegetable" van and distribute it to the local dealers throughout San Diego and Southern California. This usually involved him working well into the night. The rest of the warehouse stock was delivered by various road and rail routes to the main distribution hub in Chicago.

Carlos had been given a photograph of Mitchell, together with his address. He was expected to follow Mitchell as he left the warehouse, trail him as he drove around San Diego delivering his stock and, if necessary, follow him to his home address at the end of his shift. It was up to Carlos to select a time and place where he could confront Mitchell and kill him. Carlos was also expected to leave the body in a place where it was easily found so that the killing would be reported in the media. This was to make sure the rest of the warehouse staff heard about it.

If Dwayne had not been with him, Carlos would have tried to persuade Mitchell to leave town and not come back, as usual. But that was no longer an option. He would have to kill Mitchell in cold blood, a prospect he hated.

Early that afternoon, Carlos sat in his car across the road from the warehouse exit. Light cloud cover provided him with some protection from the incessant sun, but nothing could protect him from the inane observations of his companion. Dwayne was some way through his latest conspiracy theory when he suddenly interrupted himself. "That's him, that's Mitch," he said. Carlos saw a white van reverse out of the warehouse, turn onto the road and drive off. Dwayne started the engine and followed the van.

It wasn't long before the van pulled into a suburban garage on the road into the city centre. Mitchell, a casually dressed, fortyish Mister Average got out of the van carrying a paper parcel and walked into the garage office. One minute later he came out of the office, empty-handed, climbed into his van and drove off.

Approximately two miles later the procedure was repeated at a drive-in liquor store close to the city centre.

In the city centre Mitchell made numerous calls at bars, nightclubs, food stores and restaurants, the size of his parcels noticeably larger than those left in the suburbs.

And so it went on, street after street. The large number of deliveries gave Carlos the impression that the whole of San Diego was using. At one point he asked Dwayne how often

Mitchell made these deliveries. "Every day," Dwayne drawled, "but a different area each day...roughly a week's supply each drop."

After about four hours Mitchell drove into a large parkland area and pulled up beside a park bench on which sat an attractive blonde woman gaudily dressed in orange shorts and a red blouse. As Mitchell exited his van, the woman unwrapped what turned out to be sandwiches and potato chips. Two bottled drinks also appeared from her bag.

When Mitchell and the woman started to eat, Dwayne suggested Carlos should buy pizzas and doughnuts and coffee from a nearby mobile vendor.

"This place is called Balboa Park," Dwayne announced. "Favourite place in the city."

Carlos concentrated on his target. Mitchell and the woman seemed to be totally relaxed in each other's company, talking, laughing, smiling, touching. Carlos was disturbed by the scene. Here was what appeared to be a hard-working man meeting his wife for a shared meal break. So the man was on the take – nothing unusual about that, and the cartel could easily afford to lose a few hundred dollars. Mitchell did not deserve to die because of it.

Soon Mitchell was kissing the woman goodbye and hurrying back to his van. The woman smiled as she waved him off. Carlos fought against feelings of sympathy and envy, and the desperate urge to abandon his task.

Even Dwayne seemed affected by the couple. "Nice...real nice," he said, as if he rarely experienced the unsung beauty in everyday life.

From Balboa Park, Mitchell drove west until he arrived

in the dockland area. Dwayne, acting as though a tour guide, announced that it was the home base of much of the US Navy. Scores of aircraft carriers, battleships, cruisers and thousands of naval men and women were stationed here. He pointed out a famous old aircraft carrier called Midway which had now been converted into a museum.

Mitchell spent a long time in this area, leaving many large parcels along the way. "Now we know why they call them the *high* seas," Carlos said in an attempt to lift his own mood.

Dwayne said, "Uh?!"

It was about nine o'clock in the evening when Mitchell made his last call, an innocuous-looking door into a rundown brick warehouse, now a clandestine gambling den according to Dwayne.

When Mitchell emerged from the warehouse and drove off, Dwayne didn't follow him. Mitchell was on his way home, Dwayne explained, and home was a flat in a crowded tower block, which was an unsuitable place to do a hit. Carlos agreed.

Dwayne drove Carlos back to his room for the night – an apartment close to the warehouse on the industrial estate.

Before he went to sleep that night, Carlos decided that he must kill Mitchell early in his round tomorrow because he could not bear seeing Mitchell with his wife again.

The following morning Carlos tried to psych himself up with repeated cups of coffee. He had spent much of the night trying to think of ways to avoid killing Mitchell and get away with it, but he had failed to find the answer. At this moment he found no consolation in the fact that by obeying orders and returning to Tijuana, he was advancing his chances of a future trip through the tunnel, one that could bring him his freedom.

Dwayne picked him up at midday and soon they were sitting in the car outside the warehouse, waiting for Mitchell. Carlos opened his window to dispel the nauseating smell of Dwayne's stale deodorant. There was little conversation.

When Mitchell's van eventually emerged from the warehouse, it headed in a different direction from that taken yesterday. Soon it pulled into yet another suburban gas station and Mitchell took his parcel into the building.

Carlos surveyed the scene. There were no motorists at the gas pumps and only one or two women walking in the street. Carlos looked at Dwayne. "This is as good a place as any," he said. "When I leave the car, keep the engine running, and when I get back drive away slowly and in the opposite direction to our arrival. Don't drive straight back to the warehouse – we'll head back there later."

"Okay," Dwayne said, shuffling his body into an alert position, his tattooed hands increasing their grip on the steering wheel.

Carlos prepped his gun. Recalling his military training, he breathed slowly and deeply to help him stay calm. When he saw Mitchell come out of the gas station and head for his van, Carlos slid out of the car and followed him, walking quickly to close the gap. When there was only a few paces between them, Carlos shouted, "Mitchell!"

Mitchell turned and saw the gun in Carlos's hand. Mitchell reached behind his back and in a flash had a gun in his hand. As he raised it towards Carlos, Carlos shot him in the chest, calling on God to forgive him.

Mitchell's knees buckled, and he fell to the ground, his gun spilling out of his hand. As Carlos ran back to the car, he heard a man shout. There was no doubt the incident would make the evening TV news and tomorrow's newspapers, just as the boss had ordered.

Once in the car, Dwayne hit the accelerator and they roared away from the scene. Carlos, now feeling sick, shouted at him to slow down. The car slowing down did nothing to relieve the heaving nausea in Carlos's stomach, and now he felt his body trembling as feelings of guilt, shame and utter sadness claimed his mind.

That evening he made the return journey through the tunnel. At the Tijuana end he was met by Perez wearing a sickly smile. "Good job," was all Perez said before ordering Carlos to get on with his routine duties.

Chapter 39

Elizabeth, like most permanent residents of the Lake District, had mixed feelings about the arrival of summer. She was pleased to see the blue skies, feel the warmth, enjoy a longer swim in the lake, the extra daylight hours. But now she had to share these pleasures with millions of car-owning holiday visitors who, inevitably, made daily life in and around the towns and villages and country lanes a good deal more difficult to negotiate.

Historically, the locals had welcomed visitors or at least tolerated them. Most visitors were lovers of the outdoors – walkers, climbers, boaters, swimmers, fishers, who were careful not to damage the place they adored. But in recent years Elizabeth had noticed a deterioration in visitor behaviour, leaving locals to clean up their litter, and the Mountain Rescue teams to rescue more and more of them from the fells, where they wore inadequate clothing, relied on mobile phones instead of map and compass and walked in trainers instead of boots.

It seemed to Elizabeth that their numbers were increasing year on year, and while owners of businesses catering for tourists were pleased to see the increase, Elizabeth, like many locals, was not. This year she had decided that she would abandon her usual shopping visits to Keswick town centre and do her shopping in the outlying town of Cockermouth, whose tourist intake to see the birthplace of Wordsworth was much less than that of Keswick.

It was on such a shopping trip to Cockermouth that Elizabeth bumped into Helen. "You too?" Elizabeth proclaimed as they came together outside a chemist shop in the tree-lined main street.

Helen smiled. "Yep, Keswick is impossible these days, isn't it?"

It was a hot afternoon and they both moved under a tree to take advantage of the shade and avoid blocking the pavement.

"It's lovely to see you," Elizabeth said. "I seem to miss you every time I call in to see Ben."

"I'm very busy this year," Helen explained. "Everybody wants swimming pools these days. Good old tourists, eh?"

"A classic oxymoron if ever I heard one."

"Ben's been telling me you have been a busy girl lately. As well as writing your articles, you've been trying to solve murders, spying on suspects, buying castles in Scotland and seducing your boss."

"Guilty as charged." Elizabeth smiled. "And what about you...What have you been up to?"

"I'll give you one guess."

"Baking scones?"

"Well, yes...that and digging large holes in the ground and filling them with water. Predictably boring, I'm afraid."

"I could do with a bit of boring at the moment. Care to swap for a couple of weeks?"

"I wish I could. I could do with something to relieve the grind. Not sure Ben would agree either."

"Did Ben tell you about our last meeting? I promised to let Dominic know what he was planning next...Ben, that is...so that Dominic could ask his private detective to do the same in Zurich. Can you let Ben know that I have been in touch with Dominic, and he thinks it's a good idea."

Helen hesitated. "I'm not sure I followed all that. Sounds very cloak and dagger-ish to me."

"Oh, I'm sorry, Helen," Elizabeth pleaded. "I get carried away sometimes. Here we are having a nice chat and I'm spoiling it. Forget what I just asked you to do. I'll ring Ben tonight. How about we go and have a nice cup of coffee and talk about how strange men are."

"I'm up for that."

Just a few paces down the street, they found a coffee shop.

Half an hour later they emerged into the sunlight, having drank coffee, had a guilty slice of chocolate cake, agreed about the faults of the male of the species, put a few local things to rights, discussed when Elizabeth was going to bring Dominic to meet them, and agreed to meet in two days' time to go swimming together in Bassenthwaite Lake.

As they prepared to part outside the coffee shop, Elizabeth said, "I've just had a thought. How would you feel about having our swim in Derwent Water instead of Bassenthwaite? I've been planning to swim to Becalmed... you know, Prentice's house...to see if his laser security system works underwater in front of his boathouse. If it doesn't, it probably explains how the two wetsuit men intended to enter his property. I was going to do it on my own, but I would feel a lot safer if you came along."

"How will you know if it's working or not?"

"I'm going to dive down, swim under the boathouse door and enter the boathouse. If the alarm doesn't go off, I'll know it doesn't extend underwater."

"But what if the alarm does go off? Aren't you in danger of being caught in the act?"

"Maybe, but the boathouse is quite a distance from the house. I think I should be able to swim away and get to the shore without being seen."

"And where would I be?"

"Just behind me, keeping lookout...treading water, keeping an eye on the jetty and the garden. If anything goes wrong, we both swim for the shore. It's not very far from the house."

Helen looked puzzled. "Why don't you just ask Prentice if the system works underwater?"

Now Elizabeth looked puzzled. "Because he'll wonder why I want to know. Don't forget, Ben and I think he might have killed those two men in wetsuits."

"Yes, of course. I've been so busy..."

"And I shouldn't be asking you to get involved. You have enough on your plate."

"No...no," Helen stressed. "I would like to help. I'll come with you as long as you don't tell Ben what we're doing. He'd go crazy."

"I don't suppose Dominic would be pleased either," Elizabeth said. "But hey! A woman's gotta do what a woman's gotta do."

Helen looked at Elizabeth as if seeing her for the first time. "I think you are about to lead me astray, young woman."

Elizabeth grinned mischievously, and they both laughed, enjoying their sisterhood.

Their arrangements made, they went their separate ways, each returning to the mundane task of shopping for those essentials that keep a household functioning – a woman's endless burden since Eve met Adam.

That evening, Elizabeth went to see her parents to tell them about her new relationship with Dominic. As expected there was the usual note of caution in their mostly happy responses, followed by lots of questions about the future in general and the specifics of maintaining a relationship over distance. Elizabeth explained that a flight from Manchester to Zurich only took two hours, that she would probably be using it fairly regularly when the skiing season started in the winter (which started a whole new sub-conversation), and that their work brought them together almost on a daily basis.

She told them that Dominic had suggested they take things slowly and she pointed out that they were both mature enough to handle whatever the future may bring. This last statement brought raised eyebrows and knowing looks between her parents, but they were kind enough not to say anything.

The evening ended with Elizabeth, once again, feeling wrapped in the cocoon of love her parents always wove before she left them.

Back in her cottage, its emptiness suddenly made her feel lonely and she went to bed and wrapped herself in her own arms and cuddled herself to sleep.

The following day, as arranged, Elizabeth met Helen in a car park outside the grounds of the grand lakeside country house that Beatrix Potter's parents had rented for long summer holidays. It was here that Beatrix wrote *Peter Rabbit*, *Squirrel Nutkin* and *Mrs Tiggy-Winkle*. Although a mile's walk to Becalmed lay ahead, this was the closest access available to Derwent Water's shoreline.

Both of them had brought backpacks, which contained their towels, goggles and swim hats. Hanging from the backpacks were pairs of rubber flippers to be used for extra swim speed. Both were already wearing their swimsuits under their clothes.

It was only a short walk from the car park to Derwent Water and soon they set off walking along the tree-lined western shoreline of the lake. Even though Elizabeth was focussed on the task ahead, she could not help being distracted by the beauty all around her. She had fallen in love with this walk as a child and it still held her in its thrall.

As she weaved her way along the path, around and under the ancient gnarled, grotesquely shaped trees, never more than a few paces from the water's edge, the gentle sun-kissed waves flashing like diamonds, mysterious islands out on the water, she realised it had lost none of its fairy-tale atmosphere. It was no wonder that this area had inspired Beatrix Potter to write her magical children's stories.

Twenty minutes later they arrived at a location close to High Brandelhow jetty, where the ferry makes one of its eight stops around the lake. It was from here they intended to start their swim to Becalmed. They could see the house, about 400 metres away, which they planned to approach from an angle, with some overhanging trees offering visual protection.

After donning her swim gear, including flippers, Elizabeth led the way, slowly wading into the cold water. When chest deep, she paused and waited for Helen and they both did some warmup exercises before setting off.

Elizabeth went ahead, with Helen a few metres behind. They covered the first 200 metres, using their front crawl, the flippers aiding their speed. But as they drew closer to the house, they switched to breaststroke, which caused no splashing and was therefore much less visually noticeable.

When they were about fifty metres from the boathouse, Elizabeth stopped and waited for Helen. Elizabeth asked her to stay put and keep watch while she went on alone. Elizabeth also pointed out some large overhanging trees ahead and to their right which they should both head for in an emergency.

After receiving a thumbs-up from Helen, Elizabeth set off for the boathouse. When she reached it she found she was breathing quite heavily. She put it down to tension rather than poor swimming technique, and decided a short rest was called for. While treading water she was pleased to see that the bottom of the boathouse doors were about an inch above the water level, no doubt due to the dry summer weather. This would make it easy to dive under them.

With a final look all around her, Elizabeth took a deep breath and dived down. Although the visibility was poor underwater, she saw the boathouse door above her and, with a few flicks of her flippers, moved forward and underneath the door.

As she swam forward she saw the bow of Prentice's boat in the dock a short distance ahead. She veered to the left and came up against the concrete side of the dock wall. She edged her way along it until she reached an aluminium ladder bolted to the wall – the way to the surface.

She started to climb the ladder, relieved that no alarm had sounded. When she reached the top, she just had time to register that it was quite dark inside the boathouse when there was a rush of air and something black slapped her in the face and struck her forehead a sharp blow. Shocked, she fell back into the water. Although shaken she soon gathered herself and headed back towards the boathouse doors, intent on escape. At the doors she stopped and took a deep breath to aid her dive under the doors. It was only then that she noticed a pungent smell in the air.

Elizabeth turned and peered inside the boathouse. She was trying to see the thing she suspected of flying into her face. It was not far away, now perched calmly on the boat's structure. The strikingly handsome black villain stared coldly at her, now apparently indifferent to her presence. A relieved Elizabeth relaxed and started to enjoy having such a close encounter with one of her favourite birds. The cormorant had always been one of Elizabeth's favourites in spite of the smell of its acidic droppings.

It must have been chasing a fish and followed it under the boathouse doors, and it had yet to work out how to make the return journey, Elizabeth reasoned. No doubt it, or Prentice, would eventually solve its dilemma in the next few days.

Elizabeth swam back to the aluminium ladder and climbed it again until she stood on the concrete dock. Moving along the length of the dock, walking backwards because of her flippers, she came to the door leading to the outside. She tried the handle and was astonished to find that the door opened. She closed it again, quickly, and stared at it in disbelief. Why would a security conscious man like Prentice leave the door open? Was it simply a one-off oversight, or was it deliberate? Suddenly, it occurred to her that Prentice might have been working in the boathouse in the last few minutes and had just popped back to the house for some reason, leaving the door open for his return.

She needed to get out as quickly as possible. She turned and shuffled her way along the dock, banged her shin as she raced down the ladder and flung herself into the water. A few strokes, a dive, and she was out in the lake again.

Swimming away from the boathouse as fast as she could, she kept expecting to hear a shout or something worse coming from the house behind her. On reaching Helen she ordered, "Head for the trees" and struck off in their direction.

Helen followed obediently and, being the better swimmer, soon drew up alongside Elizabeth. She shouted, "What's wrong?"

"Don't ask." Elizabeth gasped. "Just swim as fast as you can and take cover behind the trees." Elizabeth was desperate to see Helen safe, even if she herself got caught.

Helen's deceptively smooth but powerful crawl soon took her well ahead of Elizabeth and a few minutes later she was safely out of sight behind the overhanging trees. She trod water and held on to one of the overhanging branches while waiting for Elizabeth.

Elizabeth arrived doing a ragged-looking breast stroke, her face a mixture of guilt and relief. As she drew alongside Helen, she managed a tired smile. "Sorry about that," she breathed.

"Tell me about it later," Helen said, putting a motherly arm around Elizabeth's shoulders. "Let's get back to dry land."

Together, they pushed off and swam slowly and calmly alongside each other, hugging the shoreline until they reached their point of entry. They waded ashore under the gaze of a party of passing walkers who stopped, as they all do, to watch these crazy women who dared to swim in such cold, deep water, then proceeded on their "sane" activity of carrying heavy backpacks to the top of a steep mountain.

They hurriedly dried themselves and dressed, keen to keep the effect of the cold water at bay, then collected their gear and started to walk back to the car park. "I didn't hear an alarm?" Helen queried, wondering why it was necessary to make their hurried getaway.

Elizabeth explained about the door being open and the possibility of Prentice returning to the boathouse at any moment. She went on to tell Helen about her heart-stopping encounter with the cormorant. Eventually, they both started to see the funny side of their adventure and they arrived back at the car park laughing like naughty schoolgirls.

As they said their goodbyes and walked to their cars, Helen turned, put her finger to her lips and said, "Remember, not a word to Ben or Dominic."

Chapter 40

"Get back to your regular duties," Perez had ordered when Carlos returned from his trip through the tunnel to San Diego. Within days of his return, Carlos was involved in a high-speed, heart-thumping car chase through the streets of the city as he fought to avoid an attempt on his life. His pursuers turned out to be yet another pair of drugged-up young hoods, probably on freelance hire, spraying bullets everywhere while following him in a souped-up, overpowered old car which they couldn't handle.

As the chase progressed, terrifying Carlos and the people in the streets they hurtled through, Carlos began to realise the limitations of those chasing him. Their erratic driving and shooting said it all.

Rather than stopping and getting involved in a grim shoot-out with them, he decided it would be less stressful to give them the slip. The downside of this was that they would live to try again, but that, he decided, was a problem for another day.

In an area of the city he knew well, including the fact that there was a big gas station around the next bend, he raised his speed and was able to turn into the gas station before his pursuers had rounded the bend. He sat in his car like a regular customer queueing at the pumps and watched them drive past. Then he drove off in the opposite direction and made his way home.

Home was now a small apartment above a hardware store in a busy city centre street. He had chosen the location and layout carefully. The well-lit city centre street allowed him to see any vehicle or person who appeared in front of the property during the night, whereas the unlit suburbs were places of darkness and danger. The city centre streets were also patrolled by police, unlike the suburbs.

He accessed his apartment via a fire escape at the rear of the building, where there was also enough space to park his car. He had bought the car with money from the sale of his old motorhome.

The rear of the property was unlit, but he had used the darkness to his advantage by rigging up a simple trip wire which activated small but noisy bells at the bottom of the fire escape. A laser beam security system which he had installed at the top of the fire escape activated an alarm within his apartment and also switched on two powerful outside lights which lit up the fire escape. These lights could also be manually activated from inside the apartment. He set both systems in action every night before going to bed and so far had been lucky to be woken up just once by the bells due to a wandering cat.

The Chinese owners of the store and the apartment had also installed a laser security system at the front of the building, which, luckily, provided Carlos with yet more security without having to pay for it.

As time passed, and the Tijuana violence continued unabated, the odds on Carlos's security systems remaining untested had worsened.

The inevitable test arrived on a cool night, with clouds hiding the moon and creating a darkness more dense than usual. Carlos had lived through another stressful day and was in a deep sleep, dreaming of playing kick-the-ball with his young sisters, when he heard distant bells. His brain tried to fit the bells into his dream, but it struggled to find a way. The struggle woke him up.

As soon as reality dawned, Carlos leapt out of bed, grabbed his gun from his bedside table and carefully approached the bedroom window. In the darkness he could just make out two figures walking up the fire escape. They had not been deterred by the ringing of the bells. This suicidal action made Carlos think they were probably the same two hoods who were involved in his recent car chase through the city.

Whoever they were, they were amateurs, Carlos concluded. He switched on the powerful outside lights and watched them freeze, as most dumb animals do when dazzled by light. To encourage them to abandon their mission, Carlos quietly eased his window open and fired two shots above their heads, close enough for them to hear the terrifying displacement of air as the bullets flew past.

In their panic the two men started running up the fire escape, then stopped suddenly, looked at each other and swore. Carlos found himself smiling as he watched them collide with each other in their haste to turn and retreat down the fire escape. Within seconds they were gone, leaving their expletives floating in the dark air.

With the floodlights still on, Carlos descended the fire escape, replaced the trip wire and checked the bells. Unsurprisingly, nobody in the neighbourhood left their homes to see what had happened, shots in the night being a normal background noise in Tijuana.

Carlos returned to his flat wondering how long his luck would last. He knew that one day, or night, somebody would send an efficient professional to take him out.

As a precaution, he spent the rest of the night curled up on a chair in the corner of his bedroom.

The next attack came just a few days later and it caught Carlos by surprise. He had always assumed that no one would attempt to approach him from the front of the building. To do that they would have to enter the hardware store and risk being seen by the owners or the police who patrolled the streets regularly. There was also the alarm system to deal with.

He was, therefore, always relaxed when he was in his living room above the front of the store. He was relaxed that morning, sitting at the table, drinking a coffee, when a tornado of noise and mayhem came crashing through his front window. Shards of wood and glass sprayed across the room, showering him with their sharpness. A hammer hit of adrenalin shot into his heart, making him gasp. He dived under the table, automatically felt for his weapon but didn't find it, having left it in the bedroom.

From under the table he could see where the bullet had struck the wall after flying past him. He realised the bullet, no doubt from a rifle judging by the damage it had caused, must have been fired from across the street at the same elevation as his apartment. Now he cursed himself for not having considered the potential danger from windows above the stores across the street.

As he lay waiting for the next shot, he guessed that the first bullet had missed him because it had struck the central wooden structure in the window, which had slightly deflected it. This would also explain the large amount of wooden shards and the activation of a loud alarm which now blared incessantly. His luck was still with him.

The next shot never came and after lying still for about five minutes, he crawled to the window and looked out. Two police cars stood in the street, one outside the hardware store and the other one across the street outside a fast food store. A number of police officers filled the street in between. Carlos assumed that his attacker had fled the scene on seeing the police arrive.

Carlos took a deep, tension-releasing breath and sat down on the nearest chair. It was time to move, he realised. Two attacks in quick succession meant he had at least one determined enemy who knew where he lived. It was also very likely that his Chinese landlord would want rid of him because of the damage to their property and possible danger to themselves.

Carlos had always thought of himself as strong, capable of dealing with anything life threw at him, but the sickening nature of his work, the fact that he was trapped in it, the constant fear for his life and now the attacks on his home ground had taken their cumulative toll. He now felt defeated.

It was time to escape completely, he decided, not just move to another location. In spite of the risks, he had to plan an escape and take his chances. His dream of a better life in the USA had become a nightmare; it was time to abandon it, to head home, back to Guatemala to find his mama and sisters. If the cartel sent people to look for him, he had friends who would help to hide him. He might be clutching at straws. It might all end in a bloody death. But he would die at home among his family, not alone in a dark alleyway in Tijuana.

Suddenly the blaring alarm stopped, and Carlos heard footsteps outside his door. He took a deep breath and prepared himself for a long session of questioning by the police.

A week after the last attack, having already made some escape plans, including mapping out a complicated route back to Guatemala to avoid interception by the cartel and costing the merits of hiring a reliable motorhome versus buying an old one, Carlos received bad news from good people and good news from bad people.

The bad news was, as expected, a request from his Chinese landlord to vacate the apartment. The good news, though he didn't immediately recognise it as good news, came from his nemesis – Perez. With a scowl on his face, he told Carlos that he had been ordered to fly from Tijuana to Chicago, there to make his way to the cartel's distribution hub and report to the boss – Mr Tony Marcelo.

He would receive further instructions when he got there. Before he could go he would have to wait for two or three weeks until the cartel's travel department had finished creating the documentation necessary for such a trip. This included a passport and other documents which would prove that Carlos was an honest citizen with a history of honest employment and a good reason to make his business trip to Chicago.

At first Carlos had been horrified by the news. He was becoming more and more embedded in the cartel, and he was being moved even further away from Guatemala. But then it dawned on him that the trip might present him with better opportunities to escape and his escape would be into the USA, where he could lose himself in its vast space and huge population. All he had to do was be brave enough to take his chance when it came.

He knew, however, that life rarely panned out like that, particularly not his life, which so far had been little more than a grim story of survival. The unknown reason why he was going festered all day and night in his mind, worrying away at his shredded nerves. Why had they chosen him? What did they want him to do? One thing was certain – it would not be anything that contributed to the wellbeing of his fellow man or woman.

Despite all this, Carlos could not help but look forward to making his first flight, and to seeing Chicago – things beyond the dreams of most Guatemalans.

He used the waiting time to read up on Chicago. He learned that it was the USA's third largest city, that it was 1,700 miles from Tijuana and that his flight would last about four hours and end at O'Hare International Airport.

Chicago was the main hub for much of the nation's infrastructure, be it rail, road or river, and was well known for international finance, for being the home of McDonald's and lots of other established companies, and for being the home town of Barack Obama.

Nearly 3 million people lived there, made up of an equal three-way split between white, Hispanic and Black. It seemed to Carlos that these folk had not been getting along so good because the crime rate was higher than either New York or Los Angeles, which were bigger cities.

Somehow, somebody had counted up all the shootings in a year and come up with 4,500, and all the murders in a year, which came to 750. They also claimed to know that there were over 100,000 gang members in the city and that they were mainly fighting over control of the drug-selling territories, with most of the drugs being supplied by the Sinaloa Cartel. When Carlos read this he began to mentally speculate what plans the cartel might have in store for him. The more he thought about it, the more he became determined to make his break for freedom as soon as he got there. It was now or never.

Chapter 41

After Elizabeth's last meeting with Ben, she phoned Dominic to tell him of Ben's plan to look for crimes involving big money over the past fifteen years and went on to suggest that Dominic's private detective might also do this because of Zurich's financial reputation.

Dominic had agreed it was a sound idea and confirmed that the detective had yet to come up with any other relevant information.

While they were talking, Dominic suddenly changed tack and said that he was desperate to see her. Eventually, he came up with the idea of spending the next weekend together in Zurich, where they could go shopping for skiing equipment in preparation for the season ahead. Without hesitation, Elizabeth agreed to go.

Now, as the evening started to draw a dark curtain across Bassenthwaite Lake, Elizabeth was busy putting the finishing touches to her packing. For a moment she was reminded of the excitement she felt as a schoolgirl packing for her first ever school trip abroad, though what lay ahead would, no doubt, be much more exciting than walking in the Pyrenees with school friends.

Back then she had made a bet with herself as to how many times during the week she would argue with Kathleen

Palmer. This time she had made a bet with herself as to how many times during the weekend she would make love with Dominic. *We might even reach double figures.*

She was under no illusions about Dominic's main reason for the weekend, and she had no intention of trying to foil his cunning plan. Okay, they might drag themselves outside for an hour or two's shopping, but she was convinced that the bulk of their time would be spent in Dominic's apartment enjoying long spells of indolence interspersed with regular carnal activity.

She was flying from Manchester Airport tomorrow morning, the Friday take-off contributing to as long a weekend as possible. She had also arranged to visit Ben for a quick check on progress before she flew out.

As usual, Helen was already out at work when Elizabeth arrived to see Ben. He answered the door in his dressing gown. "Sorry about this," he said, indicating his gown as he led the way through to the conservatory. "One of the perks of working from home."

"All you need is a pipe and you'll look like Sherlock Holmes," Elizabeth joked as they settled in their usual chairs.

"I wish I had his investigative powers," Ben moaned. He sounded almost serious.

"Been struggling, have you?"

"Yes, but I'm used to it. I set myself these long, tedious tasks, so I can't complain when they inevitably reveal nothing most of the time. I'm like the proverbial periodical cicada which lives in the dark earth for seventeen years then crawls into the light for just a few days. What joy those days bring. They make all the previous effort worthwhile." Ben glanced at Elizabeth. "Do you think I'm nuts?"

"Yes! I do," Elizabeth emphasised. "But I'm really glad you're on our side."

"Thank you, Watson."

"Do I take it you have nothing new to tell me?" Elizabeth went on. "How about the gun? Did you hear anything from the American National Tracing Centre?"

Ben shook his head. "Not a thing. I think we need to get in touch with the tracing centre for tracing tracing centres."

"You sound a bit disheartened?"

"Not disheartened – frustrated. I found a few big money crimes that might warrant further investigation then I came across one that fit our scenario perfectly. A big fraud case, lots of money lost by investors, money still missing, fraudster gone missing or dead, the sort of wealthy clients who could afford to hire bad men to find the missing fraudster. I thought I was really onto something at one point, but further investigation proved I was on the wrong track."

Elizabeth leaned forward. "I'd like to hear about it."

"It was a fraud case from about eight years ago. Such a big case that I'm surprised I didn't think about it sooner. You might even remember hearing about it on the news yourself, though you would have been a teenager at the time. The case was in America, but it made news around the world because it was one of the biggest Ponzi scheme frauds ever discovered..."

"Please remind me what a Ponzi scheme is," Elizabeth said. "I've heard of it but..."

Ben pushed his glasses higher up his nose. "It's a financial investment scheme that promises higher than average profits for the investor. Because of this it attracts large numbers of investors. Each year, as promised, the scheme pays out higher than average profits. The investors are happy and spread the word and so more and more people invest and the scheme grows and grows.

"What the investors don't know is that their money is not being invested in stocks and shares or anything else. It is simply being transferred by the fraudster's investment company into his personal bank account.

"The fraudster then pays profits to the people who joined the scheme *early* with the money invested by the *later* investors. It works perfectly as long as there is a steady stream of new investors topping up the fund.

"These schemes usually collapse when a large number of investors ask to withdraw their original investment pot at the same time. This particular Ponzi scheme, which had been running for nineteen years, collapsed in 2008 when the massive financial crash hit America and panicked investors queued up to withdraw their investments.

"They are called Ponzi schemes because the first man to run one, in the early 1920s, was an Italian con-man called Charles Ponzi."

Elizabeth frowned. "How on earth did they get away with it for nineteen years? Don't they have auditors and people like that checking their books every year?"

"That's true, but the trouble is the people who start Ponzi schemes are usually already running honest investment companies and are well known and trusted within the industry. They tend to be tempted into crime when they see their business shrinking and look for ways to increase it. This can be due to personal greed or when they give in to the pressure to keep important clients happy. The point is that they are clever enough to make the books look convincing and nobody, including auditors, suspects them of running a dodgy business because of their good reputation. There can also be an element of corruption involved, where the auditors turn a blind eye to the scam in return for a share of the cash.

"In the case I'm talking about, there were even bosses of other investment companies feeding some of their clients' money into the scheme for a cut of the pot."

"Remind me never to invest in the stocks and shares market."

"I agree. The cleverer the people, the bigger the crime. These money people caused the big crash that we are all still suffering from."

"So what made you think this Ponzi scheme has a connection with Charles Prentice?"

"Because the fraudster who ran the scheme, Ernest Cotton, apparently committed suicide to avoid going to prison. He left a note to say so. It was found in his car, which was parked on a bridge above a river. But his body was never recovered from the river. Although it is probable that he did commit suicide, a lot of people, including angry investors, believe he faked it and is still alive and hiding out somewhere. The money he defrauded from them, estimated by the financial authorities to be about $15 billion, is still missing. You can imagine the rest."

Elizabeth hesitated. "So you thought our man Prentice

might really be Cotton, who is being pursued by hit men acting on behalf of angry investors?"

"That's right. And the missing money would explain why they want to question him before they kill him."

"But now you don't think Prentice is Cotton?"

"Right again. The thing is I read all this information without seeing any photographs of Cotton or Prentice. Then I saw photos of Cotton in some newspapers. I don't suppose you are familiar with Fred Astaire. Well, this man is white, slim, about five foot nine inches tall, dark smooth hair, immaculately dressed in dark suits, white shirts, patent leather shoes and elegant ties – a typical executive businessman out to create the right impression. I haven't seen Prentice, as you know, but you described him to me as a bear of a man, with wiry, curly grey hair, a grey moustache and beard, some sort of scar on his face, and shabbily dressed. You said he looked like a weathered lumberjack rather than an executive."

"What a good memory you have, Ben. They certainly don't sound like the same person, I have to admit, but don't forget a few years have passed and people can change a lot, particularly when they want to hide their previous appearance. Prentice certainly does look bulky, but that could be the baggy clothes he always wears, and he is not big in the tall sense. I would guess he is about the same height as your man Cotton."

"Okay, but there's a lot more that doesn't match. Cotton had a blonde wife called Susan; Prentice's wife is dark-haired according to you, and she is called Barbara. Now, I know women are always dyeing their hair and you can easily change your name, but the thing is Cotton's wife was left behind when he disappeared and she still lives in America today, claiming to know nothing about her husband's criminal activities. And they had no daughter, no children at all."

Elizabeth nodded her head. "Not looking likely, is it? There is of course the possibility that Prentice has teamed up with Barbara and her daughter, Claire, in recent years and they have agreed to play the part of wife and daughter to help him stay undetected." She paused for a moment. "Actually," she went on, "that could explain why I haven't seen them behaving like a normal happily married couple."

"Good point, Elizabeth." Ben scoffed. "I too have never seen married couples arguing or looking miserable in each other's company." He stared at her over the top of his glasses, a slight smile on his lips.

Elizabeth gave him a scowl. "Cynic!" she snarled.

"Then there's the language and the accents. Apparently Cotton was a born and bred American. It is very hard to imagine that an American could pretend to be Oxford English over a long period of time without giving themselves away. There are so many different words in use and the accent is so hard to copy accurately."

"But if you remember," Elizabeth countered, "I told you that Prentice's English accent was *very* posh, and you said it could mean that somebody not used to using it was trying too hard. And I remember mentioning the famous English novelist Sir Hugh Walpole to him and he hadn't heard of him. I was really surprised at that."

"Now whose got a good memory?" Ben acknowledged. "You've made two good points, but they are not definitive proof of deception. As to Walpole, I'm no longer surprised by people's ignorance of the arts. Ask people who Shake-speare is, and many will say he's a manufacturer of fishing gear. Anyway, I think you'll agree that at the moment, on the face of it, we don't have a match."

"Agreed," Helen said. "On the face of it. But I still think it would be worth spending more time on this case until we can conclusively discount Mr Cotton. Meanwhile, I'll bring all this to Dominic's notice when I see him this weekend and see what he thinks."

"Don't forget to tell him there are two people here waiting to meet him."

"Will do," Elizabeth said as she rose from her chair and prepared to leave.

They made their way to the door and Elizabeth stepped outside.

"Jetting off for a weekend in the Alps, eh?" Ben observed with a smile. "You are going up in the world, Elizabeth, literally and metaphorically, and it's great to see."

Elizabeth gave Ben a daughterly kiss on the cheek. "Thanks, Ben. See you soon."

Chapter 42

The Swiss reputation for time-keeping was well deserved. The plane left Manchester Airport on time and arrived in Zurich airport on time. The ultra-modern airport processed Elizabeth within half an hour and soon she was sitting beside Dominic in a taxi heading for Zurich city centre just six miles from the airport.

Elizabeth couldn't remember much about those six miles. Her eyes rarely took in the views through the taxi window because they were closed for most of the journey as Dominic wrapped her in his arms and kissed her constantly. If they did speak during the journey, she couldn't recall a word. All she remembered was strong arms, warm lips and a pleasant smell of soap.

Dominic had already told her to prepare herself for a big contrast to her life in the countryside, so when the taxi dropped them off into a river of passing people and traffic, she knew they were close to his apartment in the historic Old Town area of the city, a place he described as a tourist hotspot, full of tourist attractions, bars and restaurants, and a good place to do business.

Holding her hand, Dominic led her through the crowd and stopped outside an old four-storey building with two doors fronting onto the pavement. He opened the second door, which turned out to be the private entrance to his ground-floor apartment.

As she had expected from such an organised and efficient person, Dominic's apartment was neat and tidy, sparsely but elegantly furnished with the emphasis on comfort, as demonstrated by a large, deep-cushioned sofa positioned in front of an ancient fireplace. Elizabeth had a feeling that they might be spending a lot of time on that sofa, and reckoned she might become familiar with the gnarled wooden beams which she now noticed on the low ceiling.

After a brief tour of the apartment, which was much more spacious than her cottage, Dominic invited her to sit in the lounge while he went to the kitchen to make coffee. Soon he presented her with coffee and snacks, and they sat facing each other, each grinning stupidly at the other in between sips.

The perfect host, Dominic asked her if she would like to rest after her journey, and when Elizabeth declined he suggested they took advantage of the sunny afternoon and went for a walk along the bank of the river, which ran through the centre of the city. *So much for non-stop action on the sofa.* She realised that he was doing what any gentleman would do in the circumstances – avoid grabbing her as soon as she's through the door – but who cares about manners when you want to be grabbed?

However, appetites of another kind were soon being satisfied as the delightful walk along the riverside ended at a pavement cafe, where they enjoyed ice-cream smothered in flaked chocolate. Here, Dominic announced that he had booked all the weekend's meals at nearby cafes so that neither of them wasted precious time in the kitchen. Elizabeth expressed her approval while feeling slightly disappointed that more potential sofa-time was to be spent out of the apartment. Double figures now looked extremely unlikely.

After their walk they returned to the apartment to freshen up and relax and finally she got to sample the luxurious softness of the sofa together with the more exciting softness of Dominic's lips.

However, as nature took over and ardour increased, she felt that Dominic was deliberately holding back. Her answer came when he looked at his watch and said, "We need to go. I've booked a table for six o'clock."

"Do I need to change?" Elizabeth asked as she sat up and rearranged her clothes.

"No, it's an informal cafe just around the corner. I thought you would prefer that kind of place, and the food's good." He sounded a bit unsure of himself, as if waiting to hear if he had done the right thing.

"Sounds perfect," Elizabeth said. "Let's go."

The street around the corner turned out to be called Augustiner-Gasse Street and it was straight out of an old European fairy tale. It had a gentle curve in it and a fairly steep uphill slope, its narrowness emphasised by tall, multi-coloured buildings on both sides, the buildings old and crooked and leaning, with sagging bay windows randomly sticking out at all levels like bulbous staring eyes. The street was cobbled and traffic free, allowing the numerous cafes space for outside tables, and boards with handwritten menus and pots of flowers. Informal flags and bunting added yet more colour and atmosphere.

Elizabeth expected Hansel and Gretel to appear at any moment as Dominic guided her into his chosen cafe.

The food and wine were forgettable, not because they were bad, but because they played second fiddle to the simple joy of just *being* with Dominic.

An arm-in-arm stroll back to the apartment felt dream-like, the air in the canyons of the narrow streets still warm, holding a slight scent of cigars and flowers. Old couples still sat on benches holding hands and small birds pecked among the cobbles, saving waitresses from sweeping up. Once inside the apartment nothing was said as they headed straight for the bedroom.

Eleven o'clock next morning saw two satiated creatures drift into the lounge and flop into armchairs. Coffee was sipped carefully, and words were whispered huskily, and slowly the world took shape again and choices needed to be made.

To Elizabeth's surprise, Dominic revealed that he had indeed planned to go out in the afternoon to buy skiing gear for Elizabeth. After last night Elizabeth felt somewhat relieved to go along with his plans.

The next surprise came when he told her that although skiing gear was readily available in Zurich, he preferred to buy in a ski resort town called Amden, which was a forty-five-minute car journey away. Here he still had retail contacts from his days as a ski instructor who would offer him a bigger choice and a better deal than the Zurich shops. It also presented an opportunity to take a look at the 900-metre-high beginners slope he planned to use to teach her when the winter snows came.

An hour later, sitting in the car en route to Amden, nibbling at a croissant picked up at a patisserie close to Dominic's apartment, Elizabeth felt that now would be a good time to discuss Ben's news with Dominic. It would leave the rest of the weekend free for more uninterrupted personal fulfilment.

"I called in to see Ben just before I left," Elizabeth started. "He and his wife, Helen, are keen to meet you next time you fly over."

"Yes, me too," Dominic said while continuing to concentrate on the road ahead. "Has he found anything worthwhile lately?"

"I think maybe. But he doesn't. It's a big fraud case that happened about eight years ago. He said it made international news. I couldn't remember it, but maybe you can, being older and wiser than me at the time."

"Fire away," Dominic invited.

Elizabeth swept some croissant crumbs onto the car floor. "It was a multi-billion dollar Ponzi scheme fraud in America run by a man called Ernest Cotton, and..."

"And many people think he faked his suicide and disappeared with the money."

"Wow! It must have been a big case."

Dominic continued. "I was married then and moving in my wife's family circle, which of course involved little else but discussions about money. If I'd still been a ski instructor, I might not have picked up on it. It was really big news in Zurich, being a financial centre. A few months after the event, a rumour went around Zurich that Cotton had been seen in the city. People were prepared to believe it because of its dodgy banking reputation, but when my wife queried it with her father, he dismissed it, saying it was just another rumour, probably started by a newspaper editor looking to increase circulation."

Elizabeth went on to explain all the reasons why Ben eventually decided that Cotton and Prentice could not be the same man, then told Dominic about the alternative scenarios she had put forward which might mean that Cotton and Prentice were the same man, adding the proviso that she had not seen photographs of Cotton yet.

"Assuming your theory is right about Cotton teaming up with a new woman," Dominic said, "the fact that Barbara is American might mean that he teamed up with her in America before coming over to Europe. Incidentally, why would Cotton, an American, pretend to be an English oil executive when it would have been easier to play the part of an American oil executive?"

"Beats me. Perhaps he thought it would provide an extra layer of disguise, but in reality he probably wishes he hadn't bothered because it's harder than he thought."

Dominic braked hard when a motorcyclist cut in front of him to avoid an oncoming car. He continued as though nothing had happened. "Remind me to phone the private investigator before you go. He spent some time interviewing the gardener who Prentice employed, and still employs, at his Zurich house. The detective didn't report anything unusual regarding the three of them, but now I'm wondering how long the gardener has been employed there. If it's less than five years, then he wasn't there when Prentice arrived in Zurich, so he doesn't know if Prentice arrived in Zurich accompanied by the two women or whether he was on his own. If we need to trace the history of these two women in order to solve our mystery, then we need to know on which side of the Atlantic to start our search."

Elizabeth sighed. "The plot thickens."

"It certainly does," came an unexpectedly enthusiastic reply from Dominic. "If Prentice does turn out to be Cotton, it will be a story the world will want to hear. It's massive. You could write a bestseller about it and I'm just beginning to wonder if my old father-in-law could have had a part to play. Now that would be fun if we were able to expose him and his cronies."

"Really?"

"Yes, really. Remember it was him who dismissed the rumour of Cotton being seen in Zurich. Was he covering for Cotton? And Prentice does his routine banking through one of the banks in ex-father-in-law's group. Perhaps there's more that goes on behind those scenes. It might all be wishful thinking, but if it's true..."

"Is Prentice's house very far from your apartment?" Elizabeth asked.

"Not particularly – two or three miles. It's in a green suburb called Fluntern, where most of the rich people live. Why?"

"Oh, it's not important really. I just thought, if we had time, I would like to see it. Blame Ben and his methods. He's always talking about getting to know every detail about the person you are investigating."

"Okay. We'll do it tomorrow. I had no special plans for tomorrow anyway. If you're interested, there is a large zoo close by. We could go there at the same time?"

"No zoo for me, thanks. I prefer my animals in the wild."

"So do I."

A natural silence fell between them, the subject of Prentice apparently exhausted for the time being. After a while, without taking his eyes off the road, Dominic leaned over and took hold of Elizabeth's left hand. He raised it to his lips and kissed it. "I love you, Elizabeth," he said in a flat, matter-of-fact tone. "Get used to it."

"I will," Elizabeth replied in an equally flat tone. "Thank you."

They continued to hold hands until Dominic's was needed on the steering wheel, and they spent the rest of journey talking about the passing countryside.

When they reached the town of Amden, Dominic drove straight to the large retail outlet where he planned to buy the skiing gear for Elizabeth. He expressed surprise when he noticed no vehicles in the car park and when he found the entrance door closed and read the sign on the door, he returned to the car with a sheepish look on his face. "They're closed for their annual holiday. I'd forgotten they always close for a month in the off season. Sorry, I've brought you all this way for nothing."

"No need to apologise," Elizabeth said. "It's been a nice journey and you still have the learner's ski slope to show me."

Elizabeth was actually relieved to see Dominic make a mistake. He was human after all, not the super-efficient dynamo she had thought. It had been difficult up till now to think of him on equal terms because of their previous boss-employee relationship. Now, she felt, this small episode had helped to bring them closer.

The rest of the day was spent over a light lunch and a long walk to see the ski slope on which he was going to teach her. The height of the slope was very similar to the high places in the Lake District, so Elizabeth felt confident she would cope when the time came.

After a leisurely drive back to Zurich, they changed and went out for dinner in another unassuming cafe that Dominic had booked. Good food and wine and conversation was enjoyed, then it was time for bed.

Another slow awakening the next morning saw them eventually emerge into the sunlight just before lunch-time. More croissants were nibbled on the short drive across town to the suburb of Fluntern, where the number of properties decreased but their size increased, the classic leafy retreat of the rich.

"Here we are," Dominic said as he stopped the car. "Home of the Prentices."

Elizabeth could see nothing but a formidable cast iron fence with a high, dense hedge behind it.

"We need to walk around the perimeter," Dominic advised. "There's always a few small gaps in these hedges to look through." With that, he stepped out of the car and led the way.

"It's a substantial plot, about 6,000 square metres, but the old house itself is not too extravagant, probably six bedrooms and an annexe for the staff. Lots of garden. No point going to the front gate – the drive curves so you can't see the house."

"Seems to me it's all about privacy and security," Elizabeth said. "It's got Prentice written all over it."

"Ah, here we are," Dominic said, stopping to look through a small gap in the hedge. He stepped aside and offered his space to Elizabeth. "Take a look."

Elizabeth peered through the gap. All she could see was a small section of a large old house built of stone, with big chimneys, windows with drawn curtains, a gravel surround and a large area of lawn. "Does the lawn go all around the house?" she asked.

"Yes. More security, I suppose. The occupants would be able to see anybody approaching from any direction."

"Well, there's not much to see, is there?" Elizabeth stepped back from the gap. "And I'm not sure I've learned anything, but it does make me understand why he went overboard about the location of Becalmed. There's no comparison, is there? The only view here is a hedge."

"Have you seen enough?"

"Yes, thanks. I hope I haven't wasted your time."

"Not at all, darling, not at all. Time spent with you is never wasted." He grinned mischievously.

Elizabeth studied him. "You lying swine. That was as genuine as a politician's promise." She took a swipe at him, and he grabbed her arm, and they embraced, and laughed, and returned to the car.

"While we are in this area, I'm going to show you something that I think will surprise you," Dominic said as he started the car. "You don't mind visiting a cemetery, do you?"

"Not at all, as long as I'm not expected to stay."

A few hundred metres later, Dominic swung the car through some imposing steel gates and parked shortly afterwards within the cemetery walls. "It's just a short walk from here."

Elizabeth walked beside him as they passed scattered, weather-beaten headstones watched over by towering beech trees. Dominic stopped suddenly in front of a headstone, alongside which stood a sculpture depicting a seated man holding a book and a cigarette. "Did you know he was here?" Dominic asked.

Elizabeth started to say "who" at the same time as trying to read the name on the headstone. She went noticeably still as the chiselled words made themselves known. "I had no idea he was here," she whispered. It was a long time before she was able to say anything else as an unexpected wave of emotion swept through her, bringing tears to her eyes. She stood and stared and waited for it to pass.

"Are you alright?" Dominic asked, noticing the change in her. "I didn't think you would be upset."

"I'm fine...I'm fine." Elizabeth sniffed. "I'm not upset, just...I don't know..."

Dominic put a protective arm around her shoulder. "I thought, as a fellow scribe, you might be interested, but I didn't expect this."

"A fellow scribe?" Elizabeth searched for her handkerchief. "I don't think writing an unpaid column in a small town's weekly paper qualifies me as a scribe at all, never mind including me in the same literary arena as James Joyce. He was...is...an international giant." She paused for a while as she gathered herself. "But I am so glad you brought me here.

Thank you." She leaned over and kissed Dominic on the cheek.

"Phew! You had me worried there," Dominic said. "I didn't know anyone could get so emotional over a complete stranger from another era."

"But that's the thing," Elizabeth insisted. "He is not a stranger. Great writers like him speak to all of us. They are never dead, not to me anyway. They live on in their creations. I think that might explain why I was so emotional; for a while I felt I was in his presence, the presence of a very rare human being."

"Do you like classical music?"

"Yes, love it…most of it."

"Remind me never to take you to Vienna. All those great composers buried there – we would need a suitcase full of handkerchiefs."

Elizabeth appreciated that Dominic was trying to lighten the tone, but she didn't want to leave the subject yet. "Do you know why he is here, in a Zurich cemetery, rather than a Dublin one?"

Dominic hesitated. "All I know is he lived here for a few years with his wife and children, and he was having an operation in the local hospital, for an ulcer I think, when he went into a coma and died in the hospital. Apparently there was only one person at his funeral."

"How sad. And I see he was only fifty-eight. Can you believe he made his great reputation having written only three novels and a collection of short stories and poems?"

"Goes to show that quality is better than quantity. I read somewhere that he was a socialist, a loony lefty like us, so I'm happy to have him here. Apparently he gets lots of visitors now – coachloads – so they make up for the past indifference."

Elizabeth turned to go. "This was a lovely surprise, Dominic. And don't worry about Vienna. I'll switch to tissues – they're much lighter to carry."

Dominic gave her a squeeze and kept his arm around her all the way back to the car.

Back at the apartment the afternoon saw plenty of sofa-time interspersed with snacks to keep their strength up and conversation to keep their business going, and ended with showers and a change of clothes before venturing out for their last dinner together.

At dinner, Dominic opened the conversation with, "I'm so glad you like classical music. You can support me when the neighbours bang on the wall because I have it playing so loud."

"I'm surprised we didn't already know that about each other," Elizabeth said. "I'm looking forward to making more discoveries about your wicked ways."

"It is very important, though, that we share lots of interests together. These things can make or break a relationship, believe me." Dominic was wearing his serious face.

Elizabeth assumed that he was referring to past experiences with his wife and thought it best not to venture into that minefield. "So," she said, "you tell me your favourite composer and I'll tell you mine."

And once that conversation got going, it lasted for most of the evening.

After dinner they went to bed early, ostensibly because Elizabeth had planned to catch an early morning flight back to Manchester, an imperative that soon lost its impetus once they were under the duvet.

The next morning, in the plane flying back to Manchester, Elizabeth did an action replay of the weekend in her mind. It had been altogether wonderful, she decided, and though they had not managed to reach double figures, she now knew that Dominic was true to his recent observation that "quality is better than quantity".

Chapter 43

Back in her cottage Elizabeth grabbed a quick breakfast before heading for her computer. She and Dominic had forgotten to spend some time online to look for newspaper articles about the Cotton fraud, with the intention of seeing photographs of him, just as Ben had done. In the circumstances she forgave herself and Dominic for the omission on the grounds that they had had more urgent things to do with their time.

It didn't take her long to find a couple of eight-year-old British newspaper reports about the fraud, which included photographs of Ernest Cotton. Smartly suited with slicked back hair, it was impossible to associate the man before her with Charles Prentice. She could see why Ben had ruled him out. However, she still felt it right to continue investigating Cotton until it was proved beyond doubt that he and Prentice were not one and the same man.

She quickly read the articles and found nothing she didn't already know. She shut her computer down, wondering why the British Press needed to add what they considered to be humour to even the most serious stories. One headline read: *Cotton pulls wool over investors' eyes*; another read: *Cotton in-vest fraud*.

She sent a brief email to Dominic enclosing copies of the two newspaper reports with photos and asked for his comments. She would have liked to extend the email with more personal stuff, but she was running late with her weekly article for *The Tribune*.

Forcing Dominic out of her mind, she started on her latest Welcome to the Lakes article. This one was about Geoffrey and Linda, two young school teachers from Leicester looking for their first jobs. Linda had managed to find a position in the tiny school in Bassenthwaite village, a few miles from Keswick, a position only available because of retirement after thirty years of service, a fact that the unambitious Linda found attractive, hoping to do likewise in the safe and secure quietness of the area.

Geoffrey, on the other hand, who had been the main driving force behind their move to the Lake District, had yet to find a position in the area. A keen fell runner and man of action, he gave Elizabeth the impression that he was not in a hurry to find a position because he was having the time of his life running around his beloved fells.

They had been very lucky to move into a rarely available rental property in the heart of Keswick, which the retiring teacher had obtained for them using her local contacts.

On completion of the article, Elizabeth emailed it to Sue Burrows, with a copy to Ben, who almost never altered a word.

She took a tea break outside, on the steps outside her front door, where she enjoyed the sights, sounds and smells of her delightful surroundings. Two red squirrels were chasing each other high in the branches of one of the massive trees surrounding the garden; was it aggression or courtship? Nearby fields sent her the sounds of cattle and sheep and some sort of clanking farm machinery, and also rewarded her with the familiar faint but welcome smell of the animals' droppings.

Tea break over, she went back to her computer and did some research work for Dominic, looking for a large holiday property in the Lake District for a Dutch family currently living in Switzerland. Their main priority was seclusion, preferably in a remote location.

Her search revealed that there were plenty of large, secluded houses for sale, but none, as yet, in a remote location. The rich of the past had made sure they were separated from the poor by surrounding their houses with acres of land, usually covered by dense trees and all encircled by high stone walls.

Elizabeth paused for a moment and wondered if she was judging the rich too harshly. What would she do if she became rich? Would she not wish to put space between herself and the poor? The honest answer was yes, she would, if the poor were the kind who spoiled the environment with their litter and anti-social behaviour.

Perhaps she *was* being a bit too harsh on the rich. However, her saving grace was that she would not exploit the poor to make herself rich as many of them had done.

Enough of this. Let's get back to my job of exploiting the rich of today.

She worked well into the night to catch up on things and found herself eating her dinner, a microwaved ready meal, just before midnight. Soon afterwards she climbed into bed to the accompaniment of a hooting owl. Here she curled up and hugged herself and thought of Dominic and went to sleep with a tiny smile still on her lips.

The following day she drove around the western region of the Lakes to take an initial look at some of the houses she had listed as suitable for Dominic's Dutch family. One on the outskirts of the village of Lorton and another near Ennerdale were judged as worth another look.

Back in her cottage, after finishing some paperwork, she was about to pour herself an evening glass of wine when the phone rang. It was Ben.

"More information about Ernest Cotton," he said. "I'm not sure it takes us much further, so don't get excited. But first of all, did you have a good weekend in Zurich?"

"It was wonderful, Ben. I'll give you details when I next see you. I told Dominic you were keen to meet him, and he was just as keen to meet you, so watch this space."

"Good...good," Ben acknowledged. "Right, back to Cotton. I've been concentrating on the two years following Cotton's disappearance to see what happened to the other people involved in his company, and to see if there had been a trial of some of them in the courts. It turns out that he had a sister, Sophia, and a nephew, Anthony, who worked with him in the company. Anthony went on the run but was caught and tried and sentenced to five years in prison. His sister has not been seen since. The police don't know if she went on the run on her own and is still living somewhere unknown, or if she went on the run with Cotton, or if she has been murdered by one or more of Cotton's angry investors..."

"Why is murder being considered?" Elizabeth interrupted.

"I was coming to that. Apparently Cotton also had two brothers, Beppe and Lucio, who owned successful businesses and used to invest some of their profits in Cotton's company. It is believed that they also invested large sums on behalf of some of Chicago's criminal fraternity. Their Italian names might give you a clue as to who they were involved with. Our friend Ernest Cotton was actually born Ernesto Cottone, son of a Mafia father, Angelo, who in turn was son of an infamous immigrant from Sicily called Luigi Cottone, who spread his bootlegging and racketeering empire from New York to Chicago just in time to fill the void left by the imprisonment of a certain tax dodger called Alphonse Capone."

Ben paused. "Do any of these names mean anything to you?"

"Yes, the last one – Capone. I've watched a few gangster movies in my time and Al Capone was a frequent subject. What was it they called it – the prohibition era – when alcohol was banned in America."

"Spot on. Well, the first brother, Beppe, was found murdered shortly after the trial of the nephew, Anthony. I won't go into details, but he had obviously been tortured before being killed, using a brutal method which had the hallmark of the Italian Mafia. I think this indicates that the Mafia had invested in Cotton's scheme, via his brother, Beppe, and they were trying to recover their investment by torturing Beppe to reveal where the money had been hidden. They had assumed that Beppe was in on the scam and when they couldn't torture the location out of him, they bumped him off.

"The other brother, Lucio, went missing about the same time as Beppe's body was found and hasn't been seen since. The police think he was also tortured and murdered by the Mafia and his body disposed of using one of their usual methods. So that is why the police have included the possibility that the sister, Sophia, was also tortured and murdered, particularly since she actually worked in Cotton's office, whereas the two brothers were not directly involved in the company."

"Nice family, eh?" Elizabeth said. "I can't understand how a member of a well-known Mafia family could set up an investment company and then persuade people to give him their money. Who in their right mind would hand over large amounts of money to a person with such a history?"

"Yes, I thought the same thing when I first came across it," Ben said. "There is clearly a lot we still don't know about this family."

"What about Mama and Papa?"

"Both deceased. Apparently Mama had been a well-known opera singer when young."

"Pity the brothers didn't sing as well...might have saved their lives," Elizabeth joked.

"The fact that they didn't sing tells me they didn't know where Cotton had stashed the money. Anyway, as I said at the start, I'm not sure that this information, however interesting, takes us any further forward. Now that you have this information, does it make you think that it is more or less likely that Prentice is in fact Cotton?"

Elizabeth hesitated. "I'm actually finding this all a bit hard to take in. I mean if we had been talking about a dodgy accountant or some other kind of pen pusher, I could understand it, but the Mafia and murder – it's another world. To be honest I could never see Prentice being involved in the world of gangsters you describe, but there is one thing you mentioned which might have a tiny relevance. The fact that I know Prentice likes classical music, which of course includes opera. I know, so do millions of other people, but that is all I've got from that information."

"Fair enough, Elizabeth," Ben said. "These tiny details can all add up and help to solve the puzzle."

"We are still waiting to hear from Dominic's detective about who, if anybody, was with Prentice when he arrived in Zurich," Elizabeth pointed out. "Maybe that answer will throw some light on this information."

"I hope it does. We've spent a lot of time on Mr Cotton. Let's hope it hasn't been wasted."

Suddenly, Elizabeth felt alarmed. "What if Prentice is Cotton, what then?"

"God knows!"

Chapter 44

Elizabeth parked her Land Rover outside the farmyard walls, walked through the yard and into her parents' farmhouse, giving the front door a cursory knock just to let them know she was coming in. She had got into the habit of leaving her car outside the yard because she felt uneasy about seeing it stand side by side with her father's battered old vehicle. She felt uneasy because it had only taken a few months' work for her to own hers, whereas her father had worked for so many years and so much harder for his. The fact that her parents had told her "not to be so daft" and that they were proud of her achievements made little difference; she couldn't change her feelings.

She had timed her morning visit to arrive at about nine o'clock, which is when her father usually came in for his breakfast, having been out working since six in the morning. She hoped to share a cup of tea with them while she caught up on their news and told them about her trip to Zurich. After her visit she planned to continue driving south to look at more potential properties for their Dutch client.

Sure enough, as she made her way to the kitchen, the delicious smell of bacon and toast greeted her, and the babble of voices told her that their routine was still unchanged.

"In here," her mother shouted, not realising she had already created pungent directions.

"Can you spare a weary traveller a cup of tea?" Elizabeth said as she walked into the kitchen.

"She's just out of bed and she says she's weary," her father joked.

"Unlike you," her mother said, "she needs her beauty sleep."

"And don't forget, you two," Elizabeth said in an exaggeratedly posh accent, "one has yet to recover fully from the jet lag suffered on one's recent trip to Europe."

"And one will continue to suffer if one doesn't get her backside on her chair and shut up," said her father.

"Here's your tea, love." Her mother sat down beside her.

"How did the lamb sales go?" Elizabeth asked as she lifted her cup. She wanted to talk about something far more important than her jaunt in Zurich. She knew the result of the annual late summer lamb sales was the critical factor in the success or otherwise of the farm.

There was a slight pause before her father said, "Not so good, lass."

Elizabeth glanced at her mother and caught the worry in her face just before she smiled when she knew she was being watched. "How bad was it?"

"Not as bad as some years but could have been better. Still, we had two good years before this one, so we mustn't grumble, eh?"

Elizabeth knew that her father, like most hill farmers, could make more money working in a factory for forty hours a week, but would never consider giving up the farm. Being his own boss, working in the fresh air, caring for his stock; these things were more valuable to him than money. The older Elizabeth got, the more she appreciated the sacrifices they had both made to support her through university and she wished with all her heart that she could take away the difficulties of their hard life.

"Anyway," her father said, pushing back his chair, "can't sit about here talking all day. I've got to get the ewes to new pasture, get them fit and fat for the tups." He looked at Elizabeth. "Grand to see you, lass. Tell your mam all about your weekend in...Zurich...and she'll tell me tonight, okay?"

"Have you got any new tups yet?" Elizabeth shouted after him as he walked away.

"Going to market next month. Buy some then," he shouted as he left the kitchen.

Thoughtful as ever, he had left them to talk on their own as only mothers and daughters can talk when matters of the heart are involved. Elizabeth stayed for another two cups of tea as she told her mother of her wonderful weekend and discussed future possibilities. An hour after Elizabeth's arrival, they said goodbye with loving smiles and tender, meaningful hugs.

Elizabeth drove out of the farm and took the main road running down the heart of the Lake District. Skirting around Keswick, she drove south, passing Thirlmere and the village and lake of Grasmere, before entering the town of Ambleside. Heading west out of Ambleside, she reached the sublime valley of Langdale, where the picture postcard village of Elterwater sat gazing up at the stunning sight of the Langdale Pikes – twin mountains that dominated the valley, the inspiring subject of thousands of paintings and photographs.

Within this great scoop of a valley lay many scattered groups of trees and sheltered within these trees were two relatively small mansions that Elizabeth planned to view (externally only) on behalf of her Dutch clients.

After a brief walk around the first house, which was obviously empty, she decided it was unsuitable because of the restricted view at the rear of the property.

The second house, also standing empty and looking a bit derelict as a result, was a possibility as long as the client didn't mind spending money trimming or cutting down some of the surrounding trees which blotted out the nice views they had asked for.

Like many of the larger old houses, both had been on the market for a long time, which was why she had selected them for viewing.

After the viewings Elizabeth headed for home. She had planned to spend the rest of the day on more online research and updating her current notes and records.

On the drive home she thought of diverting her route to take in Borrowdale to see if anything was happening in the vicinity of Becalmed, but eventually decided against it. She was itching to get to the bottom of the Prentice mystery, but hoping for some lucky break was not the way to go about it.

She was glad she had stayed patient because as soon as she entered her cottage, the phone rang. It was Dominic. After some affectionate exchanges, followed by Elizabeth briefing him on her morning's house visits, Dominic announced: "I've had a further report from my detective. He has spoken to Prentice's gardener, who told him that Prentice, his wife and daughter have all been resident all the time he has been there. But he has only worked there for the past twelve months. So the detective went looking for the previous gardener and managed to find him.

"The previous gardener is an old man who had worked there for over twenty years and retired about twelve months ago. The old man told the detective that our friend Prentice arrived at the house on his own and lived on his own for about six months before his wife, Barbara, arrived on her own. It was another three years before daughter Claire arrived, just before the old man retired. How strange is that?"

"It's nuts," Elizabeth said. "Maybe that's it – they are all nuts...Sorry, that's unkind."

"Who knows," Dominic said. "Maybe you're on to something. Maybe his daughter or his wife are nuts. Prentice himself is clearly not nuts. You have seen him in action, but the wife and daughter's responses to conversation have been almost comatose, have they not?"

"They have," Elizabeth agreed. "There could of course be a perfectly reasonable explanation which will turn out to be obvious in hindsight."

"Claire could have been in a coma in hospital for three years and then partially recovered," Dominic suggested. "But my guess is that Barbara is not a new wife but his new girlfriend. I can't see him risking going through a wedding ceremony."

"We could go on positing forever." Elizabeth sighed.

"Why don't I pass this information on to Ben and let him work his wonders. He's a heck of a lot cheaper than a detective and probably better than most. Perhaps he'll be able to find something revealing about Barbara or Claire."

"Smart idea, partner. Smart as well as beautiful. Aren't I a lucky man?"

"Guess so."

As they laughed together, so their conversation returned once more to personal matters.

Chapter 45

Once again, Carlos had been unable to shake off the grip of the Sinaloa. He had hoped that he would be allowed to make his own way from O'Hare Airport to the headquarters of the Sinaloa hub, during which he would have attempted to make his escape. He had even prepared himself to dodge or fight off a single driver sent to pick him up, but when he saw the two heavies carrying a card with his name on it, he knew he was trapped again. However, he consoled himself with the fact that he was in the United States and a long way from Tijuana and Perez. Surely he would find an opportunity to escape at some point.

As soon as Carlos was in the car with the heavies, one of them tied a blindfold over his eyes. Before the blindfold was in place, Carlos glanced at his watch and registered the time. To know how long it took to drive to the headquarters from the airport could prove useful in the future.

The journey only took fifteen minutes and soon Carlos was being ushered into the presence of the hub boss, Tony Marcelo, a small, sixty-something man with a pinched face, thinning grey hair and piercing black eyes. He looked like a member of the rodent family. Marcelo was sitting in a swivelling leather chair, behind a large leather-covered desk which had only two objects on it. One was a framed photograph of a large family group, presumably his. The other object was a gun.

Carlos was made to stand in front of Marcelo, on the other side of the desk. There were no introductions and no handshakes.

"Heard good things about you," Marcelo squeaked, looking up at Carlos across the desk. His voice had a strange falsetto tone and sounded forced as if it was an effort to speak. Carlos was to learn later that Marcelo's voice box had been damaged during a knife fight when he was young.

Carlos looked straight at him but didn't speak.

"Quiet man, eh? I like quiet men. Sometimes I like to make them quiet forever." He looked up at his heavies and waited for them to laugh, which they duly did.

Carlos remained silent.

"Our main man has a big job coming up. We brought you over to back him up on the job. He wants to make sure you are reliable, so he's going to take you on a few jobs, show you his ways, test you out. When he thinks you are ready, you both go on the big job. If he doesn't like you, we send you back to Tijuana." Marcelo paused, giving Carlos time to say something.

When Carlos remained silent, Marcelo leaned forward menacingly and shrieked, "Do you understand?"

Carlos almost took a step backwards when the high-pitched shriek hit his ears. "Yes, I understand."

"Good," Marcelo shouted. "He can speak...great...He has a tongue...Jesus, I've seen more life in a graveyard." He gestured to his heavies. "Get this guy outta here...Jesus...take him to see Dragan. He should be back by now...Jesus..." He waved his arms in a dismissive gesture and sat back in his chair.

One of the two heavies grabbed Carlos's arm and marched him out through the door. Two corridors later they entered a large garage full of cars and busy mechanics. Pop music blared from a wall speaker. Along one wall of the garage stood three offices, two with windows facing onto the garage floor; the third had no windows. The heavies marched Carlos across the garage and stopped outside the third office. One of them knocked on the door.

"Who?" came a deep voice from inside the office.

"It's Jack," one of the heavies said. "We've got that new guy from Tijuana. Tony sent him."

"Wait." A muffled sound of activity came through the door – doors closing, objects being moved, water running. Finally, the sound of two bolts being withdrawn and two locks being turned in the door. "Enter."

Carlos was more or less pushed through the doorway by the heavies. "Leave him with me," a voice boomed from a corner. The two heavies left the room.

Carlos blinked in the glaring light of numerous fluorescent tubes on the ceiling, obviously deemed necessary because of the lack of windows. A brief glance around the room told him that this was not an office. He took in many closed cupboards on the walls, some light machinery in a corner, two large side-by-side sinks with taps, a large table similar to a butcher's block, some randomly scattered chairs, and in the middle of the room a substantial wooden chair with wooden arms and a high back. On the chair arms Carlos noticed two leather restraining straps and a similar large strap on the chair back.

"Took me years to get this together," the deep voice

boasted. It came from the large man now standing in front of him. Fiftyish, over six feet tall, broad, hunched shoulders, short neck, shaven iron-grey hair, sunken blue eyes. Tight tee-shirt and jeans emphasised powerful muscles.

"Dragan Vasic, the mad Serbian," the big man said, grinning and holding out a large hand to shake. "Everybody calls me The Dragon. And you are Carlos...from Mexico... younger than I expected."

"Guatemala," Carlos said while shaking Vasic's hand.

"What?"

"I'm from Guatemala, not Mexico," Carlos explained.

"Who cares? As long as you're better than the last one they sent me."

"What happened to him?" Carlos needed to know.

"Returned to sender." Vasic grinned. His Slavic accent gave his words a sinister edge.

"Did you have anything like this down in Tijuana?" Vasic indicated the contents of the room with a sweep of his arm.

"No..." Carlos wasn't sure how best to answer the question, but he knew he needed to feign interest in Vasic's world.

Vasic walked him around the room, pointing as he walked. "These four cupboards – guns. This one – knives. This one – wires. This one – drills. This one – chainsaws. This one – electrics. This one – manual saws."

Carlos's worst suspicions had been confirmed. He was standing in an interrogation/torture room surrounded by all the tools of the trade. He assumed Vasic also used these tools when working on outside jobs as well.

"Which is your favourite?" Vasic asked, as casually as if talking about pizzas.

Carlos thought quickly. "Guns...yeah, guns...quick and easy...job done, no problem...yeah." He added a few body movements to accompany his words, pointing an imaginary gun, firing it and smiling as if enjoying himself. He had to pretend to be a typical cold-blooded killer; otherwise Vasic might send him back to Tijuana, or worse.

"I like wires best." Vasic grinned. "No noise...no machinery...just strength...keeps me fit. Where do you keep your stuff...if you don't have a room like this?"

"As you said, Dragan," Carlos started, risking familiarity, "I'm young. I haven't collected much stuff yet. What I have, I keep at home. When I'm as experienced as you, I will have a room like this one."

"Okay...good. Now, Tony has told you about a big job to do, yeah?"

Carlos nodded. "Yeah."

"We don't talk about this until the day of the job, okay?"

"Okay."

"Next few weeks you come with me on other jobs. I see what you do. If okay, good. If not, I train you. If you still no good, I send you back. Understand?"

"Yes."

"Okay. Now I show you where you stay. There are rooms here with everything, and there is a canteen for the mechanics – you eat there. There are security guards at night. You must not leave this building without me or special permission from the boss. Yes?"

"Yes."

Carlos was devastated. Not only by the horrors that he was going to have to endure, but also by the fact that he would be treated like a prisoner. He had assumed he would be based in a room somewhere in the city, from where he could plan an escape. He guessed, now, that some of his predecessors had tried that in the past and this was the cartel's way of stopping future runners.

Vasic herded Carlos back through the garage and down a new corridor and stopped at one of six doors along the corridor. He opened the door, went inside, ushered Carlos in and showed him that a key was present in the lock on the inside of the door. "You come see me in the morning," Vasic ordered and left before Carlos could ask any more questions.

The room was functional and well equipped, like those in a motel. Carlos dumped his luggage in a corner of the room and glanced out of the single window. He was facing a brick wall on the other side of a shadowy back lane. A cloud of deep despondency settled into Carlos's mind as he flopped onto the bed beside a wall. He lay back and closed his eyes and, mercifully, the stress of the day took him quickly to sleep.

Chapter 46

The late summer transition into autumn was not a favourite time for Elizabeth. It spoke of the decline of all things bright and fresh, of dying light and colder temperatures, and though it heralded spectacular colours, they were only temporary, a last grasp at beauty before decay set in.

Elizabeth thought of such things when she noticed the drop in temperature as she locked her car and made her way up the steps to her cottage.

Her mood changed rapidly, however, when she reminded herself that it was Friday evening, the weekend was nigh, and best of all, Dominic was due to arrive that very night. He had phoned to say that it was time he came over to meet Elizabeth's parents and Ben and Helen, with whom he would discuss the latest Prentice situation, and of course he was dying to see Elizabeth again.

He told Elizabeth he would book himself into a hotel or pub close to Keswick rather than stay with her in her cottage just in case anyone in her circle of family or friends might not approve, adding that if she was to stray into his hotel when darkness descended, nobody would know.

When Elizabeth told Ben and Helen he was coming, they were delighted, but when she told her parents, her father pointed out that it was the weekend he had planned to gather the sheep off the fells to separate the lambs from the ewes. Elizabeth knew that it was not possible to cancel his plans as he would have arranged for other farmers in the area to help him carry out the gather, which would take a whole day of hard work.

On passing this information to Dominic, he had immediately suggested that he and Elizabeth should help in the gather, which he would enjoy and could help win him some points with her father. Elizabeth had readily agreed.

She had been expecting Dominic to arrive in Keswick early in the evening and that she would be joining him for dinner in the hotel. She was changing her clothes in preparation for this when the phone rang. "Bad news," Dominic's distant voice said. He was obviously on his mobile and outdoors. "I've just arrived in Manchester. Plane delay. By the time I get a hire car organised, I reckon I won't be in Keswick until after eleven. So, *mon amour, je regrette* tonight is cancelled. What time are we due on the farm in the morning?"

"Eight thirty. It might be just as well, *mon amour*," she added. "We will both need all our strength for a long day on the fells."

Dominic laughed. "I hope we will have some strength left for later."

"I'm counting on it," Elizabeth joked. "Better let you get on. Where are you booked in?"

"The Swan Hotel, just outside Keswick."

"I know it. I'll pick you up there at eight in the morning. *Bon soir, mon amour.*"

"*Bon soir, mon amour.*"

The next morning, the sun shining through her bedroom

window and a listen to the weather forecast told Elizabeth that their luck was in. It was going to be perfect gathering weather – no rain, no mist, no wind, a nice walking temperature, even on the tops of the fells. Still, experience told her to put a lightweight waterproof jacket in her backpack.

When she pulled into the car park of the Swan Hotel, Dominic was standing waiting for her, dressed appropriately – boots on, small backpack. She had just closed her car door when his arms were around her and he was kissing her and squeezing her so hard she thought her ribs might collapse.

When he released her she looked up at him and uttered, "*Bon matin, mon amour.*"

"I am so happy to see you," Dominic said, his adoring eyes travelling around her face.

"You can't be as happy as I am to see you," Elizabeth teased.

"Oh, yes, I can," insisted Dominic. "I am so happy I could run to the top of a mountain without stopping."

"Well, you will get your chance today, running after sheep. Come on, we need to get going. They won't wait for us."

Dominic threw his hands up. "Ah, you English. You have no romance in your souls."

"I quite agree," Elizabeth said. "That is why I chose a Frenchman."

Dominic laughed. "You are too smart for me. I surrender."

"In the car," Elizabeth ordered.

They arrived at the farm just in time. Two groups of men were climbing into two vehicles. Elizabeth's father was at the steering wheel of his old Land Rover, with four men climbing in to join him. Behind him a trailer carried three excited sheep dogs, barking and tails wagging. The other vehicle was an equally battered ute, into which another three men were climbing. In the back of the ute, three more sheep dogs barked their excitement.

Elizabeth and Dominic just had time to say hello to her father and acknowledge the others with a wave before they were invited to squeeze into the ute as best they could. Elizabeth made sure she was squeezed more into Dominic than the other man, who she knew as John. She also knew the two in the front and introduced them to Dominic as they set off up the valley.

As they bumped along the track, Elizabeth explained to Dominic that the narrow valley was about three miles long and completely flanked by high fells, where the sheep were free to roam. They were driving to the closed far end of the valley, where they would walk to the top of a 2,000-feet-high fell then, together with the other young men and the dogs, walk along the top of the fells flanking the valley, all the while driving the sheep down into the valley, where the older men were waiting to push them along the valley and into the farmyard pens. There would be lots of climbing and descending to do to rescue sheep trapped in gullies or crags, and everybody would be exhausted when the job was done.

Dominic noticed that there were no boundaries on the fells, no fences or walls, and asked why the sheep didn't roam further away. Elizabeth explained that all Lake District sheep had been hefted, a term meaning that all the separate herds had been conditioned to stay within the reach of their farm by constant shepherding over the centuries and it was now instinctive within the herds, each ewe passing on the knowledge to its lambs.

It was about three o'clock in the afternoon when Elizabeth's mother brought food and drink out of the farmhouse and laid it on two old wooden tables in the farmyard. This was not an act born of many years' experience but the result of a mobile phone call from her husband telling her of his imminent arrival.

The gatherers, the dogs and the sheep arrived in a cacophony of barking, bleating and shouting. Dirt and dust filled the air, and the smell of dung filled the nostrils. Along with the other men, Dominic and Elizabeth slumped onto the wooden benches alongside the tables. They looked at each other and smiled a tired smile. Both were exhausted, dirty, dust-covered, scratched, scruffy and smelly, and apparently very happy. Some of the older men nodded, knowingly, at them.

The shepherds of the Lake District bred not only sheep but some of the greatest long distance runners in the country, Elizabeth explained to Dominic. Their legs were iron-strong after years of walking up and down the fells. Her father had been a county champion in his younger days.

After ravenously devouring a piece of homemade pie and washing it down with a bottle of beer, Dominic leaned over to Elizabeth and pecked her on the cheek. "Thank you, *mon amour*, that was a terrible but wonderful day. It was so good to be physical again, instead of sitting behind a desk dealing with documents and phone calls."

"Thank you for suggesting it," Elizabeth said in between gulping her bottle of beer. "It was great, wasn't it? My father will be so pleased you came to help; he puts a lot of store by people's actions rather than words. The bad news, however, is that I don't think I will be able to move again for a week."

After all the helpers had gone back to their farms, Elizabeth helped her mother clear up the outside tables and do the washing up. Meanwhile, Dominic had stayed outside to help her father with his other chores around the farm, making conversation as they worked away.

The day had taken its toll on all of them and when the men eventually joined the women in the kitchen, there was mutual agreement when Elizabeth's mother suggested that now was not a good time for further chat, suggesting that everybody should go home and have a deserved rest and, most importantly, take a shower.

Soon afterwards, Elizabeth and Dominic waved their goodbyes to her parents, promising to get together again as soon as possible. Elizabeth drove them back to Dominic's hotel, where she was easily persuaded to take a short break before heading back to her cottage. Inevitably, she stayed on and after luxuriating in the hotel's bathroom, where she fell asleep, was easily persuaded, yet again, to spend the night with Dominic.

Chapter 47

Narrow slices of sunshine framed the closed bedroom curtains the next morning, announcing another day of good weather. Dominic and Elizabeth stretched lazily under their dishevelled bedding. They had been invited to lunch by Ben and Helen so had decided not to bother going down for breakfast, however tempting the hotel's food was. After yesterday's herculean efforts on the fells, they decided that they deserved a few hours of utter laziness, wallowing in bed until it was time to go for lunch. However, the term "wallowing" could not be used to describe how they actually spent that time, and as the time approached to rise and shine, they wanted nothing more than a few hours rest.

When, eventually, they forced themselves to leave their bed and make their way to Ben and Helen's cottage, they were, as Elizabeth had predicted, received as if they were royalty. Introductions over, they were soon all seated in the cosy lounge with a drink in their hands. A slight smell of freshly baked scones drifted in from the kitchen.

Lots of pleasantries and humour flowed easily from one to the other, plus the kind of leg-pulling only true affection allowed. There were one or two hesitant moments, usually involving the topic of Elizabeth and Dominic's future plans, a topic which neither had yet to raise with the other since they had agreed to take things slowly.

Soon they were gathered around the dining table tucking in to a delightful lunch of French onion soup, salmon salad and lemon compote. Then they were ushered into the conservatory, where Helen served them coffee. While drinking their coffee they were entertained by the wildlife on the lawn and around the feeders. Unknown to Elizabeth, Dominic turned out to be a bit of a birder and spent some time comparing the birds outside with those found in the Alpine Valleys.

When coffee was over, Helen excused herself, knowing they wanted to discuss the Prentice situation and time was short. She had previously been informed by Dominic that he had to leave by four o'clock at the latest in order to catch his flight back to Zurich from Manchester.

Ben, now complete with reading glasses and having produced some papers and pen from under the coffee table, started the conversation. "Bit of an anti-climax, I'm afraid. I was hoping to produce the verbal equivalent of Helen's lunch, i.e. something tasty and well put together, but I'm afraid it is not to be. I was not able to source the right ingredients this time and have finished up with something resembling leftovers."

"Beautifully described, Ben." Dominic laughed. "You certainly know how to let people down gently. I take it you were unable to discover anything new about the two women living with Prentice."

"Not yet," Ben said. "And I don't hold out too much hope in the future. The basic problem is we have no sound base from which to start searching, because we don't know any true facts about them. Are their names real or false? Are they related to each other or not? Until we have some facts, we are just looking for a needle in a haystack. I could go on putting up possibilities and working from them, which is what I have been doing lately, but there are so many possibilities that it will be more by good luck than proficiency if I find something."

Dominic and Elizabeth looked at each other, their tight expressions conveying a mixture of sympathy for Ben and disappointment at his news.

"I don't think you should spend any more time on it, Ben," Dominic insisted. "You have done more work on this than any of us and we are really grateful." He looked at Elizabeth when he said this, indicating that she was part of the "we".

"Absolutely," Elizabeth affirmed. "Why don't we all step back from the whole thing for a while, clear our heads, then come back to it refreshed and hopefully full of new ideas, and this time try to share the burden more equally."

Dominic smiled at Ben. "You can see why I love her, can't you?"

"We were first." Ben smiled. "Helen and I loved her before you – so there."

Elizabeth was lost for words and was relieved when Dominic came to her rescue.

"You know what's really ironic about this. Here we are – three supposedly intelligent people totally absorbed in the life of a family two of us haven't even met, using all our mental powers to uncover who or what they are, while they have no idea that they are the subject of our investigations and are probably relaxed and enjoying a day's outing in their boat on Derwent Water as we speak."

Elizabeth had forgotten that Dominic had not met the Prentices; he had handed them over to her from the beginning and dealt only with Prentice's solicitor. "All the more reason why we should relax for a while," she insisted.

"I'm all for a bit of relaxation," Ben said. "I need to get my handicap down and my exercise up."

"It seems we are all agreed," Dominic summarised. "Shall we say no Prentice work for three weeks?"

Ben and Elizabeth nodded their agreement.

Ben put his papers and pen back under the coffee table and swapped his glasses over. "Why don't we go outside and see what the natural world is up to?" he invited, rising from his chair.

Elizabeth and Dominic followed him outside and trailed slightly behind him as he took them on a tour of the garden, pointing out the subtle changes in flora and fauna that indicated the onset of autumn.

Ben didn't mention the cooler air, but it wasn't long before he noticed Elizabeth intertwining her bare arms to keep them warm. "Time to repair to civilisation, methinks," he said as he put a hand on Elizabeth's shoulder and ushered her towards the cottage.

On their way into the cottage, Elizabeth noticed Dominic glancing at his watch. She sensed that he was keen not to leave his departure until the last minute. She glanced at her watch – just after three o'clock. She was also keen to spend some time with Dominic before he had to leave for the airport.

But it was not to be. In the kitchen, Helen had prepared four cups of tea and a plate full of scones with jam and cream, all laid out on the wooden kitchen table. "Just a little something to keep you going for the rest of the day," she said. "Best be quick before Ben eats them all."

As if on cue, Ben forgot his manners and sat down first. Without having conspired, Dominic and Elizabeth ate and drank a bit quicker than normal and by three thirty they were rising from the table, bidding their hosts a warm farewell and thanking them for their wonderful hospitality.

Elizabeth drove back to Dominic's hotel, where his hire car stood already packed and ready to go. Elizabeth parked beside it and they both got out of her car and swapped from the front seats to the back seats. Here they wrapped themselves in each other's arms and embraced as though they would never see each other again. With their heads resting on each other's shoulders, Dominic whispered, "I'm finding our agreement to take things slowly harder to justify every time I see you. How about you?"

Elizabeth sighed. "Right from the beginning I've always thought we were right for each other. I agreed to take things slowly out of respect for your greater experience. So in effect I'm just waiting for you to decide when the wait is over."

Dominic released Elizabeth from his arms and looked at her. "My heart is saying the wait is over now. But my stubborn old head is still saying it won't kill us to wait a bit longer. Better than rushing in and regretting it later. Do you understand?"

"Absolutely. I want you to do whatever is right for you."

"Thanks." Dominic sounded relieved.

"In the meantime," Elizabeth said, "it might be a good idea to think about things as if we were already committed to each other. There is so much to consider, like where we would live, the effect that would have on your business and each other's futures. And at some point in the future, I would want to consider, and I hope you would also, whether we really want to spend most of our lives buying properties for rich people. I understand it'll be necessary to carry on as we are for a number of years to build up finances for our future, but in the long run I would rather live my life doing something more worthwhile. You know where my interests lie, but you haven't really told me if you are happy doing what you are doing, and you haven't told me if you have anything you would rather be doing. Have you got any secret ambitions?"

Dominic kissed her on her cheek. "Yes, I have a secret ambition, *mon amour*, but I think you will be surprised to hear it." He paused, as if wondering whether to tell her.

"Come on, out with it," Elizabeth ordered. "I'm intrigued."

"Well…I would like to own a vineyard. But not in France or anywhere in Europe. In Australia. I saw lots of small independent vineyards when I visited New South Wales and they were all in stunning scenery close to the coast, where the climate is perfect and the sea teems with fish, and also close to the Snowy Mountains, where we could ski. The owners of the vineyards I visited were all laid back and seemed to be ridiculously content."

"You said your father hated working in the vineyard?"

"That was because he had a terrible boss who worked him like a slave. I would be the boss and I would treat any staff well. He did hate it, but he told me a lot about the processes, and I spent a lot of time in the vineyard as a child. It would be a great place to bring up kids."

Well, that's one topic I don't need to bring up. "Do you think you can be a boss and a land owner and still be a lefty?"

"In Australia, yes. Much of the land is owned by ordinary people; that is how they buy most of their houses – they buy a plot of land, hire an architect and builder and off they go. Much of the land is so cheap it is within the reach of ordinary people. In fact, I met a union leader who had bought a ten-acre plot in the middle of virgin forest for a few hundred dollars. He cleared the trees, installed a huge log cabin, a water tank, a generator, and lived happily off grid with virtually no costs."

Elizabeth had never heard Dominic speak so enthusiastically, but she could understand why. Having been brought up on a farm, she understood the call of the outdoors, the pleasure of working the land and producing something useful for your family and others. She had seen the shine in Dominic's eyes yesterday as he strode about the fells gathering the sheep. But did reality match the dream? she wondered. "It all sounds great, Dominic, but surely an established vineyard would cost a fortune."

"Big ones do, but most of them are small family-run businesses. You can make a living with only five acres and a profitable business selling to local wholesalers with only ten acres. You can buy an established vineyard complete with homestead and forty acres of land for the cost of a semi in London. Usually, they use ten to fifteen acres for the vineyard and the rest of the acres for whatever takes their fancy.

For example, you could build up a great market garden of fruit and vegetables and sell them locally."

"I like the sound of homestead. Do you mean a house?"

"Yes. It means different things in different countries. In Australia it means the house of the farmer or landowner. Some are conventional houses, but many are true to their image – large, rambling log cabins with overhanging roofs covering a veranda running all around the outside, where you can sit out in your rocking chair and watch the kids and the wildlife playing and drink your free wine until the sun goes down. Many people buy them when they retire and carry on making a few dollars until they die, then leave it to their offspring."

"It sounds idyllic, Dominic, but there must be a catch somewhere?"

"Leaving your family and friends behind." Dominic let the words sink in, then continued. "It's probably not fair to ask you at this stage, but do you think you could ever leave your parents and friends, and possibly a career in British politics, as I am suggesting?"

"Wow! That is a big question at this stage. We must be years away from accumulating enough money to buy a vineyard. Who knows how I might feel by then, or what my parents' situation will be. What I can say now is that if we do get together, you become my priority, not my parents or my hypothetical political career."

"Fair enough, *mon amour*."

"What about your parents? You never talk about them."

Dominic's demeanour changed. "They are not a consideration. They are divorced. My father took to the bottle, so my mother left him. I haven't seen either of them for years. Last I heard he was doing casual labouring on building sites in France, and she had left the country and gone to live with her new partner in Austria."

"I'm so sorry, Dominic. I can't imagine how it feels not to have your parents in your life at all."

"It's okay, *mon amour*. I've got used to it. I want to concentrate on what is ahead of us, not behind. It was a bit disappointing today to hear Ben had made no progress with the Prentice thing. We could all do with that riddle solved and out of the way, then we could get on and clarify our plans for the future."

"Amen to that."

Dominic glanced at his watch. "*Mon Dieu.* I must go, *mon amour*. I'm late. It was wonderful to see you and to meet your parents and Ben and Helen. I love you." He leaned forward and kissed her, then hurriedly opened her car door and rushed towards his car.

Elizabeth watched him climb into his car and drive quickly out of the hotel car park. She was left mouthing "I love you too" to the fresh Lakeland air.

Chapter 48

Elizabeth woke up early the following morning. She felt alert and full of purpose even though some of the night had been spent thinking about yesterday's discussion about Prentice. Ben had seemed a bit dispirited by his inability to produce information about Barbara and Claire, and later, Dominic had expressed his disappointment about their inability to get on with their lives because of the whole Prentice question.

Were they losing interest? Were they about to abandon their involvement and leave it to the police? Elizabeth felt as if some sort of crossroads had been reached, as though a decision needed to be made. She was concerned that after their three-week break from the problem, Ben and Dominic would be loath to return to the subject.

Her desire to continue to search for the truth had not waned and she knew why. She had started the whole thing off by finding the body in the river, then linking that, along with Ben, to the Prentices' obsession with security, their odd behaviour, and the fact that they couldn't find his name in the oil industry. She was the only one who had met and talked with the Prentices. She felt more personally involved than them, and more responsible for the outcome – good or bad.

She had woken up with the feeling that it was down to

her to do something to break the log-jam. All she could come up with was the simple but potentially dangerous idea of going to see Prentice and asking him, face to face, if he was using a false name. She could hear the warnings from Dominic and Ben not to do something so crazy, but they hadn't met Prentice. She was still confident in her ability to judge someone's character and, try as she might, she still could not picture Prentice as a scheming fraudster or as being involved in the deaths of the two men in wetsuits.

All through getting dressed for work and eating break-fast, she considered the pros and cons of calling on Prentice that very day. She had a Welcome to the Lakes appointment with a young couple in Grange-in-Borrowdale and her journey, via the Cat Bells road, would take her past the lane that led to Becalmed. The battle between the pros and cons kept swinging from one to the other and by the time she was ready to go to work, her mind had become a whirlpool of confusion and indecision.

With her head still buzzing, and no conclusion reached, she set off to keep her appointment. She wondered what state her mind would be in when she approached the lane. Would she dare take the risk of turning off, or would she drive straight on to Grange?

She arrived on the A66, by-passing Keswick, and shortly afterwards turned off at the signpost announcing the village of Portinscale. This always reminded her of that first day when she met Dominic in Smyth's office and drove him to his first viewing of Fell View. How things had changed in such a short time.

Soon she was driving through the narrow main street of

Portinscale village. As usual, the traffic was nose to tail, and it was particularly slow today because the vehicle directly in front of her was a large furniture delivery van, which caused extra negotiation problems on bends and past cars parked on the roadside.

Finally they broke free of the village, and she continued following the van along the twisting tree-lined road. Suddenly the van was indicating left and slowing down. To her surprise it turned into the entrance to Fell View. Had Prentice finally decided what to do with the apartments? Without time to think she found herself following the van into the grounds. The van pulled up outside the front door, where a number of men were standing, apparently ready to offload it. Two small yellow vans were also present, each with the word *Daredevils* printed boldly in blue across their bodies. Smaller print announced that it was a children's charity and gave contact details.

Elizabeth parked her car close to the yellow vans and headed for a young woman she noticed sitting in the front seat of one of them. The woman wound her window down on seeing Elizabeth approach. They greeted each other with a smile. "I was driving past," Elizabeth started, "and I saw the furniture van pull in. I live locally, so I know the building has been standing unused for a long time, and I was just curious as to what was going on. Has your charity taken it over?"

"I'm just a volunteer for the charity," the young woman said. "You would need to phone that number on the side of the van if you want information. We have all been told that the person who donated the building and the furniture to us wants to remain anonymous and receive no publicity, so we have to pass all enquiries on to our head office."

Elizabeth's pulse quickened. Prentice had rid himself of Fell View. What did this signify? Why had he donated a £3 million property to a charity and paid for its furnishing? Was he about to make a run for it? Here was the perfect opportunity to call in to see him to innocently offer any help he might need with the project. At the same time she could get a feel for what was going on in the Prentice household, and if the situation presented itself, to ask him the big question.

Before leaving the young woman, Elizabeth asked a question out of genuine personal interest. "What exactly does your charity do?"

"We provide outdoor adventure holidays for children with a disability."

"So it's similar to the adventure charity that operates on the shore of Bassenthwaite Lake?"

"Yes, but we deal with children only. The other one provides for adults as well."

"Well, good luck to you all. You do great work. I'll expect to see you and the kids tearing around Derwent Water in the near future. Thanks. Bye."

"Thanks...See you."

Elizabeth drove out of the grounds, her mind racing. Now she knew she would definitely be calling in to see Mr Charles Prentice in a few minutes' time.

The traffic had thinned slightly as she approached Cat Bells, some vehicles having veered off on the branch road across the fells to Buttermere. Soon she was driving past the viewpoint from where Prentice had first spotted Becalmed, the place he had described as "a seat in heaven". Next she was passing the former home of novelist Sir Hugh Walpole, and shortly afterwards came the sharp left turn into the lane leading to Becalmed.

Manesty Woods, through which the lane twisted and turned, had always had a slightly eerie feel about it and today, with autumn just starting to make its presence felt, was no exception. Everything seemed quiet and unvisited, either by humans or animals. A thin, damp mist loitered among the trees but not elsewhere – a location for ghosts and ghouls.

Elizabeth turned one more bend and the house appeared. She parked her car close to the gates and waited, trying her best to keep calm by using deep breathing exercises. It wasn't long before Prentice arrived at the front door and started walking towards the gate. Elizabeth left her car and went forward to meet him.

As he opened the gate, Prentice smiled. "Elizabeth! How nice to see you."

"Nice to see you too, Charles." Elizabeth tried to appear informal and relaxed.

Prentice looked a little neater than the last time she saw him, but it was as if an amateur barber had trimmed his wild, curly hair, and gone on to wash his clothes and iron them.

This time he didn't take her to the boathouse to waste time, but he did walk very slowly as he accompanied her back to the house. He ushered her ahead of him at the door and soon they both emerged into the lounge, where a smiling Barbara greeted her from the same sofa as last time and a half-smiling Claire, complete with blanket across her lap and legs, from her wheelchair. Charles motioned Elizabeth to sit in an armchair opposite Claire and he joined Barbara on the sofa. *Talk about an action replay. What do these people do all day?*

Again, there was no warmth, no inquisitiveness, no enthusiasm – just six eyes staring at her, waiting for her to explain the reason for her visit.

"Sorry for arriving without an appointment, but..."

"No need to apologise, Elizabeth," Prentice said, but left it at that.

"This is just a spur of the moment thing," Elizabeth went on. "I've just driven from Portinscale on my way to Grange and I saw a furniture delivery van turn into Fell View. Out of interest, I turned in myself and found that Fell View was being fitted out for use by a disabled children's adventure charity. It's such a wonderful thing to do I just thought I would call in and congratulate you and ask if there is anything I can do to help you with the project." Elizabeth prayed that her garbled explanation sounded genuine.

Prentice looked at her intently. "That is so kind of you, Elizabeth. But there is nothing for you to do. I handed the whole project over to the charity and I have no further input now. I'm sure the charity would be glad of any help you can offer. They are always on the lookout for volunteers."

Feeling more confident than when they last met, Elizabeth pressed on. "Did you always have something like this in mind when you bought Fell View?"

"By the way," Charles countered, "did somebody on the site mention my name to you?"

Elizabeth thought he was trying to change the subject.

"No, they didn't. They told me that the building had been donated anonymously and the donor wanted no publicity or interviews."

"Good. I hope I can count on your discretion also, Elizabeth?"

"Absolutely."

"As to your other question, the answer is yes, I did have a charity in mind when I bought the property, though I didn't have a particular one selected at the time. That is what I do most of the time. With the help of Barbara and Claire, I look for worthwhile causes around the world and use my money to help them. They call it 'giving something back' these days. But you will gather that I loathe publicity. I value a quiet life more than anything."

Elizabeth was astonished, not only by what he was doing, but also by the fact that he had opened up and told her about it. This was not a man who had killed two men, nor a man who was using a false identity to hide his crimes. If he was using a false identity, it was to avoid publicity for his charitable work. Elizabeth felt elated that she had been proven right, that her belief in her ability to judge character had been vindicated.

She now felt that Charles deserved to hear the ridiculous suspicions that she and Ben had conjured up, all due to what now turned out to be nothing but circumstantial evidence. She hoped that he would see the funny side of it and that it would be the start of a closer, more neighbourly relationship in the future.

As she opened her mouth to speak, the lounge door swung open and two men entered the room. Both had their right arms fully extended, pointing guns into the room. One of them also carried a leather bag.

Nobody cried out or screamed, their normal reactions frozen by shock. Elizabeth stared in disbelief. Men with guns? In the Lake District?

The big man with the shaven head dominated the room, the shorter, younger man stood slightly behind him. "Relax," the big man boomed. "Nobody gets hurt if you do what we say." He spoke with some sort of Eastern European accent.

By now Elizabeth had noticed how big the guns were. The little knowledge she had gained about guns during her session with Ben following her finding of the gun in the river told her that these were fitted with silencers. Why would you bother to do that if you didn't intend to use them? She tensed, ready for...

The big man stared at Charles. "We are here to ask questions, and you, Mr Cotton, have the answers, don't you?"

All heads in the room turned to stare at Charles. Elizabeth couldn't believe it. Charles *was* Ernest Cotton after all. He had gone from villain to hero to villain, all in a few crazy minutes.

Charles's face stiffened. "How did you...?"

"Get past your security? Never mind...We ask the questions."

The big man bent his knees to lower the bag he was carrying to the floor. In that moment, Elizabeth saw Charles glance at Claire. Elizabeth switched to Claire in time to see her knee blanket slide to the floor and a gun appear in her hand. A terrible thump shook the room, attacking Elizabeth's ears, shaking her to her core. She threw herself to the floor and started to roll, copying the heroes she had seen on screen. As she rolled she caught sight of the big man, slammed against the wall, his face fixed in a look of surprise, his heavy body sliding down the wall, leaving a dirty red smudge in its wake. Another roll and she saw Claire twitching in her chair, her gun still in her hand, all life gone from her eyes.

Elizabeth kept on rolling, protecting her head, and her body tensed to receive the inevitable bullet from the gun of the smaller man. But nothing happened, no shots, not even barked commands telling them what to do. She stopped rolling, lifted her head and looked around. The young gunman was kneeling to examine his partner. Charles and Barbara's heads appeared from behind the sofa. Both stared in horror at Claire, whose head now flopped to one side, her eyes staring forever into the distance. Charles suddenly looked old and shaky; Barbara, both hands to her cheeks, looked like she might scream for the rest of her life.

The once comfortable lounge, full of pleasing paintings and fresh flowers, now smelled more like a garage workshop. The luxurious pale cream carpet had started to soak up the blood seeping from under the big man's body and dripping steadily from the frame of Claire's wheelchair. And something else filled the air, something terrible and indefinable. Was it evil?

By now Elizabeth had concluded that Claire and the gunman had fired at the same time, which would explain the deafening noise in spite of the two silencers. Her ears were still ringing, and she struggled with her balance as she stood up, trembling with fear. She whispered "I'm sorry" to her parents and Dominic...

The young gunman stepped away from his partner's body, his gun still in his hand but pointing at the floor. "Everybody stand up," he ordered. "I am not going to shoot you. I need to make sure you are not carrying a weapon." His accent carried a Latino lilt, but it was not one Elizabeth could pin down.

Charles and Barbara moved shakily from behind the sofa to stand in front of it. The gunman walked up to Charles and lightly ran his hand all over his body. Next, he did the same with Barbara, who gritted her teeth and closed her eyes. Then it was Elizabeth's turn. He looked into her eyes momentarily before he started his search. For a second he was no longer a gunman but an admirer; she could have sworn she saw longing mixed with sadness in his dark brown eyes. His search was perfunctory and over in seconds.

"Okay." He stepped back into the middle of the lounge. "All sit down. My name is Carlos."

While talking he loosened the silencer from the gun and slipped both pieces into pockets inside his military-style jacket. He showed them his bare hands. "I am not here to kill you or torture you. That man over there was. His bag is full of torture equipment. We came here from Chicago, sent by the Sinaloa Cartel. Señor Cotton knows why. I didn't want to do this, but they kill me if I don't..."

Charles interrupted. "They threatened the same for me if I didn't invest their money in my company."

"So you know, Señor Cotton, I say the truth. You must know if I go back to Chicago without their money or proof you are dead, they will kill me. So I make a deal, Señor Cotton. You help me to disappear like you did, and I don't kill you."

"Nobody is stopping you from walking away now," Charles pointed out.

"That was not a good thing to say, Señor Cotton. I think you try to trick me. You know I am a stranger here. I get found in a few days. I think you must leave this country now also, because police will question you when they see the bodies. Everybody will know who you really are. You will go to prison for the fraud you did. So, when I let you go, I want you to take me with you and help me disappear in another country."

Charles looked at Barbara. "He's right; we have to go. And we don't have much time."

"What about Claire?"

"We have to go now. I will send money for her funeral." Charles turned to look at Elizabeth. "None of us can do anything if Elizabeth chooses to phone the police. She has a duty to phone the police now and report this shooting. We won't get far if she does."

Carlos shouted. "I am desperate, Señor. I have waited years for this chance. I will shoot her so she cannot tell anybody."

"No! No!" Charles shouted.

"Then we must tie her up strong and hope she is not found for many days."

Charles looked pleadingly at Elizabeth. "Can you just give us two hours start, Elizabeth? Barbara and I are ready to go now. We have cases already packed with everything we need and a pre-arranged route to get us out of the country fast. This is the first thing I always arrange on arrival at a new place."

"What about your daughter, and the house and everything?" Elizabeth realised it was a stupid question as soon as it left her mouth.

"Claire is not my daughter. She was my bodyguard – ex Special Forces. She is...was a great girl. Both her parents were dead, so she didn't mind pretending to be a daughter of mine. She came up with the brilliant idea of appearing to be my disabled daughter. This allowed her to always have a gun ready for action under that blanket, and she attached other weapons to the body of the wheelchair. As for the house. My life and my sister Sophia's life are more important, don't you think? Yes, Barbara is not my wife. She is my sister Sophia."

Elizabeth was struggling to come to terms with all the new information; she still wasn't sure who the Sinaloa Cartel were. "What about the two men in wetsuits," she blurted, "the men found dead in Derwent river. Did Claire kill them?"

"Of course not. I told you that. We knew nothing about it. Do you think we would have stayed here if we thought we were in danger? You can see now how we react to danger. We flee."

Elizabeth had to admit that he sounded genuine and that his argument was believable.

Charles continued. "Look, if you call the police now, you will be sentencing both of us to life imprisonment. I know what I did was wrong, but I was under threat from the Sinaloa and other big crime organisations who invested most of the money. So, even if I go to prison, none of this money is going to be refunded to them. The US government will claim all the money and no doubt spend it on weapons of war. I had made it my mission to make better use of it by giving most of it away to charities, some of whom work to help drug addicts. There is a lot more money left. Give us just two hours start, and it will all eventually go to charities. And Carlos, here, has a chance of a new life, rather than the death that awaits him from the Sinaloa."

The last sentence struck a chord with Elizabeth. She had seen the sadness in his eyes, and the humanity. She reassessed the situation. If Carlos had been a typical professional killer, they would all be dead now. He would have opened fire immediately when he saw his partner go down. It was their incredible luck that he was different. He at least deserved a chance at freedom.

She looked at Carlos, standing patiently waiting for her to decide his future. He looked back at her. "Please, Elizabeth, we are not bad peoples."

She had no choice now. She deliberately didn't give herself time to think about the consequences. She said, "You have two hours, then I must ring the police. Otherwise the autopsies might raise the question of the time of death."

"Thank you, Elizabeth," Charles and Barbara said in unison. Charles went on, "Can I ask you to make sure Claire has a good funeral? I will send the money for it. And can I ask you not to divulge our true identities? Just say you knew us as Mr and Mrs Prentice. Otherwise the whole world's police will come looking for us and it will be impossible to hide from all of them."

Carlos then chipped in. "Same for me. There is no need to tell them I was here. They have the killer here in front of them."

"Yes, yes," Elizabeth hurried. "Just go...quickly." She was

more worried about time passing than thinking about their requests.

Charles and Barbara left the room to collect their cases. Carlos stood waiting. Elizabeth looked across at Carlos. He lowered his eyes. Nobody spoke. *I'm standing in a room with two dead bodies and a hitman, and I am about to break the law a number of times to help an infamous fraudster escape the police. Have I lost my marbles?* She glanced at Carlos again. This time he forced an embarrassed smile.

Charles and Barbara returned with their cases. "I've been thinking," Charles said. "Technology is advancing all the time. Perhaps they can now tell almost exactly when death took place. I think we need to demonstrate that you were unable to call the police because you were confined in some way. All I can suggest is that we lock you in a toilet and take your phone off you. Or at least make it look as if this is what happened. You can then claim that it took you about two hours to force the door open and were surprised to find they had left your phone on the lounge coffee table. Carlos, come with me."

They all followed Charles into the hall, where he invited Carlos to go inside the toilet near the front door. Charles then locked the door and asked Carlos to kick the door open. The door shook with blow after blow until it burst open. The lock was still intact, but the metal in the frame had been dislodged. "That took Carlos just a few minutes, but I think it is fair to imagine that Elizabeth would take a lot longer. Do we agree?"

A chorus of yesses.

"Right, then that's your story, Elizabeth. Stick with it – they have no reason to doubt you."

What a calculating man. No wonder he's still free after all these years.

Suddenly, Charles was holding her by the shoulders and kissing her on her brow. "You might have saved our lives, Elizabeth. Thank you."

Barbara gave her a squeeze and moisture shone in her eyes as she said, "Thank you."

From a few feet away, Carlos put his hand to his heart, worshipped her with his eyes and said, "*Gracias.*"

As she watched them go, Elizabeth suddenly had the bizarre feeling that she was the owner of Becalmed, seeing off family members who had been staying a few days. But that feeling was soon replaced when she turned and walked along the hall and entered the lounge again. Like a deer in headlights, she was forced to gaze again at Claire and the gunman. They looked like victims of a power cut, their brief lights suddenly switched off, their frozen eyes indifferent to their tragedy. *Where have their memories gone? Where will my memories go? What is the point of that super computer within our heads storing millions of memories when we are all destined to be switched off?*

Elizabeth quickly turned away. She needed to get out of that room. All it offered was despondency and she had two hours to wait. She left the room and headed for the front door. Wandering aimlessly, she found herself standing at the end of the jetty, her eyes staring into space, her mind still numb with shock.

A sudden splash in front of her and she saw a male mallard, astonishingly beautiful, swim towards her and lift its head, expecting to be fed. She watched it for a long time, circling persistently, and as she did she slowly felt her mind clear. Things would be difficult for a few weeks, and she would have a lot of explaining to do, but the Prentice saga was finally over. Life would get back to normal, and she would be free to plan her future with Dominic. She sat down on the front edge of the jetty, her feet dangling over the water, and allowed herself an inner smile.

Epilogue

Over the next three months, Elizabeth survived a deluge of questions from the police, the media and her nearest and dearest. She kept all her promises and stuck to her story, and gradually the deluge abated, and she reached dry land.

Dominic, her parents and Ben and Helen were all so relieved that she had survived the traumatic event that they forgave her for taking the risk. They were also relieved that the Prentice saga, even if not solved, had moved on. Helen reported that Ben almost became a third victim as he choked on his scone when hearing the news. Ben theorised that the two men in wetsuits had been hitmen en route to kill Prentice, but had suffered an accident, possibly caused by Storm Desmond, or had a fight before reaching their target.

Later, Ben came across a biography of Cotton, written by a Chicago journalist shortly after Cotton had disappeared. Called *The Reluctant Fraudster*, among its many fascinating revelations were two which lodged themselves in Elizabeth's memory. The first was that Cotton had trained for many years to be an opera singer like his mother but had failed to reach the standard of excellence required. The second was that he had his naturally curly grey hair regularly straightened, oiled and dyed black while running his company in order to look like an American business executive rather than the Italian peasant he actually resembled. Once on the run, he had simply let nature take its course and his hair rapidly reverted to being grey and curly, thus providing an excellent natural disguise.

Ernesto Cottone aka Ernest Cotton aka Charles Prentice successfully escaped Britain with his sister Sophia via a pre-arranged fishing trawler trip from Peterhead to Bergen, Norway, landing along with 156 boxes of mackerel. (On his return to Peterhead, local skipper Hamish Kerr bought himself a new trawler.)

From Norway they made their way to Tasmania, where, using the names Simon Derwent, retired boatbuilder, and wife Sarah, retired accountant, they bought an old colonial house in the Sandy Bay area of Hobart, overlooking a yacht marina. The house had a large garden, necessitating the employment of a gardener. The gardener, Danilo Morales, also acted as chauffeur and bodyguard, and looked remarkably like Carlos de Leon.

Two years after the event, Dominic and Elizabeth, now married and living in Zurich, sold the business and the apartment and flew to Australia to start a new life on their recently purchased New South Wales vineyard.

Elizabeth's parents continued farming, content with their lot, happy to live amongst the Lake District's breathtaking beauty, secure in the knowledge that their beloved daughter would, one day, return with her husband, unable to resist the call of the fells.

About the Author

Michael Wood has combined a career in industry with that of a freelance writer, contributing feature articles and short stories to newspapers and magazines.

His previous novels – *The Fell Walker, Climate Change,* and the *Fell Walker's Legacy* have achieved wide acclaim, and are all set in the beautiful locations in which he has lived – The English Lake District, New South Wales, Australia, and Scotland's Isle of Arran.

Printed in Great Britain
by Amazon

23681480R00192